THE DOUBLE SPLIT EXPERIMENT

W. BRADLEY DANBROOK

FriesenPress

One Printers Way
Altona, MB R0G 0B0
Canada

www.friesenpress.com

First Edition — 2024

ISBN
978-1-03-831978-4 (Hardcover)
978-1-03-831977-7 (Paperback)
978-1-03-831979-1 (eBook)

1. *Fiction, Science Fiction, High Tech*

Distributed to the trade by The Ingram Book Company

For my inspirational mother, Carol.

PART ONE

CHAPTER 1

Richard York staggered through the dark alleyway behind the downtown restaurant. He stumbled and fell down hard onto the gritty pavement. His head smashed the ground first with a sickening thud. His limbs were all splayed at different angles, jutting from his torso. A trickle of blood dripped from the corner of his mouth. He lay motionless for an indeterminate amount of time. The late *spring* air was thick and still. Up above, in the night sky, a sharply pointed crescent moon shone down. It hung far above his head like a deadly scythe blade. An unusually bright Venus shone nearby. A police siren blared in the distance.

Inside the loud steak house, his colleagues continued their sumptuous meal. Populated with business clientele and celebrating patrons, the atmosphere was convivial. His co-workers were celebrating an office birthday that Friday night.

A slim mid-twenties account manager carved into his thick, well-charred New York striploin. The succulent flesh was bloody and chewy. He spoke in an offhand manner. "Has anybody seen Richard?"

A beautiful blonde woman in a bright yellow dress spoke up. "I think he must have headed home, he looked pretty tired."

Another male co-worker named Charlie responded, "Yeah, what else is new. I don't know what's up with that guy. All I know is, he'd better get his shit together if he wants to keep his job. He hasn't landed a new account in months, and he's going to lose the ones he already has."

Richard's body lay perfectly still on the dirty ground. His tired, bloodshot eyes eventually opened slightly. He glimpsed a beautiful girl with long shimmering blonde hair standing above him. She wore a knee-length puffed-sleeve blue dress with a pinafore worn over the top, and a white sash around the waist. A yellow-gold eight-pointed star pendant adorned her delicate neck. She held a red balloon on a string in her left hand.

He sputtered out a question, "Who are you?"

The radiant girl smiled beneficently. "I am the dreamer, and you the dream."

He puzzled over the cryptic answer. "Then I'm still dreaming?"

The bemused girl giggled. "No, silly. You have finally awakened from your long slumber. You must hurry and plan your escape. There is little time left for you, for all of you."

Richard's eyes closed. He opened them again, and the girl was gone.

Richard heard the staccato sound of high heels on **pavement**. A beautiful blonde woman wearing a tightly fitting yellow dress looked down at him. "There you are! We thought you'd gone home."

Richard stared at her face with confusion. He struggled to find the words. "I...I came out to get some air, and...I guess I must have fallen down."

His co-worker Maria helped him to his feet. "Okay, let's get you home, we can share a cab." Richard was in no position to argue. He slowly pulled himself up. He held her delicate, soft arm until they reached the main street.

Maria flagged down a cab. They climbed into the back seat and the cab drove away. Richard slumped down on the seat. He surreptitiously glanced at Maria's large chest. He looked out the window to see a fire-engine red Ferrari race by. It was followed by a slower moving white VW Rabbit.

Maria asked, "You're near the Old Mill station, right? You're closer than me." Richard nodded. Maria's tone became more serious. "Are you okay, Richard? I mean...are you drinking too much?"

Richard shook his head. "No, not really. It's more that I can't sleep. I'm lucky if I can get two hours a night. I...don't know what to do." The cab drove along through the city as they sat in awkward silence. Richard looked out the window. "Here's my place now."

Maria helped him out of the cab. "I could come up. Are you okay?"

Richard squeezed her hand warmly. "I'll be fine. I really owe you... and if you wouldn't mind not telling anybody at work about this?"

Maria gestured at her lips. "It'll be our little secret. Now you try and get some sleep, mister." Maria returned to the cab. It drove away into the sultry late spring night.

Richard fumbled with his keys and entered his house. He fell hard to the floor in the hallway. He laboriously got up and found his bedroom. Richard kicked off his shoes and collapsed on his bed.

A sharp sliver of daylight shone through the black drapes. The dark red walls of the bedroom slowly grew brighter. Richard's body was contorted across the now too large king-sized bed. The blue sky and white cloud motif bedsheets were tangled around his legs. A smear of dried blood stained his pillowcase. A shrill alarm rang from the alarm clock. Richard bolted upright, as if electrocuted. He shook his head to clear away the thick cobwebs.

Suddenly the image of a young blonde girl emerged in his mind. Like the shadowy images from a strange dream, he struggled to recall it with any clarity. He finally resigned himself to the fact that he would never know for certain, whether or not the memory was real or imagined. He slumped to the floor and stumbled to the bathroom. He used the toilet and flushed. Slowly he raised his heavy head to the mirror. An unfamiliar image stared back from the looking glass. He continued to stare at the face, but it was unrecognizable. Richard's mind was dull and unfocused. Every night he consumed a peculiar combination of sleeping aids. His insomnia was a debilitating disease, slowly eating away at his meagre life. His mundane existence was now completely overwhelming. His tenuous grip on reality was slipping away.

Richard was an unremarkable, slender man in his late forties. His physical fitness had suffered as of late, due to his constant lack of sleep. Deep wrinkles etched his wide, expressive face. His shoulders and back bowed with fatigue. He was six foot tall and had thick, dark hair. His warm, hazel eyes still occasionally sparkled with a mischievous wit. His style was understated. He normally wore a dark grey business suit, with a light brown shirt and a black-red-and-gold-striped tie.

Richard's wife, Elizabeth, had left him two years ago, after the unpleasant incident in their bedroom. He came home early one day to find her gyrating on top of his work associate Howard. The troubling image burned into his memory like a white-hot fire brand. Sadly, Richard might have forgiven the indiscretion, but Elizabeth seized upon the event as a catalyst for change. She was an intelligent, playful blonde psychologist with a keen sense of humour. She possessed a wicked streak that Richard found completely intoxicating. The injurious blow to his psyche never properly healed. His marriage was never as strong as he had imagined. In his mind, his insomnia, and the resulting mental deterioration was to blame. In his heart, he understood that his own deep insecurities were the true cause.

Richard spent his weekend in his usual manner, alone and in his house. After making a strong pot of coffee, he sat down to his laptop. He searched through his ex-wife's social media accounts. It was a self-designed, well-rehearsed process designed to torture his soul. It accomplished its intent, as he was thoroughly disheartened by Elizabeth's newfound happiness. Her account was overflowing with joyful photos of herself with her two perfect children.

Eventually he slammed shut the device. The highlight of Saturday night was a Thai food delivery. On that night, he finished off two bottles of shiraz. It contributed to a difficult, sleepless night. He replayed his interaction with Maria from the office endlessly in his mind. Mostly he watched TV and read comic books.

He arrived for work on Monday morning, exhausted and twenty minutes late. He snuck in the stair entrance to avoid detection. He scurried past his co-workers with his head down, clinging tightly to his travel mug. Richard worked as an advertising executive in a towering downtown Toronto skyscraper on Bay Street. His tenure there was now a decade long. Aldebaran Advertising was a massive multinational corporation, begun a century ago. The massive yellow eight-pointed star corporate logo shone at the top of the imposing building. Richard loved the complex, ever-changing nature of the business. He found the work of subtly manipulating the masses fascinating.

He sat in his large, heavy black leather chair, and took a large swig of strong coffee. The dark elixir jolted him alert. His twenty-third-floor window mirrored an almost identical office in a reversed image building across the street. He stared out the window at a similar man sitting at a similar desk. He scrutinized his seemingly parallel self.

His promotion two years back resulted in a new office, added pressure, and a substantial pay raise. It was a huge step up the corporate ladder, and far removed from his former chicken-coop cubicle existence. Richard continued to stare absently out the bay window, unwittingly replaying the image of his wife on top of his friend. It was like a rerun of a popular old TV show, persisting forever in syndication. It was the cause of many sleepless nights and weary days. He watched as a large black raven, uncommon in the city, tapped persistently on the glass.

His assistant buzzed his intercom. "Richard, Barry's on the way in… and he's on the warpath."

"Betty, can you stall him?"

At first there was no answer. "Richard, I'm Alice, Alice Liddell. Don't you remember what happened to Betty?"

Richard was at a loss. He had no recollection whatsoever. "I have no idea what you're talking about…so you're not Betty?"

Alice answered quickly, "Honestly, Richard, you need to get a good night's sleep. I'm Betty's twin sister. She was killed in that freak accident last month, I can't believe you don't remember. It was in all the newspapers. She was hit by a meteor, just walking her dog in the park...really tragic. Don't you remember the funeral?"

Richard was very apologetic. "I'm so sorry...Alice, I haven't been myself these days, of course I remember."

His answer was a lie. He had absolutely no recollection of the described events. He snapped out of his reverie at the entrance of his boss.

"Rich, did you finish the DMT project I asked you about?" His boss, Barry, was an excitable middle-aged man with furtive, beady eyes and thick, wavy grey hair. He wore an expression of perpetual worry and doubt.

Richard looked up with exasperation. "Yeah, Barry, remember we talked about this? Roger has to finish the layout first."

Barry looked puzzled and nodded in agreement. "Right...right, okay get it to me when you can. Oh, and don't forget about that Swedish account, you know, the one with that couple, and the home saunas." Barry walked out aimlessly.

Richard's work had definitely suffered since the breakup with his wife. His boss and co-workers were sympathetic, but patience was wearing thin. He pondered the possibility of some sort of miraculous escape. He imagined himself a hopeless prisoner, incarcerated within his own troubled mind. The idea consumed much of his dwindling supply of energy.

✷

Edward B. Lytton was a neuroscience professor at the University of Toronto. His tenure was into its tenth year at the hallowed institution. He had few friends at the campus, and was glad of it. Now fifty-one, he had been married only once. It was short-lived and ended in bitter disappointment. He was a heavy-set man standing at an impressive six foot three. His thick, floppy black hair was constantly in need of a wash. His large dark eyes glowered with a malevolent intensity. Edward had little interest in lecturing, a trait obvious to his unfortunate students. Eclectic research was his escape. His latest scientific theory met with general disdain from his peers. Its outrageous content made its eventual publication all the more noteworthy. His innovative research into the subject of sleep deprivation was widely ridiculed as quackery. Others had declared his motivations and methods as decidedly haphazard. Although his professional reputation was in disarray, he was able to retain his teaching position. His sanity was maintained by his one steadfast friend Max Thule.

✷

Samantha Steffen was an understatedly attractive actress in her early forties. She wore her blonde hair shoulder length. Her shy smile belied a fierce inner determination. She worried unduly about the feelings of those around her. Her chronic insomnia made her life even more challenging. She was usually lucky to manage three hours of sleep a night. Samantha's life had not gone according to plan thus far. She had never married, but had been in several serious relationships. She longed to find meaning and purpose in her life. Her career so far had fallen well short of her expectations. She had moved from Vancouver to Toronto several years ago. The move was easier since she had few close friends in the former city. No major acting roles had come her way, and she was growing more demoralized by the day. The odd commercial, and some extra work barely covered the bills. Samantha often wondered if she had chosen the wrong path in life. However, quitting was not an option. Her stubborn nature would not allow it. Her financial nest egg from a small inheritance was nearly depleted. She considered quitting acting for an unfulfilling full-time office position. She was slowly sinking into a deep dark hole of despair. Samantha yearned for some form of escape.

Samantha was adrift that morning. She was awake most of the night, tossing and turning. After finally falling asleep at 4 a.m., she awoke around seven. She started a pot of coffee and took a shower while it finished. She chose a mint green skirt and a beige blouse to wear out. She sipped at a mug of coffee in front of the TV as she watched the morning news. She finally left her downtown apartment to wander the city.

The unusually thick, humid spring air that was stifling the city was dissipating. A midnight downpour the previous night removed the unwanted moisture from the air. She came upon her familiar haunt. Samantha entered the busy Starbucks coffee shop. Her eyes immediately met those of her favourite barista. She ordered her usual, a venti caramel macchiato. She waited patiently until he handed her the beverage. He was a young East Indian man, with thick, wavy black hair, creamy coffee-coloured skin, and large, deep, expressive brown eyes.

"Here you are, pretty lady. How are you doing today?"

Samantha bashfully smiled and accepted the drink. "Oh, you know, I'm okay."

The barista was interrupted by a co-worker. "I'm sorry, I'd love to talk, but we're so busy."

Samantha thanked him, smiled, and walked away. She sat down in the busy establishment. The intoxicating scent of strong coffee awakened her senses. She was reading an old tome from her university days by Jean-Paul Sartre. While there, she had haphazardly pursued a philosophy program. She placed the thick paperback down beside her tall white coffee cup. It was partly for show, to project an image of intelligence and depth. She understood the complex work only superficially. It was a foolish ruse. Every person around her was lost within their own self-absorbed world, staring intently at their phones and laptops. She breathed in the invigorating bouquet of the pungent coffee. Her cell phone rang.

"Sam, it's Arturo...great news, looks like you got the job for that sci-fi thing you auditioned for. I can never remember the name of it. Anyway, it's a decent part, and it might be recurring."

Samantha was jubilant but fought to contain her enthusiasm. "Arti, are you sure? I really didn't think I had a chance. You should have seen the other girls there. Some of them were gorgeous. I still can't believe they wanted me."

Her agent gushed. "Don't be ridiculous. You are gorgeous, honey. Now, don't forget, they want you there bright and early tomorrow morning at 6 a.m. Can you learn your lines by then?"

"Oh, of course," Samantha responded enthusiastically.

Arturo continued, "I'll leave the script at the front desk, I'd give it to you myself, but I've got to be somewhere. Sandra will be here. Go get 'em, tiger!"

She ended the call with her face beaming. Samantha allowed herself a moment of celebration and stood up confidently from her chair. She strode out of the busy coffee shop with a newfound sense of hope. She walked confidently along the busy city street towards her agent's office. A bright red Ferrari zoomed by her, as she tried to cross the road. The driver of the sportscar caught her eye and winked mischievously. She stood on the precipice, looking for a break in the traffic. An old yellow Volvo wagon stopped. The driver was a large, heavy-set man with dark, floppy hair. He smiled at Samantha and gestured for her to cross.

✷

Richard stared up intently at the clock on his wall. He agonizingly waited for the hour hand to reach five. He breathed a heavy sigh as the workday finally ended. It had been another difficult, unproductive time at the office. He fell asleep from sheer exhaustion several times. Richard left the office and headed for the Bloor and Bay subway stop. He shielded his eyes from the still very hot sun beating down. The streets were packed with myriad office workers rushing to get home.

He waited only a moment for his train to arrive. The passengers inside were stuffed like cattle in a boxcar. He fought his way inside. The acrid stench of body odour permeated the thick hot air. He fought to retain awareness of his surroundings as he clung precariously to the greasy metal bar above. He absently gazed around at the ocean of weary bodies doggedly making their way home. The empty groping eyes of strangers stared back into his own. The artificial fluorescent light flooded the train as it raced through the subterranean realm. Richard instinctively looked away to avoid eye contact with the faceless masses. The train suddenly flooded with sunlight as it emerged from its tunnel. His eyes squinted to adjust to the bright setting sun. His eyes caught sight of a large white rabbit hopping quickly on the ground by the track. A large, menacing black bird swooped down toward the fleeing creature. The rabbit jumped down a deep hole at the last second, narrowly evading its prey. He disembarked from the train, and moved heavily up the stairs to the street.

Richard's home was situated two blocks north of the Old Mill subway station. It was a quiet, old neighbourhood, full of mostly second-generation immigrants of various ethnicities. The streets were populated with large old trees lending both shade and precious oxygen. Richard entered his house and collapsed on the sofa after grabbing a cold Sleeman beer from the fridge. He stared up at the ceiling and closed his weary eyes.

He awoke with a start after dozing off for twenty minutes. Richard barely retained the home after the difficult divorce proceedings. The mortgage payments, now a sole burden to bear, were punishing his bank account. He considered taking in a boarder to defray his costs, but decided against it. He was far from destitute, thanks to a frugal nature. He grabbed a frozen lasagna from the freezer and tossed it in the oven. The thought of another sleepless, dreamless night filled him with an encroaching dread.

Richard remembered his boss mentioning an important account. He retrieved his laptop from another room he used as an office. He sat down again on the sofa and turned on the computer. He opened up the file on the DMT account, and then the Swedish homes sauna account. Richard tried in vain to work on the project. His body grew slack and he fell back on the sofa.

He suddenly awoke with a start, a beautiful girl with long shimmering blonde hair stood above him. He recognized her immediately as the girl he had seen outside the restaurant. She girl smiled, turned, and walked away. Richard immediately stood up from the sofa and followed her. The young girl broke into a run. Richard pursued, running faster and faster down the endless hallway. He ran faster and faster, falling farther and farther behind. Eventually he reached out and grasped at empty air. His tired body slammed onto the floor.

✸

Dr. Lytton met with his close friend in the cafeteria that morning. The campus was bustling at the end of the spring semester. It was an unusually warm spring in the city. Ed strolled into the noisy room and waved at his friend sitting at a nearby table. Ed wandered over to the serving line to examine the menu options for the day. He made his selection, paid for his food, and walked over with his tray. He sat down opposite his colleague.

"Max, how close are you to getting that paper ready for publishing?"

His friend Dr. Thule was working on some similar speculative scientific research. "Not very close...I don't even know how you got that gibberish of yours in print." Max was a frail, bespectacled man in his early fifties. He was five foot nine, and 150 pounds at most. His thinning patch of dark hair was slicked back from the middle of his head. He was a tightly wound, meticulous, serious man.

"Gibberish? That's a little much, you're supposed to be my friend."

"Only because nobody else wanted the job." They both smiled as Ed picked at the meatloaf and vegetables he had chosen. Ed's scientific paper concerned the effects of massive doses of DMT, and the hallucinogenic compound ayahuasca on the pineal gland. It was a decidedly obscure field of study. Ostensibly, he was attempting to discover a cure for insomnia, but his true intent went far beyond this. His research focused on the strangely singular pineal gland, situated deep within the central region of the brain. His secret research uncovered a myriad of previously unknown complex associations related to this gland. Ed was obsessed with unlocking the shrouded mysteries of this anatomical structure. The metaphysical nature of his research fascinated the scholar. In addition to his scientific bent, Ed possessed an abiding obsession with the occult from an early age.

Ed had attracted funding from a few pharmaceutical companies interested in sleep deprivation research. His work on this particular branch was into its fifth year. He knowingly crossed a moral boundary two years back when he secretly experimented on live animals. It began with mice, and then testing with live, illegally obtained primates. He was certainly not about to share these results with anyone except his trusted friend Max. Should his research become public, not only would he have lost his position at the university, he likely would have ended up in jail. He remained a scientific outcast despite his recent improbable publication.

Max looked up from his unappealing bowl of macaroni and cheese. The colourless mass was glutinous and bland. "Wish I'd got the meatloaf; this stuff is inedible." His face was gaunt and lined with deep wrinkles. He wore a permanent expression of concern. "You know you'll never get federal approval for human trials, it's way too risky. What is it you hope to accomplish anyway?"

Dr. Lytton pushed a greasy lock of black hair from his forehead. He was only half listening to Max. He gazed imperiously at the lesser beings scurrying around him. He had no answer to Max's question, or at least nothing he could divulge. He could not explain to even his trusted colleague his grandiose dreams of godhood. He feigned a response, "Who knows? Why does anybody do anything? I guess it's just always been an interest of mine...if that makes any sense."

Dr. Thule nodded in agreement, but really had no idea what his friend meant. Max suspected a great deal, but kept his serious misgivings to himself.

✷

Samantha rode the Bloor subway line over to her agent's office on Bathurst Street. She walked in to the small, cramped office.

A frumpy middle-aged woman with bleached-blonde hair looked up happily. "Arti told me you were coming in. Here you go. Looks like you finally got your big break!"

Samantha appreciatively accepted the brown manila envelope. "Well, I wouldn't go that far, but yes, I am excited!" She opened the envelope and immediately began reading over the lines. She spent the rest of that day floating on air. The fantastic news from her agent filled her with an uncharacteristic buoyancy. There was also a certain degree of performance anxiety. She knew the first day on set would be excruciatingly awkward. She did not relish the thought of meeting an entire new cast of actors.

She wandered the city for hours, and treated herself to a lunch downtown. She sat down at the busy Pickle Barrel restaurant. She ordered her favourite: a Reuben sandwich with French fries. She pulled out the script and began memorizing her lines for the next day. As the sun slowly set, she returned by foot to her apartment. She lived in a fashionable uptown neighbourhood. Samantha exited the elevator of her high-rise building at Yonge and Eglinton. It featured artisanal bakeries and cheese shops, none of which she could afford. She spent a lot of time in the cavernous bookshop next to her building.

She opened the door to her claustrophobically small, one-bedroom apartment. Decorated haphazardly, it reflected the disjointed chaos of her mind. Samantha loved movies, and she watched a lot of TV. A dozen old movie posters, mostly from the 1960s and 1970s, plastered the walls of her apartment. They recalled a timeless and carefree youth.

Her bedroom walls and ceiling were painted sky blue. An old stuffed toy pig sat on a plush chair in the corner. A smartly dressed frog and a fish, sat on the bed. They both wore matching red livery long coats. She still clung tightly to the three remnants of her childhood. Her bedroom featured the posters from several old Disney classics.

She suffered from extreme insomnia, and her movies had proven good company in the dark times of her depression. She had visited her doctor to address her sleep deprivation problem. He was reticent to prescribe any strong drugs that might actually work. She had tried the usual remedies, but they left her feeling flat and listless. An ingredient in the sleeping pills seemed to prevent dreaming. She believed that her dreams were a vital aspect of her mental health.

Samantha sat down on the sofa and flipped on the TV for company. She barely even noticed the program. She got up and poured herself a glass of Merlot and sat down again. She pulled out the script from her purse and read her lines. She felt herself getting comfortable with the character and her part. She took several gulps of wine as she imagined herself being introduced to the cast. She fervently hoped that it would be a casual, friendly atmosphere. The star of the show was a very famous, extremely attractive actress. The rest of the cast was comprised of mostly unknown actors, like herself.

She picked up her phone to check for any new messages. There were none. She half expected a text from her agent, explaining that the casting director had changed her mind, and that she was not getting the part after all. Samantha always prepared herself for disappointment. She found it a useful defensive attitude for life in general. Some would have called her a pessimist, but she considered herself merely a realist. Samantha's eyes began to blur as she put down the script. She finished her goblet of wine, switched off the TV, and headed to bed.

Richard awoke on the floor of his bedroom. He glanced up at the red numbers of the clock on his nightstand. It now read 3 a.m. A panic set in as he saw his hope of a few hours of sleep slip away. Richard heard a faint noise at the window of his bedroom. He got up to see the cause of the disturbance. He looked down to see a large black raven pecking insistently upon his window. The bird stopped and stared up at him, perhaps hoping to gain entry. Richard scowled at the bird and banged hard on the window. The bird ignored him and continued its tattoo upon the window. The staccato sound filled him with a strange dread. Richard left his bedroom to escape the annoyance. He routinely switched on the TV to divert his thoughts. He absently began flipping through the channels. He watched an old sitcom from the sixties. It seemed to exist perpetually in reruns, like some unending dream. He then found an interesting program he knew entitled *Outer Edge*. It was halfway through a new episode. He sat drowsily attempting to discern the plot, as his head flopped forward in exhaustion. He figured out that the sci-fi plot concerned interdimensional travel. He considered the idea laughable, but entertaining.

✷

Dr. Lytton sat staring at the walls in his eclectically decorated office. During this part of the year his professional obligations were few. The semester was nearly over, and he had only one class to teach before exams. At this point in his career, he didn't even bother to prepare for his lectures. The material was so familiar, he could have recited it in his sleep. His mind drifted away from the concerns of the day. He conjured up the image of a very attractive assistant professor he met earlier that day. She was tall and trim with long dark brown hair and black-rimmed glassed. He fantasized about meeting her and sharing a coffee. He imagined the pretty young woman being fascinated by his research, and eventually falling deeply in love with him, enthralled by his pure genius. It was a pathetic dream that played out often in his mind.

Despite his advancing years and waning libido, he still hoped for romance in his life. His efforts in this regard were misdirected and vague. He also preferred to rely on fate, rather than a prescribed scientific algorithm to find love. The very idea of debasing himself by submitting to an online dating service was anathema to him. He very much enjoyed working at the university, and being around young people. It provided him with an illusion of vicarious hope and vitality. He enjoyed the interaction with the bright, vibrant young women attending the lectures he taught. He desperately longed for one of them to fall prey to his academic charms. It had happened once before, twenty years ago, and it ended badly for both parties. The ill-fated marriage lasted only two years. Ed dated a few women colleagues, but his arrogance stood in the way. Only a docile, not yet formed personality could accept his monstrous ego. Edward began to recede into the non-threatening world of imaginary romantic encounters. He malingered and moped within his large inhospitable psyche. The darkness buried deep within him grew more malignant with each successive moment of isolation.

✷

Samantha opened her eyes as she heard the top-forty music blare from her bedside alarm clock. She glanced over at the time. The red numbers on the screen showed 4 a.m. She pondered whether or not to hit the snooze bar a few times, but thought better of it. She reflected upon the fact that she had managed four hours of precious sleep. She would have preferred much more. With a full understanding of the daunting day ahead, she leapt out of bed and headed to the bathroom. After a quick shower, she made herself a cup of coffee in the kitchen and prepared herself. She marshalled her entire reserve of confidence as she left the apartment.

The city was quiet and still at that early hour. A few early morning delivery trucks roamed the streets. She looked up to see a bright half-moon, and a clear starry sky. Samantha drove to the site of the studio by the lakefront. The dawn light slowly appeared in the eastern sky. She easily found the old, repurposed brick factory. A collection of expensive foreign vehicles sat outside. Over the entrance, a faded yellow eight-pointed star was barely visible. Almost a century earlier, a painter had carefully put it there. Her old, rusty white VW Rabbit appeared conspicuous next to the shiny new vehicles. She pulled her phone out to check for new messages as she walked towards the studio.

Samantha walked into the cavernous space. It was the third season of the series. It was a surprise hit, as it began with low expectations. The obscure, intellectual subject matter appealed to a highly devoted fan base. She had crammed for her audition a week ago by binge-watching the entire show. She felt groggy and slow-witted.

The director approached her as she entered the building. "You're Samantha, right? Come on in and meet the cast and crew, we're just doing a read-through on the new script."

Samantha tried her best to feign interest in the show. "It's an honour to finally meet you. I mean, I know you were there at the audition...but, you know what I mean. I'm a big fan of the show. I still can't believe I'm here."

The stocky, middle-aged man was a well-established, well-respected Hollywood heavyweight. His thick, chunky hands seized hold of her shoulders. He led her into the belly of the building. She was slightly dizzy from lack of sufficient sleep, but she was accustomed to the feeling. His groping fingers dug into her waist. She considered the inevitable manhandling an unavoidable job hazard. The unwanted physical intrusion made her skin crawl. She said nothing and soldiered onward.

✷

Richard heard the piercing shriek of the alarm clock. He turned it off and quickly put on a small pot of coffee. He showered, shaved, and dressed for work. Any nocturnal occurrences were wiped from his mind. He left his house and briskly walked the two blocks to the subway stop. Richard felt exhausted as he hung onto the metal bar in the subway. It was another unusually hot and humid late spring morning. He arrived for work twenty minutes late. He carefully eluded the notice of his boss Barry. He greeting the receptionist Alice as he passed by her into his office. She eyed him with a sympathetic, but chastising look. He sat down in his big, heavy black leather chair. He flipped on his computer and began the daily password ritual. He secretly kept a notebook with the thirteen different passwords beneath his desk. He scanned absently through the twenty-one new emails received. His weary mind wandered away to the TV episode he had watched the previous night. He daydreamed about the seductive raven-haired woman in the lead role of the sci-fi show. He imagined somehow meeting her in an elevator and catching her fancy.

The shrill ring of his phone harshly interrupted his blissful diversion. He despised the painful, intrusive sound. As a senior account manager, he interacted only with the most influential clients. In his twenties he had toiled furiously to attain his present position.

His boss, Barry, spoke on the phone. "We're meeting after work on Friday night. Where do you want to go?"

Richard was indifferent, but attempted to feign interest. "Is everybody going?"

Barry replied, "It will be the usual crowd. We'll probably end up where we always do, Baton Rouge."

Richard's mind immediately returned to the humiliating events of the previous Friday night, at that very establishment. He considered himself fortunate that Barry was not in attendance that evening. Richard was interested in only one particular woman in the office. Richard was appreciative of Maria's assistance in the alleyway that night. He found her completely fascinating. Maria was an extremely desirable woman. Her cascading blonde hair flowed gently over her feminine shoulders. Her curvaceous body moved with a languid grace. Her sparkling blue eyes twinkled with wit and adventure. To Richard's amazement, she was not married or attached. She was ten years younger, which seemed a reasonable age gap to Richard. He would not have dated a woman twenty years younger. He often imagined a perfect romantic encounter with Maria. He hoped that the unfortunate rescue outside the restaurant the other night would not diminish him terribly in her eyes. He prayed that this night would bring precious sleep.

✸

Ed returned home after an uneventful day at the university. His small, comfortable bungalow was centrally located in an Italian neighbourhood on College St. West. He loved the vibrant, ethnically diverse atmosphere. Excellent restaurants were all within easy walking distance. His house not in poor shape, but needed many improvements. Edward was far too engrossed in his research to bother about home upkeep. A strange collection of prints decorated his house. They were mainly portraits of eclectic people. His bedroom was painted his favourite colour, dark red. It was a hue not usually conducive to restful sleep. Artwork by Salvador Dali, Mark Ryden, and Shawn Thornton hung throughout the house. The iconic portrait of a playful Albert Einstein, sticking his tongue out, hung proudly on the bedroom wall. Facing Albert was the menacing, glowering face of infamous English author Aleister Crowley. An enigmatic photo of an angelic blonde goddess named Maria Orsic adorned the prime position over the bed. Her strangely serene eyes were at once calming and frightening. A portrait of the obscure theosophist Madame Blavatsky hung in the corner. Edward had great admiration for them all.

Ed sat down wearily on the comfortable brown leather sofa in his living room. He reflected upon a thoroughly uneventful, uninteresting day at the university. The highlight was his conversation with Max. He dined upon a baked, frozen pizza and diet soda while watching TV. He was not a heavy drinker, but definitely was a coffee addict. He flipped through the channels, looking for something that caught his fancy.

He watched an interesting sci-fi show called *Outer Edge*. Ed cleaned up his food and dishes and made his way to the basement door. The stairs led down to a dark space with a heavy black padlocked door. He walked down into the darkness. Ed fumbled for the key in his pocket and unlocked the thick steel barrier.

CHAPTER 2

Samantha wore her blonde hair in an old-fashioned-style flip at her shoulders. Her sparkling blue eyes flashed with mischief and intelligence. She shunned the spotlight in her daily life. It was an incongruous quality given her line of work. She often pondered the wisdom of her career choice. She drifted accidentally into acting, after unsuccessfully trying a dozen other lines of work. She studied random humanity and philosophy courses at university, with no clear goal in mind. She once thought about teaching, but found the idea of returning to school unpalatable. Her first job after university was in a real estate office. She was an abject failure at sales. She lacked the obligatory outgoing personality. Had she not landed this present role, she likely would have given up on her dream. She approached her new challenge with complete conviction.

Following the unpleasant encounter with the lecherous director, Samantha wandered over to the craft-service table. She filled a plate with cheese and crackers, having skipped breakfast. She smiled at the young girl hurriedly replenishing the food. The challenges of the craft-service job were well-known to her. It was her first real job in the TV industry. Samantha sat down nervously at a table with a dozen other snacking cast members. She hated being the new kid at school.

The boisterous director, Harvey, made matters more difficult by singling her out. "This is Samantha, everybody, she'll be playing the new character Eve in the next episode."

She nodded meekly, like a stranger wandering into a backyard family reunion. Thankfully, the busy gathering barely noticed the newcomer. The exception was the female lead in the series, who fixed her with a powerful gaze. The imposing actress was named Selena. She was a black-haired seductress with luminescent emerald green eyes. Her body seemed to glow with an iridescent, unearthly light. She wore a tightly fitting red-leather skirt that accentuated her curvaceous frame. Her eyes penetrated deeply into Samantha for several moments. Samantha felt the powerful depth of her gaze, and looked away in fear.

The assembled cast spent the rest of the day reading and rehearsing the script. A walk-through of the scene was scheduled for the next day. The pace of the popular show was frenetic, and Samantha definitely felt the pressure to perform. The cast finished up for the day and prepared to leave. Samantha quietly drifted over to the craft-service table, and began filling a napkin with meat and cheese, hoping nobody would notice. She had little food at home, and her bank account was nearly empty. Tragically, she did not hear the woman who walked up behind her.

"Planning a midnight snack?" Selena had slyly sidled up, gently touching her back.

Samantha jumped and dropped the stolen food, only adding to her complete humiliation. She instinctively reached down to gather the scattered food. Her face was flushed with embarrassment. She realized the folly of her actions and struggled for an explanation. "It's for my dog…he just loves cheese." The stammering excuse fooled nobody.

The raven-haired beauty moved around to face her directly. Keenly aware of her prey's weakness, Selena pounced. "No…I don't think so. You don't actually have a dog. How sad. When you get caught in a lie, you really should just own up to it. Anyway, whatever. Take what you want, they just throw it out at the end of the night."

Samantha hurriedly moved away from the table, attempting a gracious exit but failing. "Is it that late? I really need to get home and learn my lines."

Selena simply observed her coldly. "You know I could help you."

Samantha shook her head and scurried away like a frightened mouse. She grabbed for her phone in her pocket. She pretended to make a call, actually calling her own number at home.

✷

Richard spent another dreadful night in bed passing in and out of consciousness. He would fall asleep intermittently, only to be shocked awake by increasingly bizarre, disturbing dreams. The concoction of sleep aids he consumed each night caused vivid, jarring dreams. He continuously experimented with various dosages and combinations. He imbibed a very high dose of melatonin that night. His present mental state was dull and unfocused as a result. Richard laboriously prepared for another workday. He left his house in reasonable time. Thankfully late spring heat wave was dissipating. The subway train was slightly less busy that morning. He gazed absently out the window and noticed a white rabbit hopping madly across the ground. He wondered if it was the same rabbit he had seen earlier in the week.

He arrived at the Bay and Bloor subway stop and walked to the towering skyscraper with the yellow eight-pointed star. He said good morning to the very attractive receptionist Alice as he walked into this office. He collapsed in his heavy black steel and leather chair. He struggled to regain his professional demeanour as he heard his boss heading towards his office.

Barry burst in with his usual bluster. "So you're on for tomorrow tonight, right?" He stared at Richard with expectant anticipation. "Be at Baton Rouge steak house, the one on First Street, by six. How's the presentation coming? I'm not worried, I know you'll nail it champ. You do know you have to nail it, right? We really need this DMT pharmaceuticals account, and don't forget about the Swedish one either." He turned abruptly after barking out the instructions.

Richard nodded his weary head in agreement, even as he searched his mind for an excuse. He desperately wished to solve the puzzle of his insomnia. He spent the morning frantically searching the web for some new miracle cure or experimental drug. He felt his hope withering away. Suddenly an obscure article caught his eye. It was written by a local professor named Dr. Lytton. Richard delved deeper and found the professor's work promising. The research featured audacious, ambitious ideas that intrigued him. He had fallen victim to quackery and false expectations many times. Richard closed the professor's article on the screen, but saved it. He focused on completing his important upcoming presentation.

✷

Dr. Lytton opened the heavy black steel door and entered his secret laboratory. He carefully locked the door behind him with a thick bolt. Ed abandoned the university lab a few years back, for the privacy of his own workplace. At great personal expense and danger, he had meticulously constructed his own laboratory. He was now venturing far beyond the bounds of conventional sanctions and experimentation. He had crossed many moral boundaries as well. The use of live animals was a prickly ethical thorn bush at best. He was certainly not able to justify such wonton abuse with his feeble funding from the university. Of course, his colleagues had no idea what he was actually doing. Nobody, not even his trusted friend Max knew of his ultimate goals. Edward existed on the very precipice of legality and reason.

Perhaps foolishly, Edward chronicled his devious experiments via laptop camera. Edward conceitedly spoke directly into the camera, as if staring in his own movie. He began his experiments. "Last subject, number 23, effects of massive injection of DMT, melatonin, and ayahuasca simultaneously."

Ed began experimenting first on rats a year ago. He used various combinations of the compounds, attempting to find the perfect mixture. DMT, or Dimethyltryptamine, is a naturally occurring compound that exists in many plants and animals. Ed had seen it used by many cultures as a psychedelic. He was convinced that a certain level of DMT saturation in the pineal gland of the brain, would initiate a qualitative transformation of consciousness. He was attempting the mythical quantum leap to a different state of reality. His approach was part alchemy, part science. His ultimate goal was to achieve an entirely novel state of consciousness. He wished to extricate himself from vulgar physical reality. Ed dreamed of existing within Karl Popper's visionary third world of pure, objective thought. His experiments thus far had yielded only meagre outcomes. He could not publish any of his groundbreaking results. Given the unorthodox nature of his work, secrecy was utmost. Ever-increasing dosages had caused no ill effects. The elusive omega point remained just beyond reach. Success would change everything, and bring perfect clarity. He realized that simple rat experimentation had inherent limitations. He finally obtained live monkeys on the black market. This was the subject of his new slate of experiments.

Ed increased the dosage to over 10,000 mg of DMT, melatonin, and ayahuasca. The doctor had constructed a terrifying contraption with restraints to secure the wretched creature. The animal screeched in blind horror as the procedure began. The heavy metal and leather straps dug deeply into the primate's limbs. Blood trickled down its matted hair. A steely helmet with prodding metal thorns held the cranium tightly in place. The sieve-like steel hat had many apertures. Ed carefully administered a massive syringe full of a cloudy fluid. Its tip dripped as he moved the device into place. With a violent plunge, the doctor penetrated the soft flesh of the creature, just at the back of the brain. Again, the tortured monkey let out a fearful scream of abject pain. Ed did not enjoy watching the sadistic torture the wailing creature endured. He rationalized the heinous act in the name of furthering scientific truth. He knew only a conscious subject would produce meaningful results. He studied the combined effects of the compounds with great interest. The beleaguered, listless monkey was still alive, yet transformed in significant ways.

✷

Samantha drove herself home from the studio that evening. She opened the door to her cramped apartment. The crushing embarrassment of her recent encounter with Selena still stung. She removed the pilfered snacks from her pocket in disgust. Samantha walked to the bathroom. As she looked in the mirror, she realized that her dirty-blonde hair was in severe need of washing. The image that stared back at her was somehow unfamiliar. Her thin, taut body was damp with desperation sweat. She quickly started the shower, and removed her outer clothing. Samantha felt slightly better as the streaming hot water flowed over her body. The experience helped to wash away the day's unpleasantness. She stood motionless for several minutes enjoying the calming warmth of the water enveloping her completely. She closed her eyes and allowed her mind to wander off.

She conjured up an image of the young East Indian barista naked with her in the shower. She felt his well-muscled body slowly caress hers. He felt his hands move down from her shoulders to her waist. His large, strong hands moved ever downward over her wet, warm body. Suddenly the jarring image of Selena entered unbidden into her mind. Her bright emerald eyes burrowed deeply into her thoughts. Samantha opened her eyes, finished showering, and attempted to forget the unpleasant mental intrusion.

Samantha exited the shower and dried herself off. She realized immediately the importance of making peace with Selena the next day. The aggressive woman made her very uncomfortable. Yet the star of the show demanded respect, even fealty. Selena had managed to crawl under Samantha's skin, and discovered her weak underbelly. Samantha's ever-present anxiety grew more debilitating each day. She put on some comfortable flannel pajamas with a red-and-white polka-dot mushroom motif. Though exhausted, she was much too unsettled to sleep. She walked out to the living room and sat down on the sofa. Halfheartedly, she picked up her script for the next day, and began rehearsing the lines in her head. Her phone on the coffee table buzzed with a new text. She picked it up absently, reading a message from a friend asking about her job. She checked for any new social media updates. She had recently tried several online dating sites, with no success. She had not dated in over a year. Her love life was a sloppy, haphazard, unfinished patchwork.

Samantha possessed a subdued, natural beauty. Her delicate, rounded face had thin tight lips and wide, expressive blue eyes. She did not easily open herself up emotionally, and her friends were few. She put her phone down on the table and listlessly flipped through the channels on TV. She suddenly stopped as a news story grabbed her attention.

The male news anchor spoke in an excited tone. "Scientists today have obtained, for the first time, irrefutable proof of the existence of a new ninth planet in our solar system. A year ago, there had been suggestions and speculation that such a celestial body might exist somewhere lurking beyond the Kuiper Belt. In other news today..."

The incidental news made little impression on her. Samantha was fascinated with the night sky from a young age. She recalled gazing up at the stars for hours, wondering at the immense, imponderable grandeur. She grew up in the small city of Burnaby, not far from Vancouver. She missed being able to see the Milky Way on clear nights.

She turned her attention back to the TV, searching through the channels for the show she was working on, *Outer Edge*. She found the latest episode, as she studied the nuances of the show and learned her lines. Her nightly exhaustion resulting from inadequate sleep gnawed at her. She soldiered on doggedly with the script memorization. She had a mere ten lines in the episode they were now filming. She wanted desperately to impress the director, despite his odious nature. Unfortunately, she soon realized that her first scene the next day was opposite Selena.

Samantha sensed something very strange about the woman. It was a feeling she could not accurately characterize, but nonetheless felt very deeply. The raven-haired star seemed well aware of her power, and exploited it to full advantage. Samantha fought to keep her eyes open. She finally turned off the TV and read her lines aloud. She continued rehearsing for another twenty minutes before giving up. She put the script down on the coffee table and prepared for bed.

*

Richard spent the rest of the day drifting in and out of consciousness. He accomplished very little actual work. He fell asleep several times in his chair. He awoke abruptly to see an almost identical figure in an office tower across from him. He noticed that the stranger seemed to mimic his own actions. He attributed the experience to a lack of sleep. Richard stared mournfully at the clock on the wall. Mercifully it reached 5 p.m., and Richard bolted for the exit. He zoomed by his co-workers, avoiding recognition. He hurried along the sidewalk as a huge flood of office workers were disgorged from the many tall buildings around him. He felt overwhelmed and insignificant within the faceless throng.

He descended into the subway station where strangers bustled and shoved for a place in line. He waited for two trains before managing to squeeze inside. The compartment was coffin-like, stifling, and claustrophobic. He could feel the hot, fetid breath of a man standing behind him. He watched as his stop arrived, struggled his way to the door, and left the train. He dashed home and collapsed on the sofa, but awoke several times before he finally made his way to bed. He forgot both to eat and brush his teeth.

Richard arrived at work in his usual dazed state the next morning. He might have slept for two hours. Already late, he decided to drive his car to work, however, he barely remembered the short trip to the office. He struggled to maintain his professional composure. He was working on his presentation, when he actually fell asleep. His head hit the computer keyboard, jerking him awake. Wearily, he opened his eyes to see the door to his office and the chairs around him slowly moving towards him. The deep purple walls of his office seemed to pulse with a strange energy. He stared up at the white ceiling that appeared to be descending upon him. Out of the corner of his eye, he spied a large white rabbit darting past the door. He was still barely lucid enough to realize that he was hallucinating. The troubling episodes were becoming more frequent. He slapped himself hard in the face. He took a large gulp of coffee. His near-comatose state persisted. He decided that his only hope was a quick nap to recharge his batteries. The office was not an option, as his boss could barge in at any moment. He could not risk the humiliation of sleeping at his desk. It would also damage his already threadbare professional reputation. He abruptly stood up and casually walked out of his office.

He breezed by the attractive blonde receptionist Alice. "If anybody needs me, I just need to grab something from my car."

The stunning, highly polished woman at the front desk nodded and flashed her pure white teeth.

CHAPTER 3

Dr. Lytton sat hunched over his desk in his dark, solitary laboratory. He continued his ethically objectionable experiments well into the night. He gathered many highly significant results. He discovered that continually increasing dosages of melatonin, DMT, and ayahuasca caused the subject to exhibit extreme cognitive dissonance. He found that the brain itself underwent an odd transfiguration. He still had no clear conception of the ultimate outcome of his scientific inquiries. He carefully recorded every piece of information transmitted from the mind of the creature. The EKG machine attached to the steel helmet recorded increasing spikes of energy. The wretched monkey went numb, and simply stared out blankly into the nothingness.

Ed believed that he had come close to achieving the Omega point. This was the singularity, the apex of saturation and effect. He studied the novel results on the computer. He was amazed to notice an almost impossibly high reading of brain activity. Ed prepared for the final, dangerous step in the procedure. He entered a code on his laptop and walked over to an elaborate piece of equipment that resembled a pair of Tesla coils. A bulbous torus-shaped device sat on top the two shiny metal columns. He slowly powered up the electromagnetic plasma-field generator. Slowly, the power level increased, as the air crackled with electricity. Ed transferred the energy from the plasma-field generator to the chair holding the experimental subject. The monkey screeched with an icy, terrifying howl. His bloody limbs strained against the leather restraints. A blinding flash of light bright as the sun emanated from the metal chair. A moment later, the entire room went completely dark.

Ed felt around in the blackness to find his way. He found a flashlight and then the electrical panel, where a breaker had tripped. Ed flipped the switch, as the dim light came back to the room. He immediately noticed something shocking. Ed ran over to the metal chair and found it empty. He reasoned that the monkey must have somehow escaped its restraints. He frantically searched the room for his missing test subject. The door to the basement being locked, there was no trace of the creature. Ed was stunned and afraid. He had at once succeeded and failed. The monkey escaped to a realm unknown to even Edward's wild imagination. Dr. Lytton sank to the cold floor and stared into the darkness. He was at once pleased that his experiment had succeeded, but confused by the unknown consequences of his actions.

✷

Samantha awoke to the sound of blaring music from her clock radio. She calculated her total time asleep at four hours. She recalled her dreams. They were a chaotic jumble of bizarre images and impossible scenes. She envisioned a strange futuristic world where she was in great danger. Her mind imagined towering black buildings with dark-hooded specters. Strange, ancient symbols and mystical g permeated her thoughts.

She picked up her phone to check for new messages. She scrolled through a series of photos posted from an old friend from Vancouver. The giggling group of older women were heaving large goblets of fruity alcohol into the camera, and smiling too broadly. She left an appropriate bland affirmation of the posting. Samantha put the phone down and rolled out of bed. She made herself a pot of coffee and sat down on the sofa. Samantha prepared for work. Her continuing inability to deal with her insomnia was top of mind. She had researched lucid dreaming as a possible cure. Despite her best efforts, she failed to find any definitive answers. She continued ingesting a cocktail of sleep-inducing formulations at bedtime, with little success.

Samantha arrived on the set of *Outer Edge* that morning, parked her rusting old car, and walked towards the brick building. She entered the dark building and met with a throng of weary-looking actors and crew.

The second assistant director hurried her into a wardrobe room. "Go ahead and pick a dress from this rack here...I think they want to see you in ten minutes."

Samantha quickly rifled through the clothes and settled on an iridescent powder-blue dress. It looked like some sort of unusual futuristic garment. She hastily dressed and saw the assistant director, Dinah. "Is this dress okay?"

The very young girl, festooned with piercings, was clad entirely in black clothes. Her heavily darkened eyes looked up with apathetic disdain. The girl shrugged and dragged Samantha to the set. "It's fine."

The director was busy barking out orders and settling the crew. "Okay, people, we're going to try this one with camera. Honestly, you should all know the lines at this point."

The first assistant director shouted loudly, "Please, everyone, settle." She waited a moment, then called out, "Sound!"

The heavy-set director then called out, "Action," and the scene began.

Samantha looked around nervously. She was very anxious, despite knowing her lines well. She still felt like an outsider, an interloper intruding on a well-knit group of friends.

The darkly seductive Selena stood opposite her, gazing intently. Selena wore a ruby red hooded cloak. She initiated the scene with her characteristic bravado. "Eve, we have to amplify this quantum-field generator, regardless of what might happen."

Samantha listened and responded in kind. "If we increase the power level too much, we may have no chance of rescuing Dorian. It might overload and destroy the entire building. Without the Perimeter Institute, all our careful work would be lost forever. He might be stuck in that alternate dimension forever." Samantha delivered her lines with cool aplomb. Her voice was strong and deliberate. She continued, "There must be another way...what if I go in after him?"

"That doesn't help us, then we just have two people MIA. We have to face the fact that we don't even know if he's still alive."

Samantha, playing the part of Eve, replied, "He is alive! I know it! I feel it!"

Selena, playing the part of Lilith in the show, finished the scene. "I want Dorian back just as much as you do, you know we'll never get the proper authorization to do this, but there is the possibility of creating a singularity. It's a long shot, but it's there."

Samantha nailed her lines, and she knew it. Both Selena and the director gave her approving glances. She relaxed a little as another actor took up the scene.

✷

Richard snuck past the main floor and scurried down the stairs to avoid detection. It was a long way down the many flights. He finally reached the floor to the underground garage. He grabbed hold of the heavy black metal door and pulled it open. He did not actually need anything from his car. It was a lie he had used before to good effect. He opened up the back door and huddled down in the back seat, with a blanket over him. He set the alarm on his phone for one hour, and turned the ringer off. He forced himself to close his eyes, trying desperately to quiet his racing mind. Flashing images of Alice and his co-worker Maria clouded his thoughts. Richard managed to get twenty minutes of half-sleep, when he heard a loud knocking. At first, he imagined he was dreaming. He sheepishly pulled the blanket away from his head to see the beautiful face of Alice the receptionist staring down at him. He attempted to regain his composure, in the face of his abject embarrassment. He pushed open the door, and struggled to his feet like a drunken frat boy.

Alice sized him up with a look of dismay, concern, and pity. Richard blurted out a half-formed explanation. "God, Alice...so sorry...I came down here to grab a thumb drive...not sure what happened...I guess I was sleepier than I thought."

Alice regarding him with cold disdain. "Yeah. Anyway, Barry was trying to get hold of you, sorry to bother you, but he asked me to find out where you were...so..."

Richard fumbled as he fought to regain some measure of dignity. "No...absolutely...my fault, of course. Maybe Barry doesn't need to know you caught me, you know, napping."

Alice nodded appreciatively, acknowledging her advantage. "Not a big deal. It stays between you and me." She turned away curtly in her snug white skirt and headed back to the elevator.

Richard unwittingly stared greedily at her perfectly toned behind. It swung gently back and forth under the tight material. Alice keenly felt the weight of his ravenous gaze. She was well accustomed to the attention, and ignored it. Her stiletto heels struck the pavement loudly, echoing through the cavernous garage.

✷

Edward finally gave up searching the lab for the primate and retired for the night. Sleep did not come easily, as his mind raced and searched for answers. Eventually he drifted off. He awoke to the sound of music from his alarm clock. He glanced at the time and rolled slowly from his bed. He prepared himself for the day. Ed was shocked by what he had seen, or rather not seen. The previous night's events swirled around furiously in his mind. He questioned his own judgment and sanity. He arrived at the university at 8 a.m., as usual. He gave a perfunctory lecture that morning, and headed to the cafeteria for some lunch with his close friend Max. He noticed his colleague in the food line. "Hey, Max, what're you having today?"

"The meatloaf looked somewhat edible. It looked good when you had it the other day."

"I went with the mac and cheese...you done for the day?"

"The mac and cheese is terrible. Don't you remember me telling you the other day? Anyway, too late now. I have an afternoon class in the physics lab."

The cafeteria was less busy than normal. They both paid for their lunches and found an empty table. The two middle-aged professors sat across from each other, picking listlessly from their unappetizing plates.

Ed looked up at Max with some hesitation. "Something happened last night...probably shouldn't be telling you this..." He quickly searched for some sign of acceptance on the face of his friend.

Max was habitually prepared for anything. "Christ, Ed. What the hell have you gotten yourself into now? I thought you would have learned your lesson."

"Max, I need to know that I can trust you with this. You know I have nobody else to talk to, nobody else would even understand what I'm talking about."

"What the hell are you trying to do anyway? It sounds like you're trying to play God. I hope to hell you haven't been messing around with that plasma-field generator." Max's frustration relented somewhat. "You crazy maniac, you know you can tell me anything...and no, I'm not going to rat you out, if that's what you're asking. Just make sure you don't make me an accessory to murder, or something worse."

Ed looked relieved. "Okay, thanks. Here's the thing, I've been doing experiments in my basement...with live subjects. Yeah, I did mess around with the plasma generator. I know I could go to jail, blah, blah, blah." Max simply stared at him in disbelief, and shook his head. Ed continued, "So, anyway, stay with me, Max. You understand the basic idea of what I'm doing, so I increased the dosages to insane levels, over 1000 mg of DMT and melatonin, and a huge amount of ayahuasca. So, I'm checking the EKG readings on the monitor, totally off the charts, ever increasing, and then nothing at all. There's a huge flash of light behind me, I look around and the damn monkey is gone...disappeared."

Max listened intently. "But why would you use DMT and ayahuasca? DMT is the active ingredient in ayahuasca. And what did I tell you about using live subjects in your insane experiments? Where did you even get a monkey? Oh, never mind, I don't want to know. So, it must have escaped while you weren't looking...unless you're trying to tell me it was magic."

"There is absolutely no way, this poor bastard was strapped in like nobody's business. He could not have escaped, he just damn well disappeared. And as to the DMT in ayahuasca, you are, of course, correct, but they act in different ways in the brain."

"I don't know what to tell you, Ed. I don't know what you want me to say...you need some help, man." Ed just stared at his friend, searching for some sign of forgiveness and understanding. Max could offer no adequate response. He picked up his tray and left the table. "I'll talk to you later, Ed. I'm actually heading over now to a TV set, down on the lakeshore. They need to borrow a piece of equipment."

Ed was left alone with his thoughts. His furtive mind was unsettled and disjointed. He had nowhere else to turn and no clear course of action in mind.

✷

Richard jolted himself awake, as if from a coma. Indistinct images from his dreams emerged from his subconscious. He looked around his office in bewilderment. He had no recollection of returning from the underground garage. Even the events therein were hazy. He had completely blacked out. The rest of that morning, and the entire afternoon, were completely erased from his mind. He stared up at the clock which read 5 p.m. The day was done, with nothing accomplished. He dejectedly shut down his computer and left the office. He remembered leaving his car in the garage, and decided to walk the few blocks to the restaurant on Front Street. It was a warm spring night, with a slight breeze. The sidewalks were busy with office workers eager to commence with weekend plans. He arrived at the restaurant and walked inside.

The trendy downtown steak house Baton Rouge was replete with rich, dark wood and soft mood lighting. The usual Friday night crowd of boisterous business people congregated inside. The restaurant exuded money, sex, and the succulent scent of perfectly grilled steaks. He sat down at the long table. There were eight in attendance from his workplace. He glanced at the menu and provided his order to the server. A moment later, his body slouched backward and his eyes closed.

Barry was staring at him quizzically from across the table. "Rich, you okay, buddy? Thought maybe we lost you there for a minute."

Richard attempted gainfully to regain his composure. He had fallen fast asleep at the work dinner, and he was not entirely sure he was not still dreaming. This was not his first time mixing up the two distinct mental states. He intuitively knew he was experiencing reality, and not a dream. He had no recollection of why he was at the restaurant. He did vaguely remember the invitation from his boss. He recalled the humiliating encounter with Alice in the underground parking garage. Blackouts were becoming increasingly commonplace.

For several awkward minutes, he felt the judgmental stares of his co-workers. His nemesis, Charlie Leach, was essentially a younger, better-looking version of himself. The newcomer was looking for a reason to attack, and replace his mentor.

Charlie surveyed him, like a tiger sizing up its prey. "You okay there, friend? We were thinking of calling for the defibrillator."

Richard felt disoriented and could offer no proper verbal defence. He felt Maria's warm body beside his. He sensed her smooth, soft thigh, barely touching his own leg. The attractive woman was perfumed and perfect in every way. She reached down and gently traced his thigh with her slender fingers. The provocative advance sent chills through his entire body.

He suddenly felt rejuvenated by the overt gesture. "Sorry, guys... not exactly sure what happened there...really haven't been feeling that hot, lately." His colleagues were accustomed to this level of strangeness. Since the departure of his wife, they all noticed a marked change in his behaviour. He gazed at Maria, who smiled back with a warm openness. Richard could not wait to leave, despite his attraction to the blonde goddess beside him. He chewed slowly on the delicious bacon-wrapped, medium-rare filet mignon. He savored the tender, sweet flesh of the steak, melting in his mouth. He took a sip of the shiraz red wine from the large goblet in front of him. The warmth of the full-bodied, smooth Australian vintage lifted his spirits and calmed his nerves.

He engaged in light conversation with Maria. Richard asked about her vacation plans for the summer.

She responded to his casual advances with a flirtatious invitation. "Our family has a cottage on a lake up in Muskoka, I go up there all the time. You should come up one weekend, it would help you unwind, forget about things."

Richard suddenly visualized an image of Maria standing on a dock wearing a tight yellow bikini. The picture stuck in his mind as he responded, "That does sound like fun. I could protect you from all the bears up there. Actually, we have a family place up there, too. I wonder if we're neighbours? I haven't been up there in years. My parents are gone. I just haven't gotten around to selling it."

"That would be cool. We're on Lake Rousseau. It would be nice to have the company, you know, there are so many things up north that could eat you up. Bears...and other things." She smiled knowingly at him.

Richard could feel his heart pumping vigorously. His felt his overheated blood flooding every part of his body. He needed to visit to the washroom to calm down, but decided to wait a few minutes.

✷

Samantha finished her part in the scene and watched the set from the craft-service table. She noticed Selena hanging in the wings and pulled out her phone to check for messages. She tried desperately to appear busy.

Selena spied her and walked over. "Nice job, you really nailed those lines."

Samantha felt typically uncomfortable as the attractive woman sidled up close to her. She could feel the warmth of her muscular thigh as it brushed up against hers. Samantha stared ahead, attempting to avoid eye contact. She feigned a smile and accepted the compliment graciously. "You guys are so easy to work with...it's a pleasure. Which scene are they doing now?" She motioned towards the set, where a massive piece of equipment slowly moved onto the stage.

Selena pointed at the machine. "Amazingly, that is actually real. These producers spared no expense. They're borrowing it from the university. It's for that scene coming up about the singularity-energy thingy...I don't pretend to understand exactly what they're talking about. You'd be amazed by how the fans of the show obsess over every ridiculous detail. If something isn't right, we hear all about it. They're just trying to see how it looks on camera. Apparently, it was easier for them to make a small donation to the university, than try and have the prop department make one."

Samantha listened appreciatively and strolled over to the set to get a better look. There were half a dozen students and a professor from the university setting up the complicated machine. The professor was Dr. Edward Lytton's friend Max. Dr. Thule motioned to the director that they were ready to proceed.

Max held the control panel for the apparatus. "Okay, everyone, stand back. I'm powering it up."

As the output of energy increased, the crackling plasma field began to expand. Shooting out spiky electric blue tendrils, the bulbous pods bristled and buzzed. Most of the crew were watching the proceedings on a nearby monitor from a safe distance.

"Max, that's looking good, can you increase the power? I really want this thing to light up the screen."

Max looked back at the director with a concerned expression. "We can go a little higher, but you don't want an overload. That would be very dangerous indeed." As requested, he dutifully increased the power level, despite his better instincts. The intoxicating allure of mingling with actual TV stars had muddled his reason. The magnificent plasma field engulfed part of the set, and throbbed with energy.

The director and crew stood transfixed by the spectacular sight. The director motioned to his crew. "Sound...and...action!" The scene proceeded for about a minute. There was a sudden blinding flash of brilliant white light, and then nothing. All those gathered stood still and silent. The plasma field had overloaded, as Max had feared.

The director ran over to Max. "Can it be fixed?"

The scientist, dressed in his best grey suit, with a bright yellow bow tie, looked downcast. "No way. Did you get what you needed for the scene? I hope so."

The stocky, sweaty director left and went back to the monitor. He began to review the footage. "What the hell? Max...get over here!"

The gaunt, bespectacled physicist complied. "What is this I'm looking at exactly?" Max scrutinized the image, attempting to process the information. "What is that there? It must be some sort of glitch?"

The director shook his head furiously. "That's no glitch. How the Christ did a monkey get in the shot?"

The crew gathered around the monitor looking at the freeze-frame image. The captured image was unmistakable and real. The video showed a blinding flash of light, and then the monkey appearing out of nowhere.

Dr. Thule attempted an explanation. He remembered his friend Ed recently explaining his own strange monkey experiment. Max tried to dismiss the anomaly. "It must have somehow run onto the set."

The director shook his head wildly. "You've got to be kidding me! I can see maybe a stray dog or cat wandering in...but a monkey?"

Max had nothing further to add. "Well, I'm not sure what to tell you, I hope you got what you needed. You know we can only lend this equipment out for the day. It's got to get back to the university right away."

The burly, boisterous director merely shrugged in exasperation. "Yeah, I get that. We'll figure it out in editing, it's just damn weird, you know? Dinah, check the building for a wild, magical monkey, see if he'll work for scale."

Max was apologetic to the director as his students packed up the equipment. "Listen, if you ever do find that poor creature, let me know first. I know somebody that would be very interested. That poor little creature must be terrified."

✷

Out of the immense, pure blackness of space, a blinding flash of light bright as the sun appeared. A massive asteroid emanated from the light of creation. Astronomers named the invading asteroid Apophis. Its full designation was Apophis 99942. It remained on the periphery of solar system, like an actor backstage awaiting his entrance. At about eighty to one hundred miles across, it was easily massive enough to erase all evidence of civilization from the earth in a collision. Yet its precise trajectory remained uncertain. It was definitely on a path that would take it very close to Earth, depending upon a myriad of factors. Chief among these was the proximity of the yet unnamed ninth planet. If the massive projectile travelled close enough to the giant mystery planet, it might receive a deadly nudge in the wrong direction.

✷

Richard sat quietly in the bustling restaurant, feeling anxious and exhausted. He reflected that the night had obviously not gone perfectly well. He thought it best to cut his losses and regroup for another night. He was still severely fatigued, and he had enjoyed several glasses of wine. Richard decided, upon reflection, that he possessed sufficient sobriety to drive home safely. He stood up abruptly from the table and gazed once again at his gorgeous blonde co-worker. "Got to run everybody. It's been a slice."

Maria noticed him get up. She brushed away the soft, flowing blonde hair from her face. She looked up at him with her cornflower-blue eyes. "Are you sure you couldn't stay a little? I don't mind driving you home." The subtle invitation hung in the air like a ripe, ruby red apple.

Although being very tempted, he thought better of it. He surreptitiously glanced down at her well-rounded chest straining against her dress. He did not wish to squander a precious opportunity. He very graciously declined. "I'm going to have to take a rain check. I'm really not feeling all that great. You understand, right?"

The dazzling, effervescent woman was unfazed by the refusal. If anything, she seemed to grow more intrigued by the deferral. She was not accustomed to rejection of any kind. "Not at all. By the way, that invitation to the cottage, consider it still open...anytime." Maria regarded him with an expression pregnant with anticipation and delight.

Richard tore himself away with great difficulty. He walked out of the restaurant into the now empty streets. He passed a few stragglers of the city as he walked back to his office building. The cooler night air felt bracing on his face. He looked up at the half moon, shining brightly next to the eight-pointed yellow-star logo adorning the skyscraper.

✷

Samantha left the busy set of the show. She walked out to her tiny white VW and got inside. She put the key in the ignition and the small engine sputtered to life. She sat staring out the window at the luminous half moon above her. The commotion from earlier rendered her emotionally and physically exhausted. Samantha was overjoyed that the workday was done. Her scene had gone very well, but the emotional effort drained her completely. Her mind was unfocused and tired. She sensed herself hurtling head-long towards some strange, unknown destination. She felt as though someone or something was influencing her will. She prayed for a full, deep night's sleep. Her narrow shoulders slouched forward. Loneliness weighed heavily upon her. She foolishly imagined that one magical person might hold the key to her happiness. Yet, she desperately wanted to believe in her own fierce independence. Samantha waited patiently for someone or something to wrest her from her passive torpor.

CHAPTER 4

The complex, myriad effects of DMT, melatonin, and ayahuasca fascinated Dr. Lytton. He had spent years studying every aspect of the compounds. Many years prior, he had travelled to remote Peru. There he had met with local elder shamans. At his request, these Indigenous adepts had dosed him with ayahuasca. The experience was spiritually and intellectually illuminating. Dark and forbidden truths revealed themselves to him.

Since that trip a decade ago, Ed had experimented on himself using the three compounds. He was searching for a magical mixture that would unlock hidden secrets. Dr. Lytton saw himself as a modern alchemist. He was continuing the work of other such pioneering alchemists such as Nicolas Flamel and Isaac Newton. The professor spent many nights attempting to synthesize this elusive elixir. He was not searching for the fountain of youth, or even a cure for disease. He was devising an exit strategy. Ed was looking for a means of cheating death itself. He made many groundbreaking and crucial discoveries along the way. Many of these revelations were too controversial for wide publication. He determined that the combination of compounds somehow worked as a gateway to another dimension. This portal was both a physical and spiritual realm, the nature of which was still undiscovered. Ed learned that the brain was far more than a simple lump of inert flesh. It was a conduit, and possessed capacities that exceeded even the most vivid human imagination. He wondered if his lost monkey had finally gained the secret knowledge that he so fervently sought.

✷

Richard walked down into the underground garage. He was careful and wary of his surroundings. He knew that assaults and robberies were uncommon in his part of the city, but not impossible. He regretted his missed opportunity with Maria at the restaurant. He was always careful to shield himself from the stinging pain of rejection. His mind was heavy with exhaustion and confusion. He climbed slowly into his classic black Ford Falcon. He drove out to the exit and paid his ticket with a credit card. He drove out onto the now nearly empty city streets. Suddenly he slammed on the brakes, as a bright red Ferrari raced by him. The driver of the sportscar, an attractive raven-haired female, winked at him as she passed. He tentatively drove along the streets until he found the avenue leading out of the downtown. Richard sat back in the well-worn black leather seat, thinking about Maria. He watched the bright city lights and billboards rush by the window beside him. He longed for an escape, a means of somehow transcending the monotonous, nightmarish grind of his life. He drove quickly towards the expressway through the clear starry night with a deliberate stomp on the pedal.

✷

Samantha was about to drive away, when a monstrous black raven alighted on the hood of her car. It slowly moved towards her and began pecking insistently upon her windshield. She peered at the unusually large bird. Its beady black eyes stared back into her. She tried to shoo it away with a wave, to no avail. It took flight as she stepped on the gas. Samantha drove into the night, replaying the perplexing event on the set earlier. The drama left her feeling perplexed and frightened.

Eventually the usual exhaustion set in, and she struggled to stay awake at the wheel. She drove through the nearly empty streets by the waterfront. The small white car made its way toward the expressway, and out of the downtown. Samantha looked up at the luminous half-moon, as she drove towards her apartment.

✷

Richard's mind raced ahead, imagining what still might come of the encounter with Maria. The soft, warm, and inviting woman captivated his mind. His constant longing motivated him to pursue the connection with her. He considered his conversation with her an important step towards his goal. He once felt an intimate bond with his ex-wife, Elizabeth. He struggled to open himself up emotionally. He believed the threat of more pain was too risky. It was better to simply skim across the surface of life, and avoid immersing himself completely.

He continued his drive home in the cool night air. He glanced around and noticed a large work van pass him. He read the brightly painted ad on the side. It read, "Wally Ross and Sons Carpenters. No job too Small or too Big." Two rotund, identical young men wearing striped shirts sat in the cab. A massive rig transporting a Caterpillar excavator to some distant work site followed close behind. Rings of smoke billowed from the truck's smokestack exhaust pipe.

✷

Samantha wound her window down to feel the brisk wind on her face. The night sky was clear and cloudless. A panoramic view of twinkling stars dangled high above her. She gazed wistfully at the display when a blinking bright star caught her attention. She continued driving along the empty avenue as the blazing light seemed to follow her. It continued to grow in intensity. The shooting star was the largest she had ever witnessed. It left in its wake a wondrous iridescent trail of cosmic dust.

She made a silent wish, just as she had done on every such occasion since childhood.

✷

Richard's vehicle whisked along the road, as a brilliant, incredible flash of light streaked above him. He gazed up through his moonroof at the spectacular sight. He always noticed shooting stars. Childishly, he still made a quiet wish on every occasion he saw one. Its blazing, sparkling tail illuminated the darkness above. The distraction was sufficiently remarkable to cause Richard take his eyes away from the road ahead for a moment. He didn't notice the other vehicle directly in his path, as he merged onto the Gardiner Expressway. His jet-black sedan careened into the side of the old white VW.

Samantha had been similarly distracted. She lost control of her vehicle, as it veered onto the shoulder and came to a screeching halt. The collision rendered her quiet and chastened. She was fortunate to avoid serious injury, she thought to herself. She sat rigidly with her white knuckles clenched onto the wheel. Samantha took several deep breaths and attempted to calm her nerves. After a few moments, Samantha noticed a black Ford very slowly pulling up behind her on the shoulder. The driver's side grille was bent in slightly. Initially she did not recognize the vehicle, but gradually she began to recreate the event in her head. She watched a tall, dark-haired man emerge tentatively from the damaged black vehicle.

Richard was dreading the uncomfortable encounter ahead. After realizing the extent of his misjudgment, he had quickly pulled off the road to survey the damage. He sat motionless for several moments attempting to collect his thoughts. He was already exhausted and frazzled before this latest mishap. He reluctantly emerged from his vehicle, noticing the damage to the car's side grille. He smiled sheepishly as he looked in her window. Samantha looked up and returned a slight grin. She emerged from the victimized white Rabbit.

Richard slowly began his apology. "So, I guess I'm the guy that tried to run you off the road." Richard examined her car for damage. "It needs to be fixed obviously, but I think you should be able to drive it home."

Samantha stood silent for a moment, scrutinizing the stranger, scanning to discern his true intent. She instinctively sensed that he was not an immediate threat. She lowered her usual defensive mechanisms. "Ah...so that was you? Were you angry or just bored?" Samantha was testing to see if the stranger had a sense of humour.

Richard smiled broadly, relieved that the woman did not seem vindictive or difficult. "Wow. I guess I deserve that. Let's start with my card, I'm going to totally take care of this, all my fault...obviously."

Samantha accepted the business card, and examined it carefully. "I guess this looks legit. I recognize this logo, the yellow star. Strange. I noticed it on an old building today."

Richard nodded. "Aldebaran corporation. I think they have a hand in just about everything. One of those multinational things. I think they're a hundred years old."

Samantha smiled. "I'm Samantha, by the way. So I was hit by Mr. Big Shot. You don't work at Walmart, you work in advertising. I guess that means you probably know exactly how to play me...if you wanted to."

Richard grinned. "Do I look like the kind of guy that would try and take advantage of a situation like this? Look at this innocent face."

"Now that sounds like a line. You should know, they don't work on me."

Richard regrouped. "No...I didn't mean it that way. So did you see that incredible shooting star? Honestly, that's why I took my eyes off the road."

Samantha began to feel more comfortable with the encounter. "I know, right? That was the most amazing shooting star I've ever seen."

Richard felt bolstered by her enthusiastic response. He sensed that this woman might be a fellow romantic. "I hope that you remembered to make a wish." Samantha nodded. Richard continued. "So, what was the wish?"

Samantha shook her head in a scolding manner. "Obviously, I'm not going to tell you...then it wouldn't come true."

Richard was enjoying the banter far more than he expected. He wished it would continue, but his nagging exhaustion soon returned. "I would love to chat here all night, but it's been a bit of a day for me. If you can just give me your information, my people will give you a call first thing in the morning, or I guess it will be Monday morning."

"Your people? Sounds impressive. These are like your minions, at your beck and call?" Richard took the teasing with good humour. Samantha reached into her purse and pulled out a card. She quickly wrote out her number, as well as some of her insurance information.

Richard accepted the card. "Samantha, you'll hear from me on Monday morning, and again, I'm really sorry about all this." She smiled and turned away. Richard called out, "It was really nice to meet you!" She stepped into her damaged car. Richard waved as she drove away. It was the happiest accident of his life, he thought. He looked up again at the stars, wondering what new path fate had in store for him.

✷

The gargantuan asteroid Apophis veered just close enough to the still unnamed ninth planet to alter its trajectory just slightly. It was now in a direct path to collide with planet Earth. It was still a few billion miles from the blue planet, and the possibility of a reprieve remained. Its course might stray away from the intended target. Gravitational fluctuations continued to push and pull upon the uninvited guest. It would arrive on the scene soon to possibly deliver catastrophic destruction.

✷

Ed arrived early at the campus on Friday morning. The grounds were nearly empty at the end of the semester. He opened the framed glass door to his cluttered office. His many academic accomplishments decorated the wood-panelled walls. Edward received his doctorate from MIT, and completed his undergraduate work in Toronto. He was a second generation Canadian, and grew up in Toronto. He excelled at university, and great expectations preceded him everywhere. Soon a debilitating procession of obsessions and disappointments followed. He became a miserable lonely genius, free to wallow in destructive, unbridled ambition. He thought himself both a pioneer and a singularly exceptional individual. Ed believed himself exempt from conventional moral and ethical mores.

Along with his impressive collection of diplomas, his office featured many bookshelves. The subject of neuroscience featured prominently. He was also favoured diverse subjects, including science fiction and philosophy. The great works of Sartre, Kafka, Asimov, and Burroughs featured prominently. Wagner played on his radio in the background. An Escher print depicting a dimensionally impossible building stood opposite a complicated, incredibly colourful Fibonacci fractal. The well-known Hieronymus Bosch triptych hung behind his brown leather tufted chair. His dank office lacked a window to let in natural light. The dark, cavelike space mirrored his dour demeanour.

Ed was grading papers when he heard an impatient knocking at the door. He called out, "Come on in." It was his only friend Max. The excitable man was clearly perturbed. He rushed towards Ed's desk and placed both hands firmly down upon it.

Scowling down at Ed, he blurted out, "Ed, in case you were wondering what happened to your magical monkey, he showed up...at least for a moment or two."

Ed looked up in utter confusion. "What the hell are you talking about? Shut that door."

Max did so, and returned, sitting down in the chair opposite. "Okay, so remember that monkey that somehow escaped your lab? Anyway, we were working on that cool sci-fi show we watch, *Outer Edge*. You remember I told you they needed to use some lab equipment? We were fiddling around with the plasma-field generator for one of the shots, and it was probably a little overpowered. That was my fault, showing off a bit, I guess. Anyway, there it is, you can see it plain as day, for a little over a second...and then it's gone. How it got there, where it went...who knows? It had to be your monkey, right? I mean, it's way too much of a coincidence."

Ed looked up in utter disbelief. "First of all, you know that there is no such thing as coincidence. Coincidence is a word that stupid people use when they fail to perceive the overall principle of implicate order that is at work. You've read David Bohm. You know this. So why are you talking this nonsense about a coincidence? Can you be sure it's the same monkey?"

Max merely shrugged. "Well, the way you described it, it sure looked like the same one. What do you think it means?"

Ed shook his head and settled back in his chair to consider what he had heard. "I would like to see that video. If it is in fact the same creature, the question then becomes, how did the little bastard get to that TV set, and where the hell is he now?"

Edward followed Max out of his office and down the corridor. They soon arrived at Max's lab. It was luckily empty of students.

Max pointed at the screen. "I managed to get a copy of the image from the show." They sat beside each other staring at an image on a monitor.

"Yeah...that does look like my monkey."

Max nodded. "It doesn't make any sense whatsoever. There's no point in even attempting to explain this, or discount it. You can't tell anybody else. You'd be a laughingstock...not to mention how illegal it is. Hopefully we'll be able to repair my generator."

"Laughingstock? I think I'm already there. My professional reputation was ruined years ago. Sometimes I wonder why they even let me teach."

"It's this magical thing called tenure."

Ed grinned. "Oh yeah, tenure. My very best friend, other than you, of course."

Max nodded. "Do you wonder where your monkey is now?"

"Where and when actually...it's the missing piece of the puzzle really. By adding the energy from the plasma field to the other compounds, this is what opens the portal—or whatever you want to call it. If only there was some way to bring that monkey back."

"Yes, but you do realize you can only learn so much from a monkey. It's not as if he's going to be able to tell you where he was."

Ed responded, "At some point I'm going to need an actual human to learn anything useful."

Max shook his head in disagreement. "Are you nuts? I assume you are referring to yourself? Nobody else would be crazy enough to actually try this...it's suicide, man!"

"Without some really useful data on humans, my work is at a standstill. As you know, I've tried this stuff before myself...just not with the plasma field."

Max remained unconvinced. "I'm not going to help get you killed. I don't want to have anything to do this."

Ed tried to persuade his skeptical friend. "Not necessarily killed. Look at the monkey, he's still alive, right? Even if it did send me someplace else, I'm finding this reality a little tiresome anyway, not to mention dangerous." Ed was only half joking. He continued on a different subject. "Did you hear about Abner in astronomy? A lot going on. First, they actually found that elusive ninth planet. Incredible! It also sounds like they found another space rock headed our way... probably will miss us by a mile...they always do, but it looks like it might come pretty close. It's been on the news, but people always get all worked up for nothing, they don't realize how truly common they are. One strange thing about this asteroid, it seemed to materialize out of nowhere."

"I did hear about that one, actually. If people knew how overdue we are for the big one to hit, they wouldn't be able to sleep at night."

Ed shrugged it off. "Nobody believes anything anymore, it's just another conspiracy theory to them, that's what they'll say. They could see that giant rock right above their heads and still they wouldn't believe it. Maybe if they make it into a TV reality show or put it on YouTube, then they'll watch...maybe..."

Max fiddled with his damaged generator. "I don't have any more lectures today. I'm going to see if I can get this thing working."

Ed examined the equipment. "Do you need any help? I'm done for the day as well."

"No, but I may call you later if I can't get this thing going. I should be all right. You go home and relax. And I mean that. No more messing with that generator of yours until we figure out what happened to that monkey. Promise?"

Ed reluctantly agreed. "Fine. But this is not over. Eventually I'm going to need your help. Anyway, it's probably a moot point, since that asteroid will likely obliterate us all soon."

Max laughed. "We can only wish!"

Ed left his friend and departed from the campus. He drove home in the busy Friday evening traffic. He noted that the volume of cars seemed greater than usual. The drivers seemed almost frantic. Cars honked incessantly as profanities flew freely. The unpleasant odour of desperation and anxiety soured the cool evening air.

✷

Richard bolted upright from his bed. It took him several moments to comprehend that it was Saturday, and that remarkably he was not late for work. He snatched three precious, uninterrupted hours of sleep, which was an incredible achievement for him. He instinctively grabbed for his phone on his bedside table. He checked to see if he had received any message from Samantha. He felt elated by his chance encounter from the night before. He thought to himself that he had never so thoroughly enjoyed a car accident. He incidentally realized unhappily that his insurance premium would rise.

There were no new messages on his phone, he noticed with mild disappointment. He dressed in casual weekend clothes. He wore old blue jeans and a yellow plaid shirt. He made himself a strong pot of boutique coffee. He saved the good coffee for the weekends. As the machine continued to drip, he called his insurance broker to explain the details of the accident. The matter was completed in a few minutes. He sat down on the sofa with his steaming, huge mug of French roast brew. He flipped on the TV to the American all-news channel. The anchor intoned, "*Today the FDA, for the first time has approved the use of ayahuasca in human clinical trials as a means of treating depression, and other similar mental disorders.*"

Richard intentionally ignored the time-wasting world of social media. He maintained only a strictly professional online profile. Meaningless connections with unknown strangers were of no interest to him. He immediately thought about Samantha. He reluctantly checked her online social presence. He noticed only a bare minimum of personal information. She seemed to be similarly disinclined to share minutia needlessly with others. She had a similar number of online friends, and her postings were sparse. She was, like Richard, putting little effort into the venture. He thought again about calling her, or texting her, but thought better of it. He did not wish to seem too eager or desperate.

Richard got up from the sofa and went to the kitchen to make himself some breakfast. He prepared a bagel with tomato and cheese. He poured himself another cup of coffee and sat down on the sofa to eat. He returned his attention again to the TV.

"*In other news, astronomers today have announced the appearance of a new asteroid, dubbed Apophis. It has entered the solar system, and it is expected to come very close to Earth.*" Richard listened with some interest. He could not stop thinking about Samantha. He finally decided to send an exploratory message. He reasoned that a casual text would be less risky than a voice call. The fear of rejection and humiliation was still very real to him. He composed the text in his head as he absently flipped through the channels.

✷

Samantha arrived at the set on a bright, cloudless Saturday morning. Her damaged white Rabbit was slower than usual, but still drivable. There was a huge dent in the driver's side by the wheel. She arrived slightly late as she glanced at her watch. She thought again about the car accident from the previous night. She was truly hoping to rid herself of the aging VW. She thought about buying a new vehicle with the pay from her present work. Samantha checked her phone as she exited the vehicle. She was hoping to hear from Richard, but there was no message from him yet. Her anticipation after the chance encounter grew stronger. She fought hard to curb her enthusiasm, as was her habit. She desperately hoped to avoid yet another romantic disappointment.

Samantha entered the dark, cavernous building with the yellow, eight-pointed star above the entrance. Script in hand, she made her way to the craft-service table to pour herself a coffee. As usual, she had not slept well. She might have slept for three hours at most. Her mind was clouded with anxiety and racing ahead of itself.

Selena, the star of *Outer Edge*, was lurking in the corner. Selena noticed Samantha and snuck up beside her. Samantha smiled at the seductive lead actress, before anxiously checking her phone for new messages. Selena queried, "Looks like you're expecting an important message…is it from your boyfriend?"

The bold question startled her. "No…not at all…just somebody I met randomly last night." She continued, as she attempted to divert the curious woman's attentions away from her romantic life, "This guy smashed into me with his car. He was pretty cute, actually, so who knows. There was this weird super-bright shooting star last night…"

Selena seemed well aware of Samantha's attempt to change the subject. She smiled knowingly. "So did you guys hook up yet?"

Samantha was aghast and shook her head vehemently. "No, of course not, we barely just met."

Selena shrugged. "If he's cute, you should definitely do him, but, I suppose, to each his own. A shooting star, eh? That reminds me, did you see the news this morning? Apparently, there's some giant comet or something heading towards us, so if you do want one last romp in the sack, looks like you only have a few days." The shapely woman, dressed in a tight red skirt and black blouse, turned abruptly and headed back to the set. Samantha was so preoccupied with her chance encounter she had completely forgotten about the asteroid that was now on everyone's mind.

Samantha examined the offerings on the craft-service table. She gazed admiringly at the fresh doughnuts, but thought better of it. Instead, she chose some cheese and fruit and piled it on a paper plate.

She headed over to the table where the lascivious director was holding court. "So this scene is where Dorian, who has been trapped in this other dimension, is brought back with the help of Eve and Lilith. You might have heard about the weird monkey that mysteriously showed up on camera, so the kicker is, we're going to figure out a way to incorporate this into the script. We actually found another monkey that looks just like that little rascal. This is weird stuff people, but it's a weird show. This is good stuff. You go ahead and tweet, post whatever...it's all good for the show. The fans love this *X-Files* stuff, they'll eat it up."

Samantha listened with particular interest. His explanation answered some of the questions she had about the commotion on set the other day.

Samantha walked away from the group and sat down. She pulled out the script to practise her lines. She had difficulty focusing on her work. The previous night's events thoroughly consumed her thoughts. As if on cue, she felt her phone vibrate, signalling a new message. As she had hoped, it was from Richard. She carefully read the text.

"Sorry again about last night. All the insurance stuff has been taken care of...we'll get your car fixed up, or get you a new one, if you wish. Let me at least buy you a coffee to make it up to you?"

Samantha read the text with delight, decoding its meaning. She decided to wait a while to respond, so as not to seem too eager and desperate.

✷

Richard was hopeful for a favourable response to his text to Samantha. He lowered his expectations as best he could. He decided to get some fresh air. He left his house and headed North on Yonge Street. After several blocks, he wandered into the massive, three-story Indigo bookstore. The huge store was busy on a Saturday morning. Richard enjoyed the calming ambience of the bookseller. He decided to research his crippling insomnia condition. He knew that the affliction would eventually kill him. He had difficulty, like most people, of conceiving of his own death. It seemed to him a very distant abstraction. Richard searched through the various sections of the cavernous store, looking for a miraculous book that might save him.

Richard eventually picked up a book entitled *DMT: The Spirit Molecule*. He randomly flipped through the pages, trying to decide if it might be useful to him. He sat down to read the book in earnest, as it seized his attention. A large, heavy-set man with long, dark greasy hair was standing nearby. He noticed the book that Richard had chosen. He wore an old, threadbare, green tweed jacket, with brown leather patches on the elbows. Underneath he wore a grey University of Toronto T-shirt with a faded mustard stain.

He studied the reader for a moment before deciding to introduce himself. "That's an interesting book you have there. I actually know the guy who wrote it."

Richard was at first startled by the unbidden intrusion. It was certainly unusual in a city of quiet, private individualists. His precious solitude having been disturbed, Richard took a moment to size up the stranger. "Really? I don't know anything about it at all. I guess that's why I picked it up." He inexplicably felt quite comfortable with the professor. He continued, "I actually have a pretty severe insomnia problem, and I'm looking at any kind of solution at this point."

Ed nodded knowingly, but proceeded with caution. "I often have difficulty getting to sleep, although it seems like you may have a more serious problem. As it happens, I have a certain degree of expertise with the compounds described in that book. I'm Dr. Edward Lytton, by the way. I lecture at the university."

The two men walked away from the wall of books together. He was still not entirely at ease with the stranger. Richard listened and then continued, "So you know all about this stuff? Let me tell you, I've been to doctors, I've tried so many different sleep aids...nothing really works. I feel like I'm living in a constant fog. Sometimes I can't remember if I'm still dreaming or awake. Anyway, if you know something that could help me, by all means, what is it?"

Ed reached into his wallet and pulled out a card with his office number at the university. Richard accepted the card and examined it. "Dr. Edward Lytton, yes, you did mention your name, but I didn't make the connection. This is kind of weird. I was literally just reading one of your articles online the other day. Your work is incredible, really cutting-edge stuff. Of course, I don't understand any of it, but it got me thinking about the possibilities."

Ed happily let the praise wash over him. He was duly impressed that the new acquaintance had such unusual interests. "Really? Well, you, sir, are in the minority. Very few could even begin to comprehend what it is I'm trying to accomplish. I wonder if serendipity has brought us together. Do you have time for a coffee? There's so much I could tell you."

Richard was not especially social, and did not make new friends easily, but he nodded his acceptance. "Yeah...I suppose I have a little time."

The two set off for the first floor, where the pungent aroma of strong coffee drew them onward. The trendy uptown bookstore was now bustling with a crowd of well-dressed weekend shoppers.

✷

After several hours, Samantha could no longer resist the urge to reply to Richard's text. Her scene was about to commence, so she put away the script. She sat down, typing away at her phone, accepting his invitation. Her message read, "*You definitely owe me coffee, at the very least. Let me know if you need any more of my insurance stuff.*"

She put her phone away after checking for any new messages. Samantha noticed a flurry of activity and voices. The assistant director Dinah, motioned for her to come to set.

Harvey, the director, was standing before everyone, urging them to settle down. "Okay, people, this is the scene with Eve, Lilith, and Dorian. Dorian has just returned from the alternate dimension." The brash, authoritarian man sat down heavily in his chair to watch the scene.

The assistant director called for quiet and called out, "Settle, people....and sound!"

The director shouted loudly, "Action!"

Selena's character, Lilith, spoke first. "Oh my God, Dorian...you're back. We really thought we had lost you for good this time!"

"I kind of thought so myself. How did you get me back here, anyway?"

It was Samantha's character Eve who responded, "It wasn't easy. Pretty much a fluke, really. The plasma-field generator we were using basically overloaded."

"So, you somehow sent the monkey to get me back? Is that it?"

Lilith answered, "We were testing the limits of the machine with the monkey. We thought if we could bring the monkey back, we could probably get you back also."

The elaborate scene was set in a dark, concrete room with computers and equipment everywhere. A massive steel chair figured in the foreground. An eight-pointed yellow star hung by the door. Several actors stood in the background. Two dark, menacing figures in black robes stood behind Dorian. Heavy black hoods hid their faces. They both held long metal shafts. An angelic-faced, voluptuous woman in a hooded yellow cloak worked on a computer in the background. Her lustrous blonde hair cascaded down onto the table.

The character of Dorian, played by an actor named Ricardo Sargento responded, "Yeah, I was wondering where the monkey came from." The character of Dorian wore a dark grey business suit, a light brown shirt, with a thin black-red-and-gold-striped tie.

Lilith asked, "So where the hell were you anyway? What was it like?"

Dorian considered for a moment, collecting his thoughts carefully. "That's the thing. I recognized you guys, but it was like the past, or a different timeline maybe. I was somebody different, but I wasn't aware of it. I had this mundane advertising job, and my wife was there, but she wasn't my wife in that reality. It looked like the same lab, but from maybe fifty years ago, but something was different, something was off. All the people were similar; you guys were there, but not quite the same. Like copies made on an old Xerox machine; little details were off, names were switched around, or the names sounded made up, as if someone had randomly just picked names from a TV show, or a book, or something. It was as if an AI computer program had tried to recreate our reality—and it was very good—but a person, only an actual person, mind you, would be able to notice the subtle differences. It was obviously created by some entity that believed the small details wouldn't be noticed. The question is, who exactly created this reality, and for what reason? Let me tell you, it was no dream, it was as real as anything I have ever experienced."

Both characters Eve and Lilith stared straight at Dorian, attempting to process the information, without saying a word. The scene ran on for a few more minutes. The director called for an end to the action. He liked what he saw, and told the actors they had done a great job. He brushed past Samantha and firmly grabbed hold of her behind. She jumped and scowled at the director. He laughed at her outrage, as he walked away satisfied, to have a cigar outside the building. Samantha stood stiffly with her arms folded in anger. Her rage-filled eyes followed the corpulent man as he waddled away.

Selena watched the blatant harassment, and seemed amused.

✷

Richard and Ed both walked up to the café within the bookstore. They each ordered, picked up their coffees and snacks, and found an empty table. They sat silently across from each other.

Ed picked up his ham and cheese breakfast sandwich and began munching on it. "If you're interested in this stuff, and I mean really interested, there's so much to tell you, and there might not be that much time."

Richard listened intently. He crunched on a chocolate biscotti, along with an enormous coffee. He took a large bite of it, and a swig of the very hot coffee. "What do you mean, not that much time?"

Ed finished chewing and responded, "You obviously haven't been watching the news. I'm referring to the giant death rock heading our way. You must know what I'm talking about."

"You mean that asteroid thing? What is the deal with that, anyway?"

Richard ate as Ed explained. "The deal is we're all screwed. I mean, not everybody, not the super VIPs, of course. If you happen to have a bunker a mile underground you might survive. It's not written in stone, of course, but it doesn't look good."

"If that's right, I mean if we're all going to be wiped out, it's weird, why aren't people panicking. You know, looting, rampaging, going nuts?"

Ed listened and smiled. "Simple...nobody believes anything is real anymore. Haven't you heard that we're actually living in a computer simulation? Everything is a conspiracy theory. You remember the year 2000 computer meltdown that never materialized? Then there was the Mayan calendar scare. Remember how the world was going to end on December 21, 2012? I'm ashamed to admit that even I was concerned about that one. People simply have Armageddon fatigue. Everything they see on TV is just entertainment—even the end of the world, for somebody—or something watching us, I guess. We live in a state of exponential change, and absolute chaos and confusion, my friend."

Richard took a long gulp of coffee, digesting both his food and Ed's ominous words. "I guess I kind of get that, after the big letdown of the 2012 doomsday thing. I understand that people aren't buying it anymore, but shouldn't the government be warning people, so they know it's real?"

Ed snickered good-naturedly. "Maybe in theory, but that's actually how we know it's really going to happen, that this one is actually going to smash us to bits. The fact is, there's nothing really to do, unless you have the billion-dollar underground bunker. What are the leaders going to say: we'll be okay but the rest of you are toast? What's the point in making everybody crazier than they already are? Anyway, as it gets closer the media will turn it into a big circus show. And yet, there is always the chance; nothing is ever absolute, so many variables. Even the most powerful computer can't factor everything in. There is always the matter of random fluctuation, the force that rules the universe."

Richard shook his head in disbelief. "But shouldn't the prime minister and the president or whatever be telling us the truth?"

Ed grinned. "It's not about truth anymore, my friend. Really, it never was. It's all about survival now, and the ones in power know it won't help them to get everybody excited. Better that they continue with their doomed lives, serving them. Schmucks like us, no offence, we might as well kiss our asses goodbye. Spend your money and have fun."

Richard sat staring out the window. He was chastened by the sobering explanation. It did nothing to alleviate his dark thoughts and anxious mood.

Edward sensed his discomfort. "Listen, friend, I'm really sorry if I bummed you out. Sometimes I can be a little callous, uncaring. I guess it comes with the territory of being a scientist. You know, we deal in cold hard facts."

"No, obviously this asteroid isn't your fault. I'm actually glad I know the truth."

CHAPTER 5

Asteroid Apophis continued on its deadly course towards Earth. It passed the outer planets and had now reached Jupiter. Astronomers and many astrophysicists the world over were busy frantically crunching numbers and possibilities. They were all hoping for some hidden, unknown variable. They searched for a loophole, or a reprieve from fate. Jupiter presented the last best chance for hope. The massive planet with its myriad moons possessed a powerful gravitational force, capable of nudging the asteroid from its current trajectory. The tiniest correction would save Earth from certain destruction.

✷

Samantha left the set and headed home to her apartment. They had only completed the one scene, so she still had most of the Saturday to enjoy. It was a cool, clear day as she drove north from the lakeside building. She felt a little hungry, so she stopped at her favourite bagel shop, Gryffe's, on Bathurst, just north of Lawrence. She parked and waited in line to enter the popular establishment.

An older Jewish woman stood in front of her speaking to her friend. "Can you believe it, Mavis? This really is the end of the world. Meh. My best years are behind me. I'm not too worried."

The other woman responded, "What about your kids? You're not worried about them?"

"I'm just kidding, I'm sure they'll figure out a way to stop this asteroid thing, they always do. And if not, I guess that's God's will. Who am I to question it?"

Samantha listened intently to the exchange. She was so focused on her work, and her chance meeting, the possible impending doom had slipped her mind completely. Her scene on the show had gone well. That was what really mattered, she told herself. There was no point in fretting over something she could not control, she thought. She eventually found herself at the front of the line, and ordered a dozen bagels and some garlic cream cheese.

She returned to her apartment and sat down with her bagels on the sofa. She began to replay the events of the morning. She felt unnerved by the lecherous director's unwanted advances. She was also very well aware that, as a minor character, she could ill afford to incur the wrath of the powerful man. She was angry at herself for not responding to the director's assault. Samantha sat down exhausted on the sofa and flipped on the TV, after checking her phone for messages. She again cautioned herself to contain her enthusiasm over Richard. Her wild imagination tended to overshoot her reality. Historically, Samantha had bad instincts with men.

She turned her attention to the news channel to divert her troubled mind. A petite, perky woman with perfect, short blonde hair and a tight red dress spoke excitedly. "This is day three of Asteroid Apophis Watch." A well-produced garish graphic display played out, replete with theme music. It showed an asteroid obliterating the Earth in a huge fireball. "We are now going live to a press conference with the president."

Samantha watched with interest, as the newly elected leader spoke slowly, carefully choosing his words. "People of the United States, and the Earth, please be assured that we are working around the clock, with top scientists from around the world to save our precious planet. We will beat this challenge, believe me."

The aged, weary-looking leader seemed overly optimistic to her. Samantha was unimpressed, and strangely unconcerned, like most of those around her. It all just somehow seemed unreal, like a popular show. The world could not really end, she thought. She assumed that the scientists would figure something out eventually, they always had in the past.

Samantha checked her phone again. She wondered why Richard had not responded to her text. She picked up the script for the next episode. She considered the fact that it might well be her last. She questioned the value of spending much time on the script. She wanted to do something other than just work, if the world were indeed ending. Yet, she did not want to end up jobless if somehow the disaster never arrived. She realized that the next episode was filming on location up north. She was looking forward to the change of pace, and staying in a fancy hotel. She had not vacationed in years. She was stuck in a comforting but deadening routine.

✷

The Indigo bookstore grew busier as the day progressed. News of the apocalyptic asteroid spread like an unknown virus through the populace. A feeling of anticipation, rather than panic, descended upon the city. The novelty of a near-death experience trumped all other concerns.

The two men continued their conversation in the bustling café. Richard remained transfixed by Edward's explanation of events. Ed was more than pleased to find an audience for his strongly held views. The two strangers were slowly beginning a tentative friendship.

Richard's phone chimed in his pocket. "I hate being one of those people that have to answer their phone all the time, but I really need to send a message, it's this woman I just met. Excuse me a minute."

Ed smiled broadly with no hint of offence taken. "Enough said, my friend, matters of the heart must always take precedence...even at the end of the world. Actually, especially at the end!"

Richard looked up, typing away with his thumbs. He explained his message. "I'm going to go out on a limb and change my coffee invitation to dinner. Probably should have just gone with the coffee date first, but what the hell, we may not have time for a second date, right?"

"You're absolutely right. You should definitely try and get to know her quickly. But listen, I know you're busy, we still have a lot to talk about, and who knows, this thing could still miss us. We're not completely doomed just yet. I have a lot to tell you about your insomnia problem. I may be able to help you there. I know this is going to sound strange, because we've just met, but why don't you drop by my place tomorrow...unless, of course, your night goes well." Ed grinned slyly.

Richard chuckled. "Let's not get ahead of ourselves here, it's just a first date. I think you are referring to a third date."

Ed laughed. "You know how these dinner dates can miraculously turn into breakfast dates. It could happen."

Richard nodded. "I think you gave me your business card; we should talk some more."

Ed took the card and wrote down his cell phone number. Richard accepted the card back and glanced at the digits. In turn, Richard offered his own business card, emblazoned with the eight-pointed Aldebaran logo. He got up from the table. "Well, okay then, it's been a pleasure. Kind of a scary pleasure. Not you, of course, I mean the dose of cold reality. Anyway...see you tomorrow, maybe."

Ed smiled broadly. "You will not be disappointed, I promise you. What have you got to lose?" He took one long last swig of coffee and tossed the empty cup in the trash. Ed sat alone, staring at a black raven, pecking insistently on the window of the café. Its tiny black eyes stared back at him knowingly.

Samantha was secretly hoping that a romance would blossom with Richard. She finished her bagel lunch and took her second mug of coffee into the bedroom. As she dressed, she heard her phone ping. She was pleased to see that she had received a new message. She excitedly picked it up and scanned it. She read that Richard had invited her to an upscale Italian restaurant. She quickly replied that she would be there at six. As soon as she had sent it, she regretted seeming overly eager. She worried that Richard would think she had been desperately waiting for his text. She reasoned with herself, and realized that she was likely overthinking the matter, as often was the case.

Samantha generally wore what was comfortable, rather than fashionable. Sifting through her closet, she searched for an appropriate dress. She wanted to look attractive, without being too revealing. She finally decided upon a sky-blue summer dress with a floral pattern. She definitely wanted to avoid her usual frumpy and plain appearance.

Thankfully, Richard had supplanted Selena in her mind. Yet Selena was growing increasingly aggressive towards her, and Samantha could see no easy solution. She continued to primp in front of the mirror. She could not clearly recall her last real date. It was long ago and utterly forgettable.

✷

Ed left the busy bookstore café after finishing his beverage. His mood was brightened by the chance encounter with Richard. He also realized that the stranger might well feature prominently in his plans. The sky was overcast with the threat of rain to come. He noticed an unusual sense of urgency in the air, as people seemed to scurry about like alarmed squirrels. The reality of what might lie ahead in their suddenly shortened future was slowly settling upon them. Ed perceived the subtle air of confusion and despair in the mist. He expected that the inevitable looting and general madness was still to come. The professor felt powerless in the face of such a biblical threat from the heavens.

Ed rode the subway back to his College Street neighbourhood. He soaked in the suddenly strange surroundings. The streets were busier than usual. Stockpiling of provisions and escape plans had begun, thought Ed. He replayed in his mind every relevant disaster movie. The cinematic view was always chaos in the face of annihilation, but in reality, the feeling was different. A sense of cynicism and jaded indifference pervaded. The people needed visual proof, and nobody trusted scientists anymore, thought Ed. Conspiracy theorists ruled many minds. Nobody wanted to appear foolish by believing once again in the improbable doomsday scenario. Still, he reasoned, there would always be the extreme survivalists. They were immune to the weary malaise that prevailed everywhere. They had solemnly accepted their doom, and were pleased to finally be proven correct.

There were stories circulating that some had fled to distant northern mountains to escape their fate. The vast majority simply continued their daily, mundane existence, stuck in an endless, scripted loop. They washed their cars and cleaned their clothes, oblivious to the fact that it no longer mattered. Most could not actually imagine their own death. It was better for some to live in blissful ignorance, thought Ed.

✷

Richard was fascinated by Ed's ominous tidings, and his sobering dose of cold reality. He followed the story on the news like most people, with only casual interest. His daily life remained unchanged by the imminent threat from above. He wondered how his actions might change, if the end was certain. Would he suddenly quit his job and travel the world, spending all his money, he thought? He reasoned that the time remaining to him was insufficient. Then again, there was always a chance of escape, no matter how far-fetched and improbable. Even at the darkest hour, thought Richard, a sliver of hope always remained. It was all a matter of imagination, and employing the entire extent of one's mind.

Richard continued to muse about his fate as he made his way home from the bookstore. He descended into the subway and rode it to the Old Mill stop. He immediately noticed a difference in the people around him. Furtive glances and suspicious gazes had replaced the usual blank expressions. He picked his phone out from his pocket. He noticed with delight that Samantha had accepted his invitation to have dinner. He had given the date a great deal of thought, and decided upon a restaurant he had often frequented. He had dined at the Italian restaurant Gamberoni with his ex-wife, Elizabeth, many times. It was located at Yonge Street and Roslin Avenue. It was one of the older places in town, and served authentic Italian dishes. It possessed a traditional, old steak-house feel, with heavy ornate chairs and red velvet walls. Richard always chose quality food over trendy style.

After showering and shaving, he picked out something to wear for his date. He had a bad tendency to overdress, so he consciously strove to look more casual. He wanted to avoid appearing stuffy and old. He decided upon an emerald green shirt with a brown jacket, but no tie. It was not a job interview, he thought. He considered the fact that in truth, it really was a sort of job interview. He found first dates to be excruciatingly stressful. It was difficult, he thought, to appear relaxed in the face of intense scrutiny.

His phone chirped. He leaned down to pick it up. It was a text from his attractive co-worker Maria. He read the text with disinterest, realizing that he had completely dismissed Maria from his mind. The text was asking him again about the weekend at the cottage. He responded politely, and untruthfully, that he had a work engagement. He wanted to remain on good terms with her. In case his date with Samantha flopped, he wanted to keep Maria as a backup plan.

Richard finished preparing for his date as he absently flipped through the TV channels. All the news programs featured non-stop coverage of the possible asteroid strike. He noted how the most strident of the American channels had altered the title of the story from "Asteroid Apophis Watch" to "Doomsday Watch."

Richard watched a reporter on location from Mumbai, India.

"Here in Mumbai, worshippers are seen praying to Shiva, god of destruction. Throngs of people have left their homes in hope of finding divine intervention. Despite the government's warnings to stay calm, here in India, there have been reports of looting and rioting, but police are still very much in control of the situation."

The camera fixed on a magnificent stone Hindu temple. The many-armed golden god Shiva seemed to dance in the bright sunshine. The submissive, huddled masses awaited her divine wisdom. It was an ancient knowledge, far older than that from the West, and far less forgiving.

✱

Ed exited at his subway stop and wandered aimlessly through the streets. There were more people about than usual. Ed looked around at the anxious faces suddenly torn away from their mundane lives. He wondered how many might actually survive. On his way home, he decided upon a visit to his friend Max. He walked several blocks to his colleague's abode. Max lived in an unremarkable urban apartment complex at Gerrard and Bay Street. Ed walked through the front door and searched for his friend's name on a large blackboard. He buzzed on the entry button and waited.

Max quickly answered, "Who is it? Is that you, Ed? What do you need from me now?"

"Jeez...can't a guy come visit his friend at the end-times of the world?"

"Possible end, get it right."

Ed listened and replied, "We'll continue this discussion when I get up there." Ed waited for the door to open and entered the lobby. He pushed the button for the elevator and waited only a few moments for it to arrive. The doors opened to an elderly woman of Middle Eastern descent.

Ed smiled broadly. "Good morning...or I guess it's good afternoon now."

The deeply wrinkled face scowled up at him. "What's good about it? How many mornings do we have left? We're all doomed you know, doomed!"

Ed's sunny smile remained, his bright mood undiminished. "As you wish! You have a nice day now!" His optimism and good nature seemed only to infuriate the aged crone. She limped away, muttering under her breath.

Ed took the short ride up the elevator and walked down the old, dingy hallway. He opened the door to Max's apartment. "Just had a brief encounter with one of your neighbours, a thoroughly unpleasant old Arab woman."

Max looked over. "That might have been Mrs. Akbar. She's sour at the best of times. I imagine she's even more difficult during an apocalypse."

Ed picked up on their earlier conversation. "Right you are, my punctilious chum. What is the latest estimated chance of a direct impact?"

"It keeps changing, and of course it depends upon whom you ask. Most people at work are pegging it at ninety per cent now."

The two old friends sat across from each other on the brown leather sofa. Max was drinking coffee. "Do you want one?"

Ed shook his head. "Probably not. I've had four already today; don't want to overdo it. Anyway, I was hanging around the bookstore, you know, Indigo, and I ran into an interesting fellow. His name was Richard. We had a remarkable conversation."

"What did you two discuss, exactly?"

"Oh, you know. Of course, the asteroid came up, but he was also very interested in my work, and how it relates to insomnia. The guy has a terrible time with it. Anyway, I invited him over to my place tomorrow."

Max was incredulous. "Do you think that wise? I mean, with the delicate nature of your experiments?"

Ed shrugged. "What's the worst that could happen? You forget, there may not be much time left. And this Richard fellow may be exactly what the doctor ordered."

"What the hell does that mean exactly?"

"Don't you worry, my excitable friend, I've got everything under control." Ed proceeded to change the subject. "I've been thinking a lot about my monkey...I mean, where exactly did he go? Where is he now?"

Max shrugged. "Maybe it was all some kind of mass hallucination? Who knows? Maybe some alternate dimension, whatever that means."

"Okay, okay. But stay with me here. What if I actually saved the little guy?"

Max scowled. "What the hell do you mean?"

"This is what I mean. That monkey, wherever he is, is not going to get blown to smithereens by that rock. Think about it!"

Max stared at Ed for a moment. "You know, you could be on to something there, that is, if he's still alive."

"That's the thing, we know he's still alive, you saw with your own eyes on that monitor. So he's somewhere, just not here, or now."

"Okay, I guess I see what you're getting at. And assuming it's the same monkey, but what's your point?"

"My point? Escape, my friend, escape from certain doom. Now we have an exit strategy, I just have to work out the details."

Max simply stared in bewilderment at his brilliant, demented colleague.

✷

Richard left his house early for his dinner date. He wanted to do everything possible to make a good impression. As he drove, his strange encounter with the professor at the bookstore revolved around his mind. Richard arrived fifteen minutes early to the uptown Italian restaurant. The city streets were busier than usual. Piercing police sirens echoed everywhere through the night air. He parked his car and exited. Richard stared up into the clearing night sky, wondering if he might spy the asteroid. He glanced down nervously at his watch. His expectations were very high. He felt exhausted as was typical, but his excitement spurred him on.

He continued to look around nervously until he spied a woman walking slowly towards him. She wore a beautiful light blue, floral summer dress. She wore white high heels as she sauntered towards him. He immediately recognized her as Samantha. She smiled broadly and warmly as she spotted Richard standing by the entrance. As she approached, Richard suddenly became anxious as to the proper greeting. Would a kiss on the cheek be appropriate at this point, he wondered? He thought better of it, and instead decided upon a gentle handshake. Her slender, small hand felt warm and soft.

Richard led her tentatively to the door, barely touching her back. "Well, thanks for showing up, first off."

Samantha drank in the stately Rococo Italian ambience of the establishment. "Wow, this is beautiful. Look at the chandeliers. I've never heard of this place."

He smiled as the host took them to a special table that he had chosen beforehand. It sat in a secluded, romantically lit alcove. The very young, dark-haired girl gave them both menus.

Samantha squinted at the menu. "It's a little dark in here, I may need help with the menu. I assume you've been here before."

Richard smiled back. "I chose this spot specially. I look more attractive in low light. All part of my grand plan."

Samantha chuckled slightly. The restaurant was uncharacteristically empty. It made them both a little ill at ease. Richard looked around the large room. "I guess people are staying in? Must be the whole end-of-the-world thing."

Samantha was very nervous, but feigned composure. "So, is this your go-to place for all your first dates?" She was being deliberately facetious and testing him.

Richard took the bait. "Yes, once you are added to my vast haram. Honestly, you are only the second woman I have ever taken here, my ex was the other."

Samantha looked up from her menu, sensing his reticence to discuss it further. "I guess this is the part of the date where we both spill all our relevant info. So, you've been married before then? We don't need to talk about it, if you don't want to."

"It feels like so long ago when we were together, but it wasn't that many years. I don't really want to get into all the gory details, let's just say things ended abruptly...and badly."

Samantha smiled with a warm, understanding gaze. "Yikes. Gory? You didn't chop her up into little pieces, did you?"

Richard smiled. "No, it wasn't like that."

Samantha continued, "You don't have to tell me your whole life story, as long as you're not still holding a torch for her." Samantha was considerate of his feelings, but wanted to know exactly where she stood from the beginning.

"I can tell you, in no uncertain terms, that any torch that might have existed, was burned out long ago. I caught her on top of my best friend...I came home early from work one day, it's such a cliché, but I guess it happens." Richard shrugged in embarrassment, having exposed a weakness.

"I think it's pretty common these days. I had one of those...not with my best friend mind you, but the same kind of thing." The two very slowly began to build a rapport, and a sense of ease developed between them.

Richard changed the subject. "What do you think about this crazy rock headed towards us?"

They were interrupted by the server. "Hi, guys, I'm Tabitha. I'll be your server tonight. The wild mushroom risotto is excellent. We also have a special on chicken parmigiana. It's really good. I eat it all the time. I'll let you guys look at the menus, just let me know when you're ready to order. Can I get you something to drink to start?"

Richard looked over at Samantha to try to gauge her response to alcohol. "Do you drink wine? Let me order a bottle." She nodded in agreement. Richard was pleased that they at least had this in common. Richard picked up the wine menu. "Do you like shiraz? This Australian one is pretty decent, it's what I usually drink."

Samantha knew the brand. "That's the one with the yellow label and the kangaroo, right? I like that."

The waitress smiled. "I'll be right back with that."

Richard deliberately tried not to notice the shapely waitress as she walked away.

Samantha grinned. "You know, I'm not one of those women who cries when her date looks at another woman, she is way hotter than me, although young enough to be your daughter, probably."

Richard laughed, carefully crafting a response. He was relieved to see how easygoing and relaxed Samantha seemed to be. "Why would I need to look at another woman? The most beautiful one is at my table."

Samantha accepted the compliment graciously. "Why, thank you. Of course, there seems to be only two women here." She returned her attention to the dinner selections. "What's good here?"

Richard studied the menu. "I'm pretty boring. I always order the same thing." He leaned over and pointed to a particular item. "The lemon veal piccata is excellent. Not everybody likes veal; I sometimes get the eggplant. Choose wisely, though. Who knows, this might be your last really good Italian meal."

Samantha ordered the wild mushroom and chicken risotto, and Richard ordered the veal piccata. Samantha understood his implication. "Right, you did ask me about the end of the world thing didn't you. It's so weird, you'd think we'd be running around like crazy, chicken with its head cut off kind of thing, but here we are calmly having dinner. Then again, it might not hit us, so what are you going to do? It's not like there's anything we can do about it."

As if to punctuate their discussion, there was a loud sound of glass shattering out on the street. It was followed by several blaring sirens.

Richard barely noticed the cacophony outside. He was mesmerized by his dinner date. He listened carefully before replying, "Strangely, the whole asteroid thing hasn't really hit me yet, no pun intended. It hasn't affected my sleep, anyway. I have a pretty severe insomnia problem."

"Really? How strange. So, we have that in common. I can never seem to get more than three hours sleep, sometimes less. You would think you'd be sleeping less with all that's going on."

Richard nodded and replied eagerly. "Really? You have insomnia, too? You certainly don't look as if you do. I mean, I always look like crap. But you? It's just a little hard to believe. The other day at work, I was so exhausted, I actually started hallucinating. Sometimes I black out for hours. Half the time, I'm not quite sure if I'm awake or dreaming."

Samantha answered, "No, mine is really bad, although I guess I haven't started hallucinating yet. Although maybe it's a little better lately. I just started on a new show. I've got one less thing to worry about now."

"Oh, you're an actress? I should have known. The first day I met you, on the road, I knew I had seen your face before. Is there something I would have seen you in lately?"

Samantha smiled broadly. "Yeah, I've done a few commercials. I did one for Canadian Tire last year. But anyway, I'm doing this show called *Outer Edge* right now. It's sci-fi, maybe it's not your thing."

"You're on *Outer Edge*? That's a really great show. Yeah, I've watched it. Who are you on the show?"

Samantha replied, "Well, of course it hasn't aired yet, they're filming the new season now."

"Wow, I can't believe I'm having dinner with a movie star."

Samantha smiled at the compliment. "Hardly! But what about you? You're a big advertising executive. How did you get interested in that?"

"I'm not sure I'd call myself big...I'm doing okay. I got a promotion a few years back. I remember watching a show when I was young. The main character worked in advertising. It seemed like a fun kind of job. You get to manipulate people's minds."

Samantha grinned. "How do I know you're not manipulating me right now, with your awesome powers of persuasion?"

Richard replied, in a completely deadpan tone, "You don't. Anyway, I've been with Aldebaran corporation for over a decade. It's a gigantic company. I think they have a piece of just about everything."

Samantha was fascinated by the subject of his work. "I know, it seems like they're everywhere. Maybe they're watching us right now."

Richard nodded in agreement. "It wouldn't surprise me, but seriously, it's a strange company. It's a German company that was started after the war by a woman named Maria Orsic. Other than that, very little is known about the firm. The upper management, their headquarters, it's all very mysterious. It's a private company, so they don't have to divulge anything to the public." Richard proceeded to change the subject. "So, are you getting your car fixed? You know it won't cost you anything. Did my guy call you?"

"Yeah, the body shop is busy though. He can't get it in until next week, by then it probably won't matter."

"Oh, there will be a next week, somewhere. Just maybe not here, and not for us."

✷

Ed and Max spent the rest of that Saturday afternoon in Max's apartment, discussing immediate plans for the future. Max was frustrated. "How did I suddenly get roped into being your personal henchman?"

Ed chortled. "Henchman? We're not exactly trying to pull off some grand heist here. Listen, you know I can't trust anybody but you. And as I explained, this might really be our only chance of escape."

Max shook his head furiously. "I know you told me your plan, but it still doesn't make any sense. And if we have to steal equipment from my lab, it is kind of a heist, isn't it?"

"I believe that technically, a heist requires an assembled team, like in *Ocean's Eleven*. This is a simple temporary appropriation. Much less complicated. We'll return it as soon as we're done. And since we're all probably doomed anyway, who cares? Haven't you heard the sirens out there? It's basically every man for himself." Max reluctantly agreed to his friend's admonitions, as he always did.

They both left Max's apartment and rode the subway to Ed's house to pick up his car. The plasma-field generator in Ed's basement was damaged in his last experiment. Ed spoke as he drove towards the university. "Are you sure you still have security access for the equipment? Has it even been repaired properly?"

Max replied with some consternation, "I have the highest security... bloody hell! Who's going to stop me? Anyway, things have become rather loosey-goosey this past week. Yeah, it actually wasn't that badly damaged; it's in better shape than yours, anyway. Between the two of them, we should be able to get something rigged up."

Ed drove his old, yellow Volvo wagon haphazardly through the empty streets. Many in the city had packed up and left, awaiting the end in some far-flung wilderness. Most had simply given up, and stopped going to work, or anywhere. Ed proceeded to elaborate on his complex experiments. "Max, you've never actually used DMT or ayahuasca before, have you?"

"You know I'm not interested in your shaman medicine-man, witch-doctor nonsense."

Ed shrugged. "It's really difficult to explain the things I've seen and experienced on these drugs to somebody who's never tried it. It's like trying to explain colours to a blind man. The things, or beings I've met, not really sure what to call them—I tell you, my friend, it's more than just a drug trip. It's another reality altogether. The problem is, it never lasts long enough. That's where the plasma generator comes into play. The intense plasma field seems to amplify the effects of these compounds upon the pineal gland."

Several police cars whizzed by them, as well as a fire truck. A huge plume of black smoke poured ominously from the top of a nearby office building. The evening air crackled with an electrical anticipation.

"They say animals know what's going one long before people do." He pointed up to the sky, and stopped the car. Vast black flocks of birds darkened patches of the sky. Suddenly a huge black raven descended onto the windshield of the yellow Volvo. It stared down curiously at the occupants and began pecking insistently upon the glass. Ed attempted to shoo the bird away with a swipe of his large hand. It finally flew away as they he slowly took his foot off the brake and continued driving.

Max nodded. "Anyway, I see what you're trying to say. I guess that's something you really need to experience for yourself. Who's to say what's true anymore? None of this whole asteroid thing seems real, for some reason."

Ed listened carefully as he drove. "You going to the university on Monday?"

"I suppose so, we should know pretty soon if we're truly doomed. I read something about the government's last-ditch effort to save us. That should be interesting."

✷

Richard and Samantha both finished their delicious Italian meals. The waitress arrived with a dessert tray. Featured prominently in the centre was a very impressive cake. It featured layers of soft white cake interspersed with sweet whipped cream and fresh strawberries. It was covered in a bright red fondant, with white polka dots of whipped cream.

Richard exclaimed, "I'm completely stuffed, although that cake does look delicious!"

Samantha grabbed at her stomach to exaggerate the effect. "Me, too. I don't think I have room for dessert, unfortunately!"

Richard picked up the cheque and paid. He left a ridiculously generous tip. The server accepted it with great appreciation. "Are you sure you meant to leave a one hundred per cent tip?"

Richard shrugged. "Of course, what does money mean at this point?"

The beautiful young girl looked worried. "Do you really think this is the end? I mean, I told my father we should be getting ready to leave the city, but he told me there was no point."

Richard replied, "Well, who's to say? Anyway, thank you for staying open tonight. It was really an unforgettable meal, as always."

Samantha was mock impressed. "Wow, do you always tip so well? You know, I don't mind paying for half."

Richard shook his head. "No, this is partial payment for me running into you, remember?"

"So, this is a simple business arrangement?"

Richard shook his head. "Not to me, not at all."

They left the restaurant with Richard gently grasping Samantha's hand. The streets were eerily empty of people for a Saturday night. They walked towards her car. The sky above grew overcast. The night was now malevolent as grey clouds churned above. A monstrous black mass of birds moved above them. Samantha gazed up into the darkness. "On the news, they say we should be able to see the asteroid soon. It will be near Mars, maybe."

"How romantic. We're so lucky to be able to see the cause of our demise hurtling towards us!" Richard continued, "Yeah…sorry, I didn't mean to ruin the mood, but it's hard not to think about it right? Why am I laughing anyway? Shouldn't we be crying? I mean, why aren't we both looting and pillaging somewhere?"

Samantha appreciated his sense of the ridiculous. "I'm game if you are. You know, come to mention it, I do need a new TV, to watch as we get destroyed. Although honestly, you really don't look like the looting type."

Richard scowled. "You don't know me…yet. I'll have you know I've been in jail for looting many times, too many to count really," he said in a facetious tone.

Samantha was incredulous. "You may be many things, but a pillaging pirate is not one of them. I bet you've never even had a speeding ticket."

Richard, as if to contradict her taunt, spied a garbage can and grabbed it high above his head. He ran towards a high-end jewelry shop and stopped. The display case was resplendent with dazzling jewels.

Samantha ran up to him, laughing. "Okay, Mr. Jewel Thief, very funny. Now put the can down. We're not robbing this place. I don't feel like spending my last few days in jail, thank you."

Richard refused to put the can down. "I'm still thinking about it. You know, risk versus reward kind of thing."

Samantha smiled and looked down at the impressive collection of gems. She admired a deep, red ruby pendant, a dark blue sapphire necklace, and an exquisite yellow diamond ring. She studied the incredible treasures, imaging how they might look on her.

Richard stood, still with the can above his head. "See anything you like?" he said in a serious tone.

Samantha looked at the sparkling gems. "That yellow diamond ring is kind of nice. Maybe not though, let's wait a bit."

Richard reluctantly put the garbage can down and they walked away laughing.

They continued strolling along the empty streets. Richard was about to grab hold of Samantha's hand, when he noticed the dirt covering his own grubby hands. "Oh gross, now I have garbage hands. Didn't think that one through, I was just trying to get you a nice pair of diamond earrings to wear for the end of the world. You wouldn't want to show up in heaven looking like a peasant."

Samantha replied, "Oh absolutely, that is definitely the most important thing. Wouldn't want to be caught dead without fancy earrings. That would be terrible!" They arrived at Samantha's car. "Well... this is me."

Richard looked at the damage he had earlier caused. "Yes, your car and I are well acquainted." He was unsure of how to proceed. He did not wish to seem forward, but he also desperately wanted to kiss her. He decided to risk it. He slowly leaned in to kiss her cheek, with a soft embrace. Samantha turned her head and kissed him strongly on the lips. The connection grew as the kiss became more passionate. Soon the emotion overwhelmed them, and they pulled away simultaneously. Their eyes locked together in a timeless moment of transcendent bliss.

Richard smiled to break the awkward silence that had descended upon them. "Wow, it will be tough to top that one...I mean ever..."

Samantha was effervescent with joy. "I would love to try, but maybe not tonight, I have to be up super early tomorrow. The show I'm on, they have a location shoot up in Muskoka, and I really need to try and catch a few hours of sleep. I'm sure you know what I mean."

"Are you implying that I might keep you up, not let you sleep?"

"If that kiss was any indication...then yes...that's exactly what I'm saying." Samantha kissed him gently on the cheek and stepped into her car. "You make sure to call me, not until later on in the day, though. I won't have my phone on set."

Richard was elated by their extraordinary kiss. "Don't worry about that, you'll see me again, very soon, I hope. Have fun in cottage country. Hope you don't get eaten alive up there. You know, bears and stuff."

Samantha started her car and drove slowly away as Richard stood watching. He walked slowly back to his own car. He stared up at the overcast night sky. The clouds dulled the view, but a few bright stars were visible. He squinted up towards Mars, searching for the huge celestial projectile headed towards him.

CHAPTER 6

Max and Ed arrived at the campus late Saturday night. It was a dark, overcast night, with the threat of rain. The university buildings were more empty than usual. Uncertainty and panic had also infected the campus. A sense of routine persisted for most people, who carried on with their mundane lives, oblivious to the dire reality around them. Most students were far too fascinated with the impending doom to concentrate on their studies. Many professors taught to nearly empty lecture halls. Some in the faculty had stopped showing up altogether. Neither Max nor Ed counted themselves amongst this group of pessimists.

The two conspirators left the car and moved stealthily toward the Physics building. They were careful to avoid the attention of security staff still patrolling the grounds. Max led the way.

"Okay, first we get the equipment, then I'll go get the van. Now we still have to be wary. Security is still working." He used a key card to enter the building. They walked through the barely lit, empty halls. Suddenly they heard footsteps. A beam of light shone against the opposite wall. Max whispered, "Quick! In here!" He rapidly swiped his card through a door security mechanism and swung open the door.

Ed was unaccustomed to such clandestine escapades. He banged his foot against the door as they entered.

A loud voice called out, "Hello? Is somebody there?" The portly, middle-aged security guard waddled down the hallway. He shone his flashlight into the room. The two intruders hid behind the door. Max was terrified as he held a finger to his lips. Satisfied by his search, the guard ambled away, muttering, "What the hell do I care? Rob the place blind if you want, won't make no difference to nobody anyhow."

Max stood up. "Well, that was close. Let's grab that dolly and load this stuff up quick."

They loaded the heavy, expensive equipment and carefully moved it to a loading bay. Max left and returned with a dark blue van emblazoned with the university's insignia. Security seemed to have gone for the night. They loaded the scientific instruments into the van. Max drove the van back to Ed's home, with his colleague following close behind in the old yellow Volvo. They arrived at the house and unloaded the equipment down into the basement. Max had never been down to Ed's very secretive lab.

"Good lord, man...this is some serious Dr. Frankenstein shit going on here. No wonder you've never shown me this place!"

Ed shrugged innocently. "A man's got to do what a man's got to do. Anyway, it's all in the name of science, right?"

"I'm sure that's just what Josef Mengele said."

"Gee, I don't think I'm quite there yet."

They continued to install the plasma-field generator. Ed was the expert in this area. "This baby can kick out ten times the power of the one I have. The trick is to find the sweet spot between frying your brain like an egg and complete escape." Max shook his head angrily. "I hope you're not considering actually doing this to yourself? You must know that I refuse to be a party to that."

Ed appeared perturbed. "Max, seriously, what difference does it make at this point? I mean if we're all soon dead anyway, what's the harm?"

Max slowly considered his words. "Well, when you put it that way, I guess it makes a sort of sense, but only if we really are doomed for sure."

"Damn right! Anyway, I'm exhausted and hungry, what say we order a pizza, and down a bottle of something."

"Do you think any place is still delivering pizza?"

"God, I hope so. If not, we might as well be dead." Ed phoned a multitude of establishments. Not one of them answered the phone. Everyday practices were falling by the wayside. They made do with stale leftovers and pantry scraps.

Following a thoroughly unsatisfying meal, they each retired for the night. Ed called out to his friend, "Are you sure you don't want to sleep in the guestroom?"

Max was already half-asleep. "No, I'm good here."

Ed retired to his bedroom after brushing his teeth. Max slumped onto the sofa and immediately fell into a deep sleep.

✱

Richard drove his car that Saturday night in a state of blissful elation. Finally, somebody had driven the painful memory of his ex-wife, Elizabeth, from his mind. He drove through the cool night air with the windows down, in no particular direction. In his mind, he replayed the memory of that perfect kiss with Samantha. He felt too energized to sleep, even if that were possible for him. He drove aimlessly through the sparsely populated streets. His mind wandered back to a conversation about Samantha's work. She had mentioned that the set was down on the waterfront, in an old, repurposed nineteenth-century factory building. The location piqued Richard's curiosity. Richard knew the city well, and drove south on Yonge Street towards the set of the TV show.

He drove up to the lot and parked. The place was empty. He emerged from his sleek black sedan, and surveyed the location. He immediately noticed the faded yellow, eight-pointed star emblazoned on the building. He thought it very strange that it was the exact same logo of the Aldebaran corporation, where he worked. He recognized the image as the star of Ishtar, and he wondered about the connection. Richard felt an odd sensation, as he gazed at the familiar motif. He experienced a sense of déjà vu, as his suddenly weary mind began to wander. He felt as though something or someone were trying to communicate some crucial piece of information meant only for him. The unsettling sensation filled him with an icy dread. His buoyant mood vanished, as the reality of his dire situation struck him hard. The idea of complete annihilation overwhelmed him. He reflected on the irony of finally meeting a possible true love, only to have it quickly snatched away. He struggled with the realization, but could not fully grasp it. His mind raced frantically, as he searched for a solution, or some type of escape. He returned to his black Ford Falcon and drove back home.

Richard opened the door to his house. He was immediately overcome with exhaustion. He struggled to regain the sense of joy he had felt earlier in the evening. He willfully forced the image of the deadly asteroid out of his mind. He prepared for bed as he thought again about his magical date with Samantha. The clouds of dread in his mind slowly drifted away. He picked up the phone from his bedside table to check for any new messages from Samantha. He decided to send a text to her. He read it over once, and sent it. He returned the phone and attempted to calm his mind. He prayed for sleep, and for a miracle.

✷

Samantha drove home that Saturday night filled with the promise of new love. She failed to notice several burning cars on the side of the street, as well as the now constant blare of sirens. She exited her vehicle and entered her apartment building. She felt as though she were walking on air. She felt truly happy for the first time in recent memory. It was such an unusual emotion for her that it felt uncomfortable. Her mind resisted the urge to feel free, and let go of the comforting routine of sadness. Her more prudent half suggested calm. Still, the childlike joy was freeing to her soul. Her happiness recalled cherished Christmas memories. She recalled a Christmas morning at the age of six, when possibilities were endless, and time stretched out before her without limit. She remembered the scent of sugar cookies baking in the oven, and wrapping paper strewn across the floor. A tall tree with brightly lit, multicoloured lights stood in the living room. She knew such unbridled passion could not last. She imagined that ruin and disappointment lay ahead, but she indulged herself nonetheless. She held very high hopes for her romance with Richard. She desperately hoped that he felt the same way towards her.

Samantha shook herself from her romantic reverie as she thought about the challenging day ahead of her. She lay in bed staring at her ceiling, daydreaming and replaying her romantic encounter with Richard in her mind. She sat up in bed, trying to calm her enraptured mind. She was far too excited to sleep, despite her understanding of its necessity. She sat pointlessly for another twenty minutes before abandoning her search for sleep. She walked out to the living room and flipped on the TV. She quickly checked on Google maps to calculate the driving time. She concluded that she had to depart from the city no later than 6 a.m.

Samantha put her phone down and absently flipped through the channels. She found her usual news channel, which featured constant news of the impending disaster. A terrifying graphic of a massive asteroid, and then a burning, destroyed planet, filled the screen. A deep voice intoned, "*Asteroid Watch. Countdown to Doomsday! Stay tuned for the latest updates.*" A commercial came on. It was an ad for the Aldebaran corporation. Samantha recognized the name as the place Richard had mentioned during dinner. She thought it an odd coincidence to see the strange advertisement, and the unique eight-pointed yellow-star logo of the company. She watched as a seemingly endless series of experts opined on the subject of their collective demise. Professors of astrophysics, sociology, economics, and others debated and explained in excruciating detail what might lay ahead. Oddly, the more she watched, the less real it seemed, as if it were nothing more than a long running episode of some tired old program.

The talking heads on TV continued, "*Here are highlights from the president's press conference this afternoon.*" The image of a gravely serious politician emerged on the screen. "*Please be assured that we are doing everything humanely possible to avert this disaster. This government is working together with experts from around the world to solve this problem. We aren't sunk yet, not by a long shot. God bless America!*" Samantha remained unconvinced, despite similar assurances from her own prime minister. He was also counselling an unreasonable calm. Samantha easily saw through their glib, empty promises. They would be soon be safe in their impenetrable, luxurious underground bunkers, she thought. She turned off the TV with a heavy sigh and returned to bed. With great effort, she forced herself to sleep.

✷

Ed bolted upright from his bed that Sunday morning. He was full of excitement and determination. He had carefully planned out the day in advance. The grim and menacing face of Aleister Crowley glared at him from the bedroom wall. Ed jumped out onto the floor and threw on his official Hogwarts burgundy robe. He bound out to the living room, where his friend Max was still fast asleep on the sofa. "Get up, sleepy head! Time's a-wasting, my friend!"

The groggy scientist sat up and reached for his glasses. "Uh...what the hell time is it?"

"It's 6 a.m. You sit still, while I brew us a pot of strong coffee." Ed walked over to the open kitchen. He set about making the coffee, as he grabbed a granola bar from a basket. He munched loudly as he spoke, "You know, what we really need is another monkey."

Max shook his head. "No...no, we don't have time for that, we could all be gone in days."

"Good point. If not a monkey, how about something slightly higher up the evolutionary ladder? Hear me out. So you remember I mentioned this guy I met yesterday, Richard? He's interested in a lot of things, in what we're doing, and I think he might be just what we're looking for here." Max watched as his exuberant colleague ran to the bedroom. Ed returned with a business card. "Yeah, here he is. This Richard, he's an advertising man, but don't hold that against him. He works for the Aldebaran corporation. That can't be just a coincidence, if I even believed in them. No, clearly, we were meant to meet. He's fascinated by my work, and apparently the guy is a severe insomniac."

Max shook his head in disagreement. "No way. If you think you're going to experiment on a perfect stranger, that's nuts!"

Ed listened, and continued. "You're right, of course, and I'm not talking about the full meal deal here, I mean we have to give him a taste first. Then, if he's okay with that, he might be ready to take the big leap."

"What exactly are you suggesting then?"

Ed took a long swig of coffee from his huge *Doctor Who* Dalek mug. He grabbed a chicken wing. "I'm not going to give him the plasma-field treatment, just my special dreamland cocktail. We'll see how he does with that first."

"Dreamland cocktail?" Max said quizzically.

"Yeah, that's just what I call my proprietary blend: extreme doses of DMT, melatonin, and ayahuasca."

"So, you want to turn him into a drug addict?"

"No, just an adept, like me." Ed finished munching on the leftover chicken and picked up his phone.

✸

Samantha was conflicted as the alarm went off at 5 a.m. It seemed foolhardy to attempt such a long drive in such dire circumstances, she thought. She immediately checked her phone for any new messages. There was a message about her schedule for the next morning. It stated that the call time was 11 a.m. She was also delighted to see that Richard had texted her. It read, "*Magical night with a magical woman. So lucky for a dumb monkey like me to meet such a wonderful person. It will not be our last. Can't wait to see you again.*"

Samantha smiled wistfully, wondering if that truly was to be their last night together. She quickly dressed and motivated herself for the challenging day that lay ahead. Selena, the star of the show had offered a ride in her limousine, but Samantha had politely declined the offer. Selena was increasingly brazen in her romantic overtures towards Samantha. The lead actress was utilizing her superior position to gain power over her. The difficult situation was growing more troublesome, but Samantha doggedly hid her displeasure.

Samantha slept a little better than usual, but her mind was still foggy. She poured herself a cup of strong coffee, and sat down with a toasted bagel and cream cheese. She flicked on the TV. The news channels continued with their relentless coverage of the impending doom. A darkly serious middle-aged male newscaster declared, "*The prime minister stated today, in an emergency session of parliament, that every possible effort was being made to divert or destroy the asteroid. He was furiously questioned by the opposition, who were attempting to ascertain contingency plans for mass evacuations.*" Samantha watched for another minute, and then turned off the TV. The news had become tiresome, she thought, like a favourite program grown stale. Samantha poured herself a large coffee in her travel mug. She put away her dishes, grabbed her suitcase, and left the apartment.

Samantha walked towards her car. She was startled as she looked up. The asteroid Apophis was now clearly visible in the sky overhead. It glowed like a bright beacon in the early morning light. Although she was clearly aware of the imminent threat, seeing the actual object was jarring. It was difficult to imagine the all-encompassing destructive power it possessed.

Samantha started up her still-damaged white VW. The long drive north to cottage country in Muskoka lay ahead of her. She gazed out her window at the chaos and confusion around her. In the span of few days, the temperament of the populace had grown desperate. People had given up hope. It reminded Samantha of a zombie apocalypse movie, or some other such dystopian horror film. Garbage was now piling up on the streets, and essential services were shutting down. Many people continued with their everyday lives. Only society's upper echelon might survive. The rest, thought Samantha, would be gone and forgotten. Considering the circumstances, the traffic headed up north was not as bad as she would have expected. Most of those escaping the city had done so earlier. The stragglers were still pointlessly pulling trailers full of useless belongings. They were told that salvation lay in the mountains, or at least in the far north.

Samantha arrived at the luxurious chalet-style Deerhurst resort in Muskoka. She arrived on time with ten minutes to spare. Except for the television crew and actors, the hotel was nearly deserted. She saw the long line of massive transport trailers containing all manner of equipment. The director, Harvey, was standing on the grand steps of the impressive building. He noticed Samantha emerge from her vehicle. He put out his cigar and walked down to greet her. He threw his meaty paw over her shoulder and hugged her close. The unwanted intimacy caused her to cringe.

"Glad you could make it, sweetie, under these circumstances. Frankly, I'm a little surprised nearly everybody showed up."

Samantha reluctantly returned his warm greeting. "Well, the show must go on."

"Indeed! Wouldn't we all feel silly if it all turned out to be a false alarm or a hoax?" Samantha glanced up at the asteroid, clearly visible directly overhead, but said nothing. She nodded in mock agreement. He continued, "Anyway, Samantha, your room is on the second floor. There's Selena, I think you're right next to her."

She was not pleased by the news of the close quarters. She was even more distressed when she saw Selena walk towards her. "Hey, Sam. Good to see you. You never know who's going to show up. Let me help you with that, it looks like we're going to be neighbours, so follow me."

Samantha could not reasonably refuse the offer for help, but was nonetheless apprehensive. She replied meekly, "Thanks, good to see you again. I just have the one bag here. You lead the way." She then retrieved her phone from her purse and sent a quick message to Richard, notifying him of her safe arrival. She dutifully followed behind the dark sultry woman as she walked up the stairs of the exclusive, five-star resort.

✷

Richard awoke to the jarring sound of his cell phone ringtone. His fitful night was plagued by disturbing, troubling dreams. He lay for a moment, ignoring his phone. He stared at the ceiling, attempting to visualize his nightmares. His mind reviewed the disparate impressions stuck in his psyche, as they slowly dissipated in the morning light. He reached for the phone, hoping to hear Samantha's lovely voice. He did not recognize the number, but he accepted the call nonetheless. It was an unfamiliar voice on the other end of the call.

"Richard, you might not remember me, the guy from the bookstore. It's Ed."

Richard was slightly surprised to hear from the seemingly random acquaintance. "Right...Ed, of course, I remember. I was just expecting a call from somebody else."

"Somebody much better looking than me, right? It's that woman you mentioned."

"Yeah, pretty much, but anyway...what can I help you with? You need some advertising? You know, I don't think there's much point now, and what exactly could you be selling?"

"Yeah, well, not selling, but I do have a proposition for you. It's more about the apocalypse thing, and I guess it has something to do with your insomnia also. I may be able to help out there, but time's a-wasting, we need to act now."

"Good point. How can I help you?"

"If you recall, I did invite you to come over today. Okay, listen. If you're really interested in my work, my friend Max and I have an idea. It might be better if you came over. It's kind of a lot, the kind of thing you need to explain in person. I swear, it will be worth your time."

Richard was a little hesitant. "Sure, I suppose I could, I don't really have anything else planned today."

"Excellent. Also...do you think you could find a Tim's that's still open? We could really use some doughnuts. I'll pay you back."

Richard smiled. "You're a doughnut man, eh? Yeah, that sounds good. I could go for an apple fritter. Oh yeah, where is it you live? I think you mentioned it yesterday, but I forgot."

"I'm at 2037 College Street. It's a yellow house with an old yellow Volvo wagon out front. See you soon."

Richard ended the call. He grabbed a piece of paper and wrote down the address. He had absolutely no idea what the professor had in mind, but he was intrigued. His insomnia had relented somewhat in the face of his possible annihilation. His phone pinged as he noticed a new text message from Samantha. "*Can't wait to see you again...just arrived at the hotel in Muskoka.*"

Richard smiled as he thought about Samantha. The image of her face in his mind chased away his fears. He sent back a quick text outlining his plans for the day. He dressed in some casual weekend clothes. He wore an old pair of jeans and a grey University of Toronto T-shirt. He shuffled off to the kitchen to make coffee. The pungent aroma and sound of the slowly dripping liquid perked up his senses. He got ready to leave. He brushed his teeth and waited for the coffee machine to stop. He grabbed a travel mug and filled it with steaming coffee, and a little milk. He locked is house and stared up at the sky. Even in the morning daylight, the asteroid was clearly visible. He pulled out the piece of paper in his pocket with the address. He got into his car and thought quickly about where to stop for the doughnuts. He started the vehicle and headed toward Ed's house.

✷

Apophis's ultimate destination was now written in stone. The gravitational forces from the many celestial objects had failed to sway its deadly path in any way. There remained one last hope, as the leaders of the world's superpowers devised a final solution to destroy the celestial invader. The plan was to wait for the very last possible minute. The entire arsenal of the world's nuclear intercontinental ballistic missiles would then be simultaneously launched on an intercept course with the asteroid. Of course, such a risky scheme was entirely untested. They were relying completely upon the impossibly complex calculations of the world's top scientists. The prospect of success was slim, but it remained the only viable option.

✷

Samantha glanced at her phone as she walked up to her hotel room. The cavernous lobby was lush and warm with the smell of cedar and fresh trees all around. She glanced up at the cathedral ceilings. The room was filled with inviting brown leather sofas and chairs, decorated with Indigenous motif blankets. A huge brightly coloured hunting scene tapestry hung on the wall to the left. She looked around to see a single staff member at the desk. Presumably, the rest had not shown up, she reasoned.

She stopped as she heard her phone ping. Selena was by her shoulder, so close that she felt her hot breath on her neck. The imposing woman leaned over. "Is that your new lover? Did you finally get lucky? That's good timing. I could really go for one last roll in the hay. This apocalypse thing makes me so horny for some reason. What about you?"

Samantha smiled and shook her head. "Uh...I don't know... maybe?" She moved away awkwardly to gain some personal space. She read a new text from Richard. He explained that he was meeting with a new friend at a house on College Street. He finished the text by stating that he would call her later to elaborate, and that he could not wait to see her.

The two women approached the front desk clerk. The young woman had short brown hair and was generously proportioned. She wore a tightly fitting blue skirt and matching jacket, with a crisp white shirt. Her face beamed with an unnecessarily bright, forced smile. "So glad you could make it up here! It's so exciting having TV people here, imagine, in our little town!"

Selena smiled graciously. She lacked genuine warmth. "Oh sure, it's so beautiful up here! So many trees! Until the space rock of doom comes, of course! Then we'll all be dead. Well, most of us, anyway."

The front desk clerk turned up the volume of her smile. "Oh, you're being silly! God would never let that happen, not to everyone anyway. Here are your key cards. Hope you don't mind carrying your own bags up; as you can see, we're a little short-staffed!"

Selena smiled ingratiatingly, rolling her eyes. "Yeah, we're big girls, we'll manage."

They each grabbed their respective suitcases and walked away. Selena remarked sarcastically, "Don't you hate those cheery religious nutjobs? I mean, please, not everyone believes in God, right? Don't force your attitudes on me, you know?"

Samantha replied nonchalantly, "I don't know, I thought she was nice. At least she was trying, right?"

The two women rode the elevator up to the top floor of the hotel. They arrived at Selena's room first. Selena swiped her card and entered. "I'll see you later." She then winked mischievously.

Samantha simply smiled in response and continued to the next room. She was relieved to be rid of the salacious woman. She swiped her own key card and entered, throwing her suitcase on the bed. She flopped down, completely exhausted by the long drive. She admired the luxurious room. She realized that it was the finest hotel she had ever visited. The room was finely appointed with dark walls, and a huge king-sized bed. The calming scent of cedar permeated the surroundings. An abundant bouquet of brilliantly coloured flowers adorned the dresser. Upon the table was a generous basket of fruits, cheeses, and crackers. It was enclosed in a yellow Cellophane wrapper. A huge painting hung on the wall above the bed. She gazed at the curious woodland scene. It depicted a white rabbit racing across a forest floor, with a massive raven swooping down upon her. A sly looking red fox sat nearby, observing the chase.

Samantha unpacked her suitcase and put her clothes in the dresser. She hung up some blouses when she heard a knock on her door. She peered through the peephole. Reluctantly she opened the door. Selena stood expectantly at the entrance, waiting for an invitation. "You want to check out the hotel? We have a little while before call time."

Samantha was guarded and hesitant. "You know, I was in such a rush this morning, I actually didn't shower yet. I may take a quick one before we have to start.

Selena smiled. "Yeah, okay...you do that." Selena turned away and walked down the hall. Samantha shut the door quickly.

The brief, seemingly innocuous encounter left her feeling uncomfortable and anxious. Samantha gazed around at the finely decorated décor. The amenities felt all the more inviting out in the wilderness. A wide, fifty-two-inch TV hung on the wall across from the bed. She flicked it on as she undressed for her shower. The constant coverage of the looming asteroid strike continued unabated.

The grim-faced news anchor intoned, "*The president of the United States has approved the final plans for the massive missile launch that will happen in mere days. This remains the last, best for hope for humanity's survival.*"

Samantha did not find the news particularly depressing, although she wondered why. She had briefly considered leaving the city and heading up north like all the other lemmings, but thought better of it. If she had not just met Richard, she might well have gone ahead with it. If it really were the end, she thought, she did not want to spend her last day on Earth scurrying around like a scared rabbit. The news continued as she left the bedroom for the washroom. The space was pristine, with both a walk-in shower stall and a jacuzzi tub beside. The gleaming white porcelain and chrome shone brightly. Thick white towels monogrammed with the hotel's name sat on a chrome shelf by the sink. A soft and inviting terry cloth robe was hung on a hook behind the door. She walked into the shower stall and turned the knob controlling the water temperature. She immediately felt the steaming hot blast of the powerful stream of water cascade over her body. The exhilarating sensation calmed her nerves. She closed her eyes and enjoyed escapist pleasure of the hot water enveloping her smooth naked body.

✷

Richard arrived at Ed's house at 2307 College Street. He was lucky enough to find a Tim Hortons coffee shop still open. Most restaurants were shut down. He knocked on the door of the small 1950s-era house, with a flat box of doughnuts in hand and a feeling of apprehension. He was plagued with strange thoughts since he had awoken that morning. It was something more than the usual pervasive dread. This was a feeling that had begun recently. It was the inexplicable sensation that everything around him was somehow unreal, and without substance. He had the strange sensation of feeling like a mindless puppet, or a two-dimensional character. Richard felt a sinister presence, beyond his understanding.

Ed answered the door, still in his wizard-school bathrobe. He held a huge mug of coffee, shaped like an enormous cylindrical robot. He warmly ushered Richard inside. "Max, please meet Richard, a bit of a kindred spirit, I think maybe. Ah, you brought doughnuts. Good man! I hope there's an apple fritter in there somewhere. Do you mind? I'm starving." He lifted open the box and grabbed hold of the fritter. Richard also helped himself. Max grabbed a lemon-filled doughnut.

Ed moved over to the living room from the entrance. Ed sat down on the brown leather sofa beside Max. Richard took a seat to their side. "Eat up and enjoy, gentleman, these might well be the last doughnuts we ever eat, which brings us to why we have invited you here, Richard."

Max chimed in, "Yes, in theory, these could be our last doughnuts ever."

Richard casually scanned the room as he listened. "So, Max, is it? Do you live here also?"

Max shook his head vigorously. "No, no, we're simply work colleagues."

Ed turned to look at his friend indignantly. "Well, I'd say we're a little more than that. We're best buddies, at least I thought so anyway."

Richard continued, "So, guys, nice place by the way, I still have no idea what any of this has to do with me exactly. I remember discussing insomnia, and the whole doomsday thing, the asteroid, but why am I here?"

Ed smiled. "Well, you're here because of the asteroid, because it might well be the end of everything."

Richard responded, "I mean, do you ever feel like this whole apocalypse thing is somehow fake?" Both scientists looked intently at him.

Ed replied, "Richard, you're not one of those conspiracy theory crackpots, are you? I mean, you do know that they actually did land on the moon, that wasn't fake, you know, despite what a bunch of kooks on the internet may say."

Richard shook his head. "No...that's not what I mean. It's like, some people are reacting like you'd expect to this end of the world thing, but a lot aren't. Shouldn't more people be going crazy about this? It just doesn't feel like the actual end of everything. I mean, why am I even here? Shouldn't I be living it up, spending all my money, that kind of thing?"

Ed took a long sip of coffee, and a bite of his doughnut. "This is delicious. Anyway, I see what you're saying, and it's not stupid. The masses have grown increasingly desensitized to this kind of thing.

Nobody wants to look the fool for believing in something that may or may not be there."

Max continued his friend's thought. "You see, the fact is, Apophis is now visible to the naked eye. Theoretically, the images you see from NASA on TV, yes, those could be faked, but we are way beyond that now. This asteroid is really happening."

Richard remained unconvinced. "Then why do I feel like I'm in some kind of stupid *Star Trek* episode, or some sci-fi movie, where the superior alien race comes to save us at the last minute? It's like somebody is watching all of this and laughing."

Ed responded, "First of all, there are no stupid *Star Trek* episodes, if we're talking original series here—maybe the tribble one—anyway, if you're speculating that some alien race sent this asteroid here to wipe us out? Logically, that scenario can't be ruled out. Although, since we'll all pretty much be dead, there will never be a way to prove it...or disprove it."

Max looked at Richard. "You have an interesting mind, Richard. The testing of humanity aspect; that is a fascinating idea." The wide-ranging conversation continued in this vein for most of the morning.

✷

Samantha enjoyed feeling the frothy warm soapy bubbles flow over her body. She closed her eyes tight as she rinsed the shampoo from her hair. She was startled by a noise. She suddenly opened her eyes. The shower curtain was flung open violently. Selena stood before her completely naked. The intruder said nothing as she locked Samantha in her powerful gaze. The hot stream of water continued to pour over Samantha. She averted her eyes from Selena's jutting breasts pointing towards her. Samantha was shocked and frozen in fear. She reached down with one hand to cover herself. She tried to hide her chest with the other arm. Selena simply smiled and calmly climbed into the shower. The larger woman seized hold of the trembling Samantha in a rough embrace. Samantha looked away and sobbed miserably. She continued her assault by grabbing Samantha's right breast and squeezing tightly. With her other hand, she reached around and firmly seized her slippery wet exposed behind.

Samantha struggled against the forced embrace. "No! Stop! What are you doing! You can't do this!"

Selena grinned broadly and said nothing. She pushed her lips aggressively against those of the whimpering woman. Samantha fought against the urge to accept the forced kiss. Their wet lips locked together as Selena's tongue shot into Samantha's waiting mouth. Her rational mind was overwhelmed by the primal, sensual pleasure of Selena's large breasts rubbing against hers. The aggressor sensed her victim's subtle capitulation. Selena suddenly reached down between Samantha's legs and gently pried them apart. She pushed two fingers deeply up into Samantha. The penetration sent a dizzying, electric shock through her body. She convulsed reflexively and went limp. Her rational sense of outrage could not contain the ever-growing, rippling pleasure coursing through her body. Samantha clenched hard on the appendage probing her. Imperceptibly, and then more quickly, her hips began to undulate against Selena's body. Automatically, she reached up and stroked the heavy breasts pressing hard on her own. Samantha lost all control of herself, and submitted to her body's lustful needs. She felt the aggressive woman again push her tongue deep into her gaping mouth, darting and exploring. She reluctantly returned the carnal gesture.

After a few brief minutes, the fiery, stolen passion subsided. The victimized woman was devastated and ashamed.

Selena looked directly into her eyes. "Now, was that so terrible?" She smiled with a lascivious, penetrating gaze.

Samantha turned off the water and glared at Selena. She shook her head in confusion and self-doubt. Her mind was dizzy, trying desperately to process what had transpired. "No! I did not invite you in! How did you get in here? How dare you!" Her face was red and puffy, as tears flowed down uncontrollably.

"It was easy. Everything is easy, you see, when you know how to play the game. I just asked the desk clerk, told her that you were locked out; these sheep would do anything for famous people. She didn't think twice, just gave me the card to your room. Anyway, you must have figured out by now, that rules, good and bad, that sort of thing, they don't apply to someone like me. I am something beyond your mere mortal comprehension."

Samantha was mystified by the woman's cryptic remarks. She wrapped herself in a robe and stormed out of the bathroom.

Selena stood, still naked, as droplets of water slowly descended down her curvaceous, slick frame. She laughed coldly. "Don't act like you didn't enjoy it. Maybe not at first, but you began to feel it, don't deny it. The great thing is, we can do that whenever we want, or at least maybe once more, before we're all wiped out by the big rock."

Samantha was apoplectic. "Absolutely not! You raped me! Don't think I won't report this!"

Selena responded in a mocking tone, "Do you actually think anybody would believe you? Especially with all that's going on? Just think of it as a going-away present from me to you. I don't need you anyway, I just wanted a taste...I'm done with you now."

Selena grabbed her clothes from the floor of the room and dressed quickly. She left the room with a parting shot, "See you on set, lover." She slammed the door behind her, laughing.

Samantha's mind raced in a chaotic frenzy of anxiety. Thoughts flew around haphazardly. She knew she could never face her aggressor again, and decided to leave altogether, regardless of consequences. She quickly dressed and prepared to leave. She grabbed all her clothes from the dresser and closet and jammed them in her suitcase. She retrieved her phone from the nightstand and placed it on her purse. She took one last look around the room and departed. She fled down the hall and waited for the elevator. She was much relieved to be alone as the car descended. Her first thought was of Richard. She had no idea what she would say to him. She struggled to collect her thoughts as she desperately fled the luxury resort.

CHAPTER 7

The three men sat in Ed's living room eating doughnuts and drinking coffee. The heavy-set scientist leaned in to Richard. He spoke with great deliberation. "Okay, Rich, you have your doubts, although I think your virtual reality conspiracy theory might be something of a long shot. What if we told you I might have an escape plan? What would you think?"

Richard seemed understandably confused. "How do you mean *escape plan*? You mean an escape from the planet? You guys have a secret rocket in the basement? Like Batman or something? That would be cool."

Ed smiled, and shook his head. "Not exactly...no. We don't have a Bat-rocket, although that is a great idea. So this is not an escape from Earth, this would be an escape from reality, or at least this particular one."

Max added his opinion. "Yes, I think it's fair to say that this one, this reality, is used up, or tainted, however you want to say it's become untenable. You know, with the destruction of humanity aspect."

Richard stared in bewilderment. "I literally have no idea what you two are talking about."

Ed, munching on his fourth doughnut, extemporized. "Richard, my boy, let me explain. You have every right to be confused. This is very much cutting-edge stuff we're talking about. Stuff that has never been done, things that have never even been conceived, but desperate times call for desperate measures and all that. Let me show you my secret mad-scientist lab in the basement."

Max laughed. "Sadly, the mad part, that's not far from the truth."

"All great geniuses have been misunderstood in their time. I'm simply the most recent in a long line of so-called mad scientists."

Max tried to calm him down. "You know I'm just kidding. Anyway, I guess we're both mad scientists, since I'm in this with you."

Richard stood up, still completely baffled. He was having second, and third thoughts about agreeing to this meeting.

Ed noticed the look of concern on Richard's face. "Listen, my friend, we're not forcing you into anything. Obviously, you can leave whenever you want. Just give me a chance to show you what we are trying to do. Don't forget, this represents an opportunity for you, first and foremost."

With that, the three men walked down to the basement. Ed unlocked the heavy steel black door, and led them into the dark, cavernous basement. "So this is it, Dr. Frankenstein's other basement. It's not much really, but it's cozy."

Richard stood gazing around at the strange place. It seemed to him, to be much larger than the room above, almost as if it did not belong to the same house. It felt like a completely separate location, both in time and space. He felt deeply uncomfortable, as if he were an intruder. "Maybe not quite Dr. Frankenstein, but close. What the hell is this all about?" Richard was becoming impatient.

Ed sensed his new friend's agitation. "Listen, Rich, I know this is a lot to take in at once. Let me try to break this down for you. I know you're a smart guy, an open-minded guy, I wouldn't have invited you here otherwise. You've read my article, or at least some of it. You know I've done extensive research on the long-term cognitive effects of DMT, melatonin, and ayahuasca. So, all of this is an extension of that research. I'm not going to bother explaining every minute aspect of my current work for the past ten years. So here is the bottom line for you.

I have somehow managed to send a living being, a monkey, to some place else."

Richard had some difficulty processing what he was hearing. "I do recall seeing something on the news the other day about ayahuasca. It's being used to treat depression? And what exactly do you mean, *someplace else*?"

Ed motioned Richard over to the computer monitor. He sat down and began to type. Soon the image of a very distraught monkey, strapped down to a metal chair came into view. Richard looked intently at the image. "What is it I'm watching here?"

Ed pointed to the apparatus behind them. "What you're watching is a monkey that is not going to be obliterated by that damn giant rock headed towards us. You see, by combining the three compounds that I mentioned, along with a massive jolt from the plasma-field generator, viola, our friend here has been transported to another dimension, presumably. The point is, he is still alive, probably. The experiment was a success."

Richard watched with some dismay and clear apprehension. "So, you're telling me this monkey is still alive?"

Ed was noncommittal. "Maybe? Just keep watching…right there… he just disappears, and believe me, we are talking into thin air. So anyway, get this, my friend Max here sees what seems to be my monkey, with his plasma generator set-up, still very much alive, out there somewhere in the ether."

Richard nodded slowly as his mind processed all the implications of Ed's words. "So, you want another monkey, is that it?"

Max laughed. "No, you see this is all very hypothetical at this point. Ed was merely seeing if you wanted a taste, of his concoction."

Richard looked aghast. "A taste of what?"

Ed jumped in, sensing that he was losing the pitch. "A taste of eternity, my friend, and of victory over death. This is an escape, pure and simple. Here's the plan. We're not talking about the complete package here the first time, just the ayahuasca, DMT, and melatonin, at a low dosage. It's a trip, I can tell you, but it's a short one, and therein lies one of the problems. It might last twenty minutes, tops. If that works okay, we'll try the big one, but we have to remember here, that we don't have a lot of time left. None of us. Last I heard, the missiles fly very soon, and if that doesn't work, which it won't...we're toast. So that's how much time we have left."

Richard listened with great interest. He was slowly warming to the outlandish proposition. "So why not use one of you guys as the guinea pig?"

Ed nodded. "Fair question. The thing is, only Max and I know how to operate all this stuff, no offence, but it would be a little tough for you to figure it all out in a few days. Listen, what I'm offering you is an opportunity and if you don't like this, turn around and walk out the door, no questions asked. But honestly, what do you have to lose at this point? In a matter of days, we'll all be dead."

Richard stood for a few moments pondering. "You know, if they are successful with the missile launch, and the asteroid is destroyed, everything goes back to normal, and I'm left a brain-dead vegetable, right?"

Ed smiled. "My friend, the people in charge of this missile launch, they are not telling you the truth. It's simply a ruse to calm the masses. The chances of success are miniscule. Your chances with us are far better, think about it."

Richard pondered his options, and slowly grew more amenable. "You must know this is crazy, but then this entire situation seems crazy. None of this seems quite real, so why not? But before we do anything, I need to call Samantha."

Ed understood. "Yes, your new girlfriend. Of course, you do what you need to do, but remember, time is running out, for all of us. Why don't we just get prepared, then you'll be able to tell her something interesting."

Richard reluctantly agreed with a nod. "Okay, I left my phone in the car...but as soon as we're done."

✸

As Samantha reached for her phone, the assistant director Dinah stopped her on the steps of the hotel. "You know you were supposed to be on set half an hour ago?"

Samantha looked down at her phone to see the time. "I'm not feeling well...I just can't be here." She abruptly turned away for her car.

Harvey the director noticed her leaving. He was chatting with Selena in the lobby over a steaming latte. He ran outside to confront the distraught woman. "Samantha, where are you going? You're supposed to be on set."

Selena sauntered outside to watch the scene unfold. She grinned slyly. "Yeah, what's wrong, Sam? You look like you've been run over by a train, what's the rush?"

Samantha stuttered out a weak response. "I don't feel well...I have to go." The burly, aggressive director chased her to her car. He grabbed her forcibly by the arm. She winced in pain and anguish. "Leave me alone! Don't touch me!" She pushed him away and climbed into her vehicle.

The furious, red-faced director yelled loudly, "You'll never work in TV again!"

Selena walked up and seized hold of the infuriated director. She stood beside the portly man. "Leave her alone, she had a bad morning and she's a little messed up. Anyway, what the hell difference does it make, you actually think anybody is going to get anything done today? All anybody can think about is this stupid asteroid. You really should shut down production, at least until we know what's going to happen."

The director nodded. "I know you're right. It's just so hard to take this thing seriously. I mean, I think I've seen this movie before, they always think everybody is going to die, but doesn't some dumb action hero always save the day in the end? I'm just waiting for Bruce Willis to show up."

Selena listened. "Well, this isn't a movie, is it? This is really happening, so I don't think your rules necessarily apply here. It is a little strange, though, it's like everybody is walking around, carrying on like zombies. Anyway, I wouldn't worry too much. As the song goes, life is but a dream."

Samantha locked her doors and sat dejectedly in the well-worn seat. Her hands clenched the steering wheel, with her head hanging down. She threw her suitcase haphazardly into the back seat. Wiping tears of humiliation from her face, she started the engine. The old white VW Rabbit slowly lurched into gear and shot back gravel as it sped from the property. Her mind raced ahead as she fought hard to regain her composure. She drove with her white knuckles clenched like a vise on the wheel. Her eyes burned with tears. She could barely make out the road ahead of her. Samantha drove her car fast along the highway. After ten minutes, she noticed a gas station up ahead and decided to stop. She pulled up to the single gas dispenser and exited the vehicle. She looked around at the ancient, weathered building. It looked at least a half-century old. Worn-out tires and rusted gas company signs littered the yard. A tired-looking dog sat by the entrance, casually watching her progress. A wizened old proprietor peered at her through the greasy window of the establishment.

Samantha finished filling up her gas tank and returned the nozzle. She suddenly felt a ravenous hunger, as her stomach groaned. She went in to pay for her gas and buy herself a coffee and doughnut. The man smiled and waved as she entered. "Just brewed a fresh pot only ten minutes ago. You go on and help yourself now. You look like you could use some pick-me-up."

Samantha grabbed an extra-large Styrofoam cup and poured the coffee. It was strong and aromatic. The familiar scent calmed her nerves. She examined the selection of doughnuts and put two in a brown paper bag.

The sleepy-eyed old man at the register smiled kindly at her. "Are you okay, miss? You look like you've had a terrible scare. Of course, with all that's going on, who could blame you? There's no charge for that, not today. In fact, you go ahead and help yourself to whatever you want in here; doesn't much matter anymore, does it? Since it's all going to be gone tomorrow...or is it the day after? I can't exactly remember."

The kindly man's breezy attitude cheered Samantha. "Well, that's nice of you. Actually, this is all I need." She managed a wan smile.

He replied, "Not at all, you help yourself. You look like you're in a hurry. You headed up to the mountains like everybody else? I suppose not, since you're going the wrong way, but I expect you know that already."

"No mountains for me, I'm just headed home."

"Yeah, times like this, you should be with family."

"Actually...I don't really have any family. My parents are gone, no brothers or sisters either, but there is somebody special."

"I knew there had to be somebody, pretty girl like you. Anyway, you take care, and God bless."

Samantha thanked the kind stranger. The random encounter boosted her spirits. She walked back to her car. She noticed a large black raven perched on the roof. As she grew closer, the dark bird began to caw loudly at her, as if warning her. Samantha was unnerved by the strangely persistent black bird fixated upon her. She tried to shoo it away, but its cry only became louder, and more insistent. Samantha struggled to comprehend the bird's incomprehensible message. Samantha climbed into the vehicle, and quickly sped away. The enigmatic bird flew off indignantly.

Suddenly she thought of Richard. She pulled over to the side of the road and called his number. It went directly to his voice mail. She thought it odd that he did not answer. Samantha started to worry, given the dire circumstances, and drove more quickly towards the city. Only her vehicle was travelling back towards civilization. Trucks and trailers overloaded with belongings headed north and west whizzed by her rapidly. She had heard that rental companies like U-Haul had long since run out of vehicles. A collective desperation and hopelessness filled the air with a wretched scent. Samantha sensed it enveloping the world like an unearthly darkness. The sordid images of her traumatic morning suddenly flooded her mind like a horrible nightmare. She struggled to banish the horrible assault from her mind. The embarrassing humiliation of the event filled her with a burning anger. Samantha felt as though she would meet up with Selena again. She imagined what she would say, and what she would do. She fantasized a terrible, violent revenge upon her attacker. She also tried to think of her wonderful night with Richard, and of seeing him again soon. The hopeful sentiment soothed her chaotic mind.

✷

Richard, Ed, and Max sat together in the dark, forbidding laboratory. Richard stared at the imposing steel chair, processing the deluge of information provided to him. He gazed around at the strange room, and its perplexing accoutrements. "Why would you have a poster of him?"

Ed turned to see where Richard was looking. "Oh, you mean Tricky Dick? Richard Nixon was an underappreciated genius. Over there is Richard Wagner. Some of my influences and people I admire. Time's a-wasting, let's get to it. Are you ready for this?"

Richard was still very apprehensive. "I suppose. You should know, I've never used drugs of any kind, not even weed. This isn't going to turn me into some kind of junkie, is it?"

Ed laughed. "No more so than me, I guess. So, you've never even smoked a little ganja? Listen, this stuff has been used for centuries, eons probably. It's practically medicinal. I'll tell you, if all the crazy people in the world tried a dose of this stuff, we'd all be better off. I'm glad the FDA is finally starting to see that. I'm going to start you off with a little ayahuasca; this is the pure stuff. It won't hurt you, there's no danger, but you will be tripping balls. Just remember to go with it, let it flow over you, don't fight it, just let it happen."

Max tried to reassure the clearly worried Richard. "Don't worry, Rich, I won't let Dr. Frankenstein here carve you up for parts."

Richard could not help chuckling. "Well, just leave me the important parts, I still have to meet up with Samantha soon, when this is all done."

The palpable tension in the room eased considerably.

Richard sat down in the heavy black metal chair. Ed returned from his desk with a large syringe. Richard rolled up his sleeve. Ed took a cotton swab dipped in alcohol and rubbed Richard's bare arm. "Now, don't worry, I've done this to myself many times. You'll feel a slight sting of course, but no worse than a flu shot."

Richard stared at the yellowish liquid within the glass cylinder. "Okay. I'm ready."

Ed admonished him once more. "Remember, like it says in *The Hitchhiker's Guide to the Galaxy*, above all, *don't panic*." Ed adopted a more sombre tone as he administered the compounds to Richard.

He struggled to maintain his composure. Slowly Richard's mind, identity, and awareness of the reality around him melted away. He was surprised at how quickly the drug took effect. As one part of his mind disappeared, other novel aspects emerged from within. Richard was no longer conscious of himself. A completely alien presence supplanted his own. It was something beyond anything he could have imagined in his wildest dreams. Cascading, rippling waves of soothing, beneficent mental sensation washed over him. A wondrous, calming liquid joy flowed over the shores of his mind. All of his everyday insecurities and worries evaporated into nothingness. His eyes remained closed, as far as he knew, but he might well have been floating on air. His visual field was overwhelmed with a dazzling, kaleidoscopic, ever-increasing display of pure colour and shape. These were not the crude and vulgar images from his reality, but rather the manifestation of the base reality, of pure being itself.

A perfect geometrically represented third world reality exploded in his brain. He could feel a billion tendrils of electricity coursing through every neuron of his brain. Richard also had the very distinct, and quite unnerving sensation that other, non-human beings were in his presence. He not could visually apprehend them, but nonetheless felt their existence. He struggled to affix some sort of description or appellation to them, but words failed. Gradually his visions transformed into a bucolic scene. He found himself staring up at a tangerine sky, gargantuan trees, and brilliant multi-hued mushrooms. He watched an enormous caterpillar wearing a smoking jacket. It wore a monocle and sat upon a huge electric blue mushroom. A young blonde girl rushed by him at breakneck speed. She wore a knee-length puffed-sleeve blue dress with a pinafore worn over the top, and a white sash around the waist. She turned slightly towards him, yet he could not see her face. She called out plaintively, "Do hurry! There is very little time left! What are you waiting for?" The strange girl stopped by a large patch of oversized red with white polka-dot mushrooms. She reached up to tear off a piece to eat.

Richard yelled loudly, "Don't eat those! They're poisonous!" The bewildering images faded away. They melted into a misty fog as his outer consciousness reemerged from within.

For several minutes, Richard stared into space, slowly processing his bizarre experience. He finally looked over at Edward. "Wow...that was a hell of a thing. I had no idea. I feel really, really good. I feel different. Are all drugs like this? How long exactly was I gone? It felt like hours."

Ed shook his head. "Just twenty minutes, my friend. Did you see the elves?"

Richard stood up from the heavy black metal chair. "Elves? Is that what you call them? There was somebody, or something in there with me...I mean, it was definitely not you guys here...aliens maybe? I really can't describe it properly. It's like they were watching me, but not in a bad way, they were just monitoring me, but I could not quite see them. Then there was a little blonde girl...I've seen her before."

Ed replied, "I just call them elves. Who knows what they really are? Just because we can't see them, doesn't mean they're not real. Anyway, the important point, is that you survived, which means we have to plan for phase two: the big escape. Next time we go the full monty, all the way."

Richard wrestled with his newly acquired knowledge. The strange, expanded state of mind induced by the drugs, altered his perspective. He was decidedly calmer, despite a future of near certain demise. His many anxieties, regrets, and petty fears melted away. Richard glimpsed a universal reality greater than anything he had previously understood. He was more determined than ever to escape his doomed fate.

✱

Samantha checked her rear-view mirror before stopping at the side of the road. Cars and trucks continued to whizz by her in the opposite direction. She pulled out her phone and tried again to call Richard. As before, the call again went to his voice mail. She did not leave a message. She generally avoided leaving messages for anybody, as she much preferred direct communication. Samantha desperately needed to hear his voice. She was mildly alarmed at how quickly she had formed an emotional dependance. The perceived vulnerability offended her sense of independence. She grew more concerned as to his whereabouts. She briefly entertained the thought of calling her agent, Arturo, but thought better of it. She imagined his chiding tone as she explained her intolerable situation on set. She didn't have the energy to absorb his lecturing.

Samantha put her phone away. She stepped out of the car to stretch her legs and collect her thoughts. The morning's traumatic events still clung closely in her mind. Her mind raced furiously, as she struggled with feelings of guilt and self-doubt. She wondered if she had somehow provoked the assault, or given Selena the wrong impression at some point. She wondered if she were to blame, and if she could have prevented the attack. Even worse, was the deep buried sense that, on some primal, physical level, she had enjoyed it. The more her anxiety grew, the more she needed Richard. Samantha looked at the bright rock hurtling towards her, high above. It seemed to be taking aim directly at her, as if to annihilate her alone. She wondered how it would feel to not exist. It now appeared larger than the sun in the sky. The long tail emblazoned the dark and cloudy sky. An eerie mist hung damply in the late morning air. She marvelled at the incredible beauty of the devastating asteroid, even as it delivered such horror. She watched the steady flow of trucks and cars headed north. Samantha wondered at the sheer futility of their efforts to escape their fate. She also recognized the implacable sense of hope, even in the face of certain demise. She returned to her car and continued driving back to the city.

Richard was still dazed by his exhilarating experience. He eagerly anticipated relaying his thoughts to Samantha. Ed looked down at him expectantly. He released his subject from the heavy black chair.

Richard slowly stood up and felt overwhelmed by a need to contact Samantha. "Guys, I need to go out to the car and grab my phone; I have to make a call."

Ed nodded. "Of course, but make sure you come back. We have much to discuss."

Richard quickly bounded up the stairs with determination. Ed glanced over at his colleague. "What do you think?"

Max thought for a moment. "I think this could actually work. I mean, I think Richard is on board, but there's no way he'll try anything without this girl of his."

Ed nodded in agreement. "Yes, we need to convince her, or rather get Richard to convince her." The two conspirators departed from the dark laboratory, pleased by the success of their endeavor.

Richard left the house and walked out to his car to retrieve his phone. He noticed that the sky had grown dark and misty, save for the blazing celestial rock illuminating the grey. The streets around the house were strangely empty and silent. Richard immediately noticed several missed calls on his phone from Samantha. He immediately regretted not retrieving his phone earlier. He was now consumed by guilt and concern. He called her immediately. Samantha heard her phone ring and pulled over. She picked up the phone and answered it, "Richard!"

"Samantha, are you okay? I'm so sorry I missed your calls. I was busy doing something here, and, like an idiot, I left my phone in the car."

"Richard, thank God! I thought something had happened to you."

"Well, I guess you could say it did. I have so much to explain, but I need to tell you in person. It's really quite amazing, I mean, what I've experienced. But enough about me, you sound upset. Is everything okay? I thought you'd be too busy to talk with your schedule. How is the filming going?"

"Not well. I'm actually headed back to the city now, something happened...something went wrong...I can't tell you on the phone...I mean, I'm okay...but I'm also really, really not okay." Samantha choked back a sob.

Richard struggled to interpret her words. He sensed the clear distress in her voice. "Okay, you said you're headed back to the city, right? Why don't you come and meet me at Edward's place, that's the guy I mentioned at dinner. He's on 2307 College Street. You know where that is?"

"I think so...can't wait to see you." She ended the call and continued driving back to the city. Samantha felt slightly better having spoken with Richard. She wiped the tears from her eyes and focused on the road ahead.

Richard put the phone in his pocket and returned to the house. He found the two scientists standing in the living room, drinking coffee and talking intently. Ed immediately noticed the look of anguish on Richard's face. "Is everything okay? You look a little shaken. I mean, other than the demise of humanity thing of course."

"Not sure. Just got off the phone with Samantha, something really bad happened to her. She left the show, it sounds like she's on the way here."

Ed nodded. "Sorry to hear about that, but you know, this might just work out perfectly for everyone." He smiled broadly, as he watched the expression on Richard's face. "To tell you the truth, I never really liked the idea of sending you out into the unknown all by yourself. That could be scary, so my idea is this, what if we send you two together?"

The daunting prospect had not occurred to Richard until then. "So you're saying you could save both of us?"

Max was not as enthusiastic. "Or kill them both...depending upon how you define kill."

Ed quickly countered his friend's dampening remark. "What difference could it make? We're all dead anyway, after tomorrow. Okay, just hear me out. We'll get everything ready for tomorrow, for you and your girl, we'll wait of course, to see how this doomed missile launch goes. Then we should have a few hours before we're all toast. Meanwhile, tonight we'll have an end of the world shindig. What do you say, Rich?"

Richard grinned. "You know what? Crazy times call for crazy measures, right? Of course, Samantha might take some convincing...it will be a lot for her to take in all at once."

"Rich, that will be your job in this plan. Max and I will take care of the scientific stuff. We're going to have to mess with the equipment to get it to work. My equipment was damaged in the last attempt, but now we have Max's generator from the university. We'll have to make it work for two people, of course. I think I have another chair down there to rig together. It will be difficult, but doable. So, Max and I will work on that, you work on her...and the food...we need some tasty food. This might well be our last meal, so it has to be good." With his speech completed, Ed filled up his mug of coffee, as did Max. The two men began deliberating as they headed down to the basement. Richard sat alone in the living room, waiting for Samantha. He reflected upon his recent bizarre, consciousness expanding experience. He sensed his life becoming increasingly strange and dreamlike.

He soon grew restless waiting for Samantha to arrive. His mind raced, as he speculated upon the nature of her troubling news. He prepared himself for the worst, and considered that Samantha had no further use for him. He flipped on the TV. Most of the channels had ceased broadcasting, save the news channels. The coverage of the impending doomsday continued relentlessly. Nothing else mattered at this point. As far as Richard could surmise, there were no new developments. The news conversation was now focused on the massive, coordinated missile launch scheduled for the next day. Experts and pundits weighed in on the possibility of success or failure of this last-ditch effort. The consensus was, that the desperate gambit held a reasonable chance of success. If unsuccessful, the asteroid would smash into the Earth an hour later. None of the experts mentioned that the very wealthy and important might well survive. They would be safe within the confines of their deep underground bunkers.

Richard heard a knock at the door. He ran to open it and found Samantha standing there. He immediately noticed the look of deep anguish on her face. He pulled her close and held her tight.

Samantha stepped back. "I know it may sound silly, we just met... but I missed you so much." She was clearly struggling to hide something, and Richard sensed it. Her eyes welled up with tears, as they flowed down her red cheeks. "Something terrible happened to me...I don't know where to start...it's so embarrassing, I'm so ashamed."

Richard reassured her, "You know, I'm sure whatever happened was not your fault. You don't have to tell me if you don't want to."

Samantha shook her head strongly. "No, I need to tell somebody. If I don't tell someone, it would be like it never happened. I'm just afraid that after I tell you, you'll look at me differently."

Richard gently caressed her shoulders. "Nothing you could tell me would change my opinion of you. I know that sounds a little ridiculous, considering that we just met. I feel like I've known you my whole life. Listen to me, I sound like a crappy Hallmark romance movie character.

I know you, Samantha, and you can say anything to me." Samantha smiled slightly. Her eyes brightened through her tears.

She walked with Richard over to the sofa and sat down. "I feel like garbage. Do you have a Kleenex or something?" Richard grabbed a tissue and handed it to her. Samantha wiped away her tears and dabbed at her nose. She looked around at her surroundings. "So you just met this guy, you said at a bookstore? And this is his place?"

Richard nodded. "You're avoiding the subject, come on, tell me what happened up there."

Samantha slowly began to relate the strange and disturbing events of the morning. Richard listened intently, fighting back his natural sense of shock and dismay. "You do realize, that you have absolutely nothing to feel ashamed about. You were attacked, you were raped. Just because it's a woman, that doesn't make it any less serious. I don't see how you could have done anything differently."

Samantha felt calmed and relieved by his empathetic response. "I know...it's just that, I feel like I should have fought back more. It's just so confusing, you know? I wonder if I somehow gave her the wrong impression of me. I mean, I don't think I come across as a lesbian, do I?"

Richard chuckled. "Yes, that's what attracted me to you. I'm joking. Of course not. You can't control how other people see you. That's not your fault. You know, I think we're all a little bit confused, and we all think we're the only ones that are. It's the people that think they're not confused. Those are the ones you have to worry about. Anyway, everybody has some weird sexual thing that's happened to them, that they're always ashamed of it. I remember that this guy at summer camp took a liking to me, who cares? I know it's not the same thing, but I just mean, everybody has these terrible things happen to them, and everybody thinks they're the only ones...but they're not."

"Okay. I actually feel a lot better. I mean, I still feel like shit, but I'll survive."

Richard replied, "At least until tomorrow, when we're all blown to bits by the killer rock!"

"Oh yeah, with all my own drama, I almost forgot about that. I'm so hungry...is there anything to eat here?"

Richard offered her the last doughnut from the box. The basement door opened. Ed looked over at her. "Sorry about that, I think we gobbled up most of the doughnuts. Anyway, we're here to talk about our situation." Ed loped across the room and extended his hand towards Samantha. "You must be Samantha. Pleased to make your acquaintance. Professor Edward B. Lytton, at your service. Any friend of Richard's is a friend of mine. And this stalwart fellow is my esteemed colleague and friend Max Thule." Max extended his bony hand towards her. Samantha smiled back and shook his hand warmly. Ed continued, "Why so glum? Is it the whole end of humanity thing getting you down?"

Samantha felt buoyed by the ebullient, gregarious scientist. "Hi, there, nice to meet you. No, it's nothing for you to worry about, it's just a personal thing."

Ed walked through the living room to the kitchen. He began to rifle through the cabinets. "Damn, we have nothing but coffee. We ate all the doughnuts...well, mostly me, and the leftovers are gone. We are definitely going to need some food. We have a long day and a long night ahead of us."

Ed looked over at Richard. "Have you brought our lovely guest here up to speed?"

Richard shook his head. "We didn't really have a chance yet...there were...other matters."

Ed looked over to Max. "I know we have a lot of ground to cover, but I'm still starving. My mind needs fuel. Any way you could get us some more doughnuts? To hell with calories! I'm eating all I want now...why not?"

Max nodded. "I doubt any place will still be open, let alone making doughnuts, but I'll give it a shot. I guess Richard here found a place. Where was it anyway?"

Richard responded, "It was at Younge and Davenport."

Ed shrugged and gave Max the keys to his Volvo wagon. He handed him a wad of bills from his wallet. "Well, at this point, money is clearly no object. Spend what you can; there should be three hundred dollars maybe in there."

Max smiled. "In theory, you're right, although, there is also the very real possibility that we could all be laughing about this in a week...like it was all just a bad dream."

"True enough, my friend."

Max left the house to begin his hunt for sustenance in the city.

Ed turned to Richard. "Any news about the missile launch on the tube?"

Richard turned on the TV to the news channels. "It looks like they've scheduled the launch for noon tomorrow."

Ed looked over at Samantha. "Okay, then, after that, if this missile launch plan fails, which it probably will, then we have I think an hour to accomplish our task."

Samantha had no idea what he was talking about, and looked at him quizzically. "Now what do you mean *task*?"

Ed returned to the kitchen and filled up his mug. He took a long swig of coffee. "Mmmm...that's the good stuff. Richard, do you mind if I try to tell your lovely lady here about our brilliant plan?" Richard agreed with a nod. Ed faced Samantha squarely. "Now I warn you, this is going to sound completely crazy, and it may well be. But just try and stay with me. Try to keep an open mind."

Ed sat down beside Samantha on the sofa. She was clearly apprehensive. Richard looked on from the chair beside. Ed proceeded to explain the details of his research and experiments over the years. Samantha listened with great interest to his explanation, her curiosity piqued. She finally spoke up. "This is really a lot to take in all at once, and you're right, honestly, it does all sound a little bonkers. I mean, is all of this actually safe?"

Richard attempted to reassure her. "Ed gave me a dose of ayahuasca and I'm still here in one piece. To be perfectly honest, it made me feel fantastic. It's a very difficult thing to explain. It's as if all my anxiety seemed to melt away."

Samantha was somewhat shocked. "That seems a little out of character, although I admit we haven't known each other long."

Richard was sheepish. "You're totally right. It's definitely not something I would normally do, but you have to admit, there is nothing normal about what we're going through, all of us, I mean."

Ed continued his thought. "Desperate times call for desperate measures."

Samantha was still very much apprehensive about the whole venture. "So, what you're actually saying, is that there is a chance we could survive this asteroid? I still don't completely understand what a mixture of drugs has to do with us escaping."

Ed nodded. "That is exactly what I'm saying. Of course, you'll have to actually see the laboratory, and all the equipment to fully understand what we're trying to accomplish. Obviously, we're going to wait until the missile launch, to see if that works, which it won't, by the way."

Richard could see the doubt etched upon Samantha's face. "You know, it is completely nuts, but everything about our whole situation is nuts. Sometimes I wonder if it's all really happening, it's like a nightmare."

Ed tried to counter her disbelief. "Oh, this is happening all right, I don't think there's such a thing as a collective nightmare, and if it is just all a nightmare, it doesn't really matter what we do, right?"

Samantha nodded. "That's a dangerous way to think, though, isn't it? That whole living-in-the-Matrix idea...that's just a made-up movie."

Ed could not help but take the philosophical bait. "You are right, of course, it was just a movie, a damn good one if you ask me, but it was based upon sound logical reasoning. Essentially, there is no means of disproving the proposition that we are all living in a virtual, computer-generated reality."

"No, I don't believe that's necessarily true. I mean to say, I understand what you're saying, but I don't think that's what reality actually is," Richard replied.

Ed nodded. "So, do you disagree that we're living in a virtual world, or do you disagree that it's impossible to disprove this proposition?"

Samantha agreed with Richard. "That's just an idea some scientists with too much time on their hands came up with one day."

Ed accepted the criticism graciously. "Maybe...maybe not, but I think you're absolutely correct in stating that we certainly can't depend upon all of this being some kind of simulation, some elaborate dream in the mind of some advanced alien supercomputer. We have to proceed as if all of this is really happening, however strange and unbelievable it may seem to us."

Richard had the last remark. "It probably seemed really strange to the dinosaurs, too, until the asteroid actually hit them and wiped them out." Ed and Samantha laughed.

Samantha stood up from the sofa. She was reeling from a very difficult, traumatic day, and her mind struggled to process all the new information. The tribulations tested her resolve to the limit. Her turbulent emotions churned and fomented inside. "I'm still starving. Do we have anything good to eat?"

Ed shrugged apologetically. "You're welcome to raid the fridge, but I'm really not much of a cook, I tend to order a lot of takeout, as you can see." Ed gestured towards his sizable belly.

Samantha rummaged through the kitchen, and finally gave up. "We'll have to rely on Max, hopefully he'll keep us alive, at least for another day."

"Yes, it would be a shame to starve to death, just before we're all instantly burned alive...except you two, of course," said Ed.

Samantha was amused. "Yes, that would be terrible, I mean, the irony. Where is the washroom?"

Ed pointed up the stairs. "The one upstairs is cleaner and nicer."

She headed up the stairs, stopping to notice the unusual images that adorned the walls. Samantha walked past Ed's bedroom, and noticed the imposing, grim visage of Aleister Crowley. She did not recognize the face. She also looked at the angelic image of Maria Orsic, her face radiant with a beneficent, calming peace.

CHAPTER 8

Max Thule drove the yellow Volvo leisurely through the nearly empty city streets. People had fled north or out west, abandoning their carefully manicured lives for a desperate escape to nowhere. Max, like most educated people, realized the futility of fleeing. The asteroid presented an all or nothing proposition. It would either wipe out most of humanity, or be obliterated completely. Sadly, Max had nobody special to contact. His parents were gone, and he had no siblings. He had been married for only a month, and then she was gone forever. He had grown accustomed to solitude and loneliness.

The downtown core showed obvious signs of disarray and chaos. Garbage pick-up had ceased. Many storefront windows were broken, their contents looted. It was not quite apocalyptic, but very nearly. There were no raging fires or angry mobs, but one could easily imagine them appearing out of nowhere. This was the last day of the living, or so it seemed to Max. To his chagrin, all stores seemed closed, shuttered, or damaged. He drove first to the Tim Hortons shop on Davenport suggested by Richard, but found it closed, utterly devoid of life. He searched desperately for a restaurant still open. Max turned around to head back, when a brightly lit beacon caught his eye. It was a red neon sign blinking the word "*Pizza*." Beside it, a smaller green neon sign flashed the word "*Open*." The discovery was like a beautiful mirage in a vast, barren wasteland. Max wondered if this miraculous sight was merely wishful thinking, rather than actual reality.

He drove over and stopped the vehicle at the curb. He walked up to the front window and peered in. The glass was slightly fogged over, obscuring his view. He spied an elderly, stocky man in a worn dirty apron, hard at work. Max opened the front door and walked in. A high-pitched small bell heralded his arrival. Max surveyed the establishment. The large wall by the entrance featured a crude fresco depicting an Italian landscape. There were three tables upon a black-and-white-checkered tile floor. An old ceiling fan slowly revolved above him.

The old man looked over with a bright and open expression. "Can I help you?" He spoke in a thick Italian accent.

Max tried his best to look friendly and unassuming. "Sorry, I hope I didn't startle you, I'm just a little surprised to see a place that's still open. Are you still making pizza? If so, could I get some for my very hungry friends?"

The weary Italian sized up the customer carefully. "You don't look like the looting type, believe me, I've chased quite a few away." As if to punctuate his remark, and provide a warning, he revealed a double-barreled shotgun from beneath the counter.

Max waved his arms in dismay. "No, no, there will be no need for that. I assure you my intentions are purely culinary."

The proprietor smiled broadly. "I can see that, but you can't be too careful these days."

Max smiled back. "No...looting and pillaging has never really been my style." He reached into his pocket and pulled out a small wad of cash. "Here, for whatever it's worth now, there's at least three hundred bucks. How much pizza will that buy me?"

The owner of the pizzeria accepted the money and placed it in the old-fashioned register.

Max sat down at one of the three the well-worn wooden tables. A white-and-red-checkered plastic tablecloth covered the tabletop.

Two glass shakers, one filled with parmesan cheese, the other with hot pepper flakes sat on top. The overwhelming aromas of melting cheese, pepperoni, and tangy tomato sauce wafted through the room. The wonderful smells made him even more ravenous.

The owner yelled over the counter. "So, what can I make you today?"

Max thought for a moment. "Well, there are a few of us...why don't you make us something you like. You're the expert. We're not picky."

"You like the anchovies?"

"Maybe on just one. I don't think everybody likes them, I know I do."

The stocky man set about expertly constructing the pizzas. He proceeded with a flawless conservation of motion. "So what are you and your friends still doing here? It looks like everyone but the thugs have left."

"Well, my colleague and I are attempting to construct a temporary interdimensional portal to an alternate reality and thereby utilize the device to transport two people to this purely theoretical dimension, and in the process save their lives."

The weary-looking pizza artist stopped his work for a moment and looked at Max. "Well, good luck with that, I guess it makes about as much sense as everything else going on. Say, you think this dimension place, you think they have pizza there?"

Max smiled, but thought seriously about the query. "You know, that is a good question. I certainly hope so. Who knows?"

"Well, if this other dimension place ain't got pizza, then I'm staying right here. How could you live without pizza? That's no life at all, if you ask me."

Max nodded. "Perhaps you're right." He sat at the table waiting for the food. He gazed out at the empty city streets. He watched as a huge black bird swooped in. It landed on the windowsill, and began to peck persistently on the glass. It stared at Max with its penetrating black eyes.

✷

Samantha rejoined the small group on the sofa, after returning from the bathroom upstairs. Ed was still slurping coffee. "So, Samantha, did you find the bathroom okay? You know, I can't blame you for being apprehensive, this is a lot to take in. What say you take a short trip, before the very long one?"

Richard looked over quizzically at Ed. "You're going to give her the same stuff you gave me?"

"Exactly."

Samantha looked bewildered. She remarked to Richard, "Well, I guess you don't seem any different; you're not brain-dead or anything."

Richard smiled. "Well, not more than usual, I guess. I'll take that as a compliment." He attempted to reassure her. "To be perfectly honest, I actually feel better than ever. It's hard to put into words exactly, but there's this feeling of wholeness. I know that sounds all new-age. It's like all my problems seem sort of trivial now. It's a whole new state of mind...a new perspective really."

"Wow. That's a lot. It's just really weird, for me; I've never even smoked a joint, if you can believe it."

Ed was clearly amused. "I definitely didn't have you pegged for a heroin addict, but not even a little reefer at university?"

Samantha shook her head. "No, I actually was pretty boring at university."

Richard replied, "Listen, I was exactly the same. I can't tell you how many times I just sat with a beer, while my friends were smoking dope. It's not my thing, either, believe me. You may be many things, but boring is not one of them. Remember, this is totally up to you. If we're actually going to go through with this crazy plan of Ed's, it just might make the big trip a little easier, I think that's what Ed is thinking here."

"What the hell! What do I have to lose? It's worth a try, and if we're really going through with this crazy plan, we might as well go all the way, right?"

Ed was clearly enthused. "Now that's the can-do attitude I like to hear. Let's get started." He stood up and put his hand to his ear. "Hear that?"

Richard shook his head. "I don't hear anything."

"Exactly. This is the first time I haven't heard sirens blaring. It means everything is stopped. It's all up to us now." With that ominous observation, they left the living room and descended into the dark basement.

Ed opened the heavy black padlocked door into the inner sanctum of his laboratory. Samantha wasn't prepared for the maelstrom of dark imagery, and strange machines that assaulted her senses, as she entered. She looked around at the dizzying array with a look of shock and apprehension. "This is certainly your classic mad scientist lab."

Ed was sombre. "We have serious work to do. Now this combination of drugs is administered in a number of ways. For instance, is commonly consumed as a tea. I'm going to give you the exact same thing Richard took, the ayahuasca. For the actual experiment, you will receive all three ingredients. This is directly injected into your bloodstream. You will be fine. Each person's experience is different, of course, but you will hallucinate. What you see and feel is different for each person. Just try to stay calm, and maintain a positive mental outlook." Ed prepared the apparatus and the compound.

He motioned for Samantha to sit down in the heavy steel chair. Her face twisted with worry and fear. "I'm sorry, this is just so strange for me, it's almost like it's not really happening, but it is. I feel like I'm going to suddenly wake up and realize it was all just a dream, you know? I know that sounds crazy."

Richard nodded. "No, you're not crazy, I've been having the same feeling, but we just have to carry on as if everything is normal, okay? Just trust me on this one."

Samantha remained unconvinced. "Richard, you'll make sure nothing happens to me, right?"

Richard held her hands tightly. "You know I would never let anything bad happen to you."

His compassion calmed her. "I'm so scared...just hold onto me, while he does it."

Ed administered his carefully measured compound. After a few moments, her body uncoiled and her mind relaxed. She slowly released her hands from Richard's. Her eyes closed and her breathing returned to normal. Samantha focused on pleasant thoughts, as her consciousness slowly drifted away into an ocean of pure nothingness.

She suddenly experienced a violent, dizzying loss of awareness. Her immediate surroundings disappeared, while her awareness of an inner reality increased tenfold. She felt a frightening sensation of her body spinning wildly out of control. Bright, ever-evolving spectrums of colour burst across her field of vision. Rivers of deep azure water, canary yellow flames, and ruby red stars flowed through her mind. Samantha felt her body immersed in the warm blue water. She floated effortlessly on the buoyant water. A dizzying pinwheel of pastel comets with endless sparkling tails danced before her eyes. Enormous blue, yellow, and red mushrooms with white polka dots stretched to the limitless sky above her. She stared at her outstretched arms that seemed to extend towards infinity.

Samantha was keenly aware of another presence in the room. She understood that it was neither Ed nor Richard. The entity was not human. Its identity was unknowable, yet she sensed a powerful and beneficent wisdom. She strained her eyes to apprehend the creature, yet it remained always beyond her sight. It was watching her intensely while it gauged her reactions. It seemed to be gently guiding her along a predetermined path. She imagined them as small, elvish creatures, with darting eyes and grinning faces. They seemed not quite alien, yet definitely not human. These were in-between beings. They were neither here nor there, and neither fish nor fowl. They were something beyond her understanding.

Slowly a novel scene materialized in her mind. She looked down at her feet and found that she was being whisked along a gleaming metal walkway. She looked around to see a strange, futuristic cityscape, replete with bulbous white cars and an elaborate pneumatic tube system. A gleaming bright emerald green building with a sharp spire shot into the pillowy clouds. She then spied an enormous grey concrete building with terrifying swastika banners hanging everywhere. She turned around to see three black-hooded menacing figures speeding towards her on the walkway. She quickened her pace, but to no avail. They pursuers grew closer. Suddenly she fell off the walkway and the imaginary scene ended. She felt herself slowly emerge from the mists of the netherworld to her ordinary reality. Her eyes suddenly shot open, as she looked around in confusion. "Good lord...I had no idea...it was incredible, troubling, but incredible."

Richard gently helped her from the chair. "Are you okay? You were gone for a while, longer than me, anyway."

"It felt like just a few seconds. I guess like in a dream."

Ed replied, "Time has no relevance in the dream world...or whatever state you want to call it."

Samantha began to relax. "I actually feel much better, calm. It's definitely not what I expected."

Ed was visibly relieved. "I'm really glad you had a good experience, but that's the point; if ordinary people knew about this stuff, Big Pharma would go broke. This stuff is better than any antidepressant crap they pump into you these days. Maybe the powers that be are finally starting to understand that."

The sound of footsteps above them interrupted the conversation. "That must be Max! God, I hope he found food." The group of three exited the basement and headed to the living room. Ed excitedly burst out in joy by both what he smelled and saw. "Max! I knew you'd come through for us. I was just hoping for more doughnuts. I can hardly believe it. Pizza! How on Earth did you find a place that was still open?"

"Cunning and skill, obviously, and the three hundred dollars helped, I guess." Max carried the four extra-large pizzas and placed them in the kitchen. The wonderful aroma of tomato sauce, cheese, and pepperoni wafted through the house.

"My God, I am hungry, like I've never eaten before! Is this what they call the munchies?" She narrowly beat Ed in a race to the kitchen. She opened up the box to a steaming hot, incredible smell. Uncharacteristically, she grabbed a slice and devoured it, not even waiting for Max to retrieve the plates from the cupboard.

Ed accepted the plate and helped himself to a slice. "You know, this really is a feast of sorts, we should make an occasion of it. This might well be our very own last supper."

Max laughed. "I suppose you will be sitting in the centre, like the Messiah!"

Ed grinned. "Well, I wasn't exactly going to say it, but now that I think of it, I am saving these two, so...maybe?"

Samantha lifted another piece of pizza. "To our saviour, the mad scientist Edward!"

They group agreed that it was indeed a special occasion. Ed declared, "Let's not half-fast this. I'm going to get out the fancy stuff." Ed soon returned to set the dining room table with his finest dinnerware. He grabbed an ornate mahogany box from a closet in the hall, and began emptying the contents. "This is a really nice silverware set that I inherited from my mom. I think it's the only decent thing she left me. She sure as hell didn't leave me any money. I don't think I've ever used it; always waiting for that really special occasion. I guess this will do. Might as well get at least one use out of them."

Everyone helped preparing the table for the end-times feast. Finally, they were set to eat. Ed picked up an old-looking bottle of red wine. "Now this is something special, been saving this one, too. This is a Chateau Latour 2007. I think it's worth a couple of grand...better be good." He walked around the table and carefully poured the entire contents of the thick, deep Cabernet Sauvignon wine into everyone's glasses. He picked up his own goblet and took a deep lungful of the exotic scent. He lifted it up to the light and swirled the expensive elixir around. He took a large mouthful and savoured the aromatic, complex melody of flavours. "Now that is not half bad. Max, my man, what is your opinion?"

Max in turn took a large mouthful and swallowed. "That is absolutely delicious, Ed, worth every penny, it's the best I've ever tasted."

They all sipped the exceptional wine and watched Ed as he lifted his glass high. "We come together on this night, on the very strangest of occasions. My friends, and it does seem strange to say that to you all, having just met Richard and Samantha, but I feel as though I've known you much longer. Fate has brought us all together, and with the help of science, we may be able to save you two from what fate has in store. Only time will tell, and of course, we may all wake up tomorrow unscathed, as if waking from some strange nightmare. It has been a pleasure to know the both of you, and, of course, my trusted friend Max, who does his best to keep me on the right side of sanity!"

"Too late for that, I'm afraid!" Max chortled good-naturedly.

Richard raised his glass. "Those are kind words, Ed. Now I can't speak for Samantha, but I know that I'm grateful to have this opportunity to survive, in some form or another. There was one thing, Ed, that I was kind of wondering about. Why can't you two join us...I mean, after we see if this thing works?"

Max fielded the query. "Unfortunately, this apparatus we have set up really isn't a push-button, automatic pilot kind of thing. It might be possible for one of us, if there's still time left."

Ed pondered the question himself. "I suppose we could flip a coin, leave it to fate. I just know I'm not going to leave my friend here alone to die, I just couldn't do it. How would he survive without me? I mean look at him, he's a hundred pounds dripping wet; any surviving marauding hordes would eat him alive."

Max laughed. "Yes, I would be easy pickings. Of course, it's a moot point, nobody would actually survive the initial blast, save of course, for the rich and powerful in their underground bunkers."

Ed and the others sat and enjoyed the delicious pizza, the incomparable wine, and the delightful company. Although Ed was not a particularly social person, he could not recall a better dinner party in his home. All thoughts of their approaching demise disappeared for a few hours. It was rather like a last supper, thought Richard. He hoped that he would not be the one betrayed.

✷

The dawn broke with the morning sun bursting forth across the blackness. The day of reckoning was upon them. The gigantic burning asteroid figured prominently in the sky, now appearing larger than the sun. It was difficult to reconcile its incredible beauty with its horrible destructive power. A loud radio alarm blasted classical music in Ed's room. The loud rendition of Mozart's "*Requiem*" seemed acutely appropriate. One by one, the gathering of friends awoke from a sound sleep. Max roused himself from the sofa, still wearing the clothes from the previous day. He headed to the kitchen to make some coffee. The aromatic, familiar scent of the fresh-brewed elixir wafted through the rooms. It energized those who were still sleepy.

Richard awoke from a long, dream-filled sleep, which was unusual for him. The heavy wine consumption made him groggy. He shuffled out into the hallway wearing borrowed pajamas. They were a burgundy-and-gold-striped pattern with a wizard school insignia on the left chest. Samantha emerged from the bedroom across from Richard. She wore blue flannel pajamas with a fluffy cloud pattern on them. She had borrowed them from Ed, a souvenir from a tryst years ago. Ed emerged like a great bear from his cave, wresting himself from a deep night of hibernation. "Nothing like a few bottles of fine wine for a great sleep. Haven't slept that well in years. How did you sleep, Rich?"

"I know what you mean. That was the best sleep I've had in...well, as long as I can remember anyway."

Ed replied, "That's good to hear." He took a long sniff at the air. "That smells good. I need some coffee. Max makes a strong brew, let's get this show on the road." The group gathered in the kitchen.

The coffee machine finished its brew cycle. Ed retrieved mugs from the cupboard and began pouring for everyone. There was not much else to eat but leftover pizza. Max removed the cardboard pizza box from the refrigerator and placed it on the kitchen island. Both Samantha and Richard helped themselves to the cold leftovers.

Ed moved to the living room, after heating up a slice of pizza in the microwave. "Let's see what's going on with this missile launch." He took a long swig of coffee and put down his *Doctor Who* Dalek mug. He flipped on the TV to the news channel. A desperate-looking anchor intoned, "The final launch is mere hours away now." The split-screen showed an elderly scientist discussing the likelihood of success. A countdown clock appeared in the corner of the screen. It showed three hours remained until the massive missile launch into Earth's stratosphere. "Eat up, people, we don't have that much time. You two finish the leftovers and get ready. I'm going to start getting set up in the basement. We have less than an hour after the missile launch."

Ed stood up and returned to his bedroom to get dressed. Max was still in the kitchen sipping his coffee and chewing on a slice of pizza. Ed returned from his bedroom to the kitchen to talk to Max. Both scientists proceeded to the basement to prepare for the experiment. Ed called out from the basement, "Call us when they're ready for the launch!"

Richard acknowledged the request and stood up. He looked over at Samantha and headed for the front door. "I wanted to take a quick look at this thing." Samantha followed. Richard opened the door to a deathly quiet street. They both looked up simultaneously at the terrifyingly close asteroid above them.

Samantha remarked, "If it weren't about to destroy all of us, I'd say it was beautiful."

Richard replied, "Not as beautiful as you." He grinned immediately. "Sorry, that was kind of corny, but you're right. It's hard to imagine something so deadly being so gorgeous."

Samantha quipped, "Just like me, deadly and gorgeous!"

Richard smiled. “Right, now who’s being corny. I’m glad you can laugh about this.”

“What else can you do? What’s the point of being miserable? It’s not as if we can stop it.”

“But we are trying to escape. Are you sure about this? Are you sure you want to go ahead with this crazy plan?”

Samantha shrugged. “What have we got to lose?”

Richard and Samantha returned to the house and sat together on the brown leather sofa, watching the news. The anchor spoke in a sombre tone. “In less than three hours, the fate of the world and all of humanity will be known. All eyes will be on the hundreds of ICBM missiles as they attempt to obliterate the asteroid. Ironically, the vast nuclear arsenal of the world may be used on this day to save life, rather than destroy it.”

Samantha listened to the newscaster. There was no new information, rather just an endless repetition of well-worn facts. “Didn’t you mention you had a brother?”

Richard nodded. “Yes, Allen. I tried to call him a few days ago, there was no service. I’m not sure there’s much phone service left anywhere. Knowing him, he would be one of the first to head for the hills, with his family. You don’t have brothers or sisters, do you?”

Samantha replied, “No, it’s pretty much just me. My parents died a while back, not at the same time; it was my father first, then my mother a year later.”

Richard and Samantha sat close, cherishing what little time they had left. Neither of them felt optimistic for their chances of survival. They both sat precariously upon the precipice of uncertainty. The impending doomsday strengthened their attachment. Soon the time had come for the final solution to save humanity. The news anchor explained that the missile launch was mere minutes away.

Richard looked at Samantha. “Do you want to get changed for the big day?”

Samantha examined her pajamas. "No, I'm good, I think. Why not be comfortable for the trip, right?"

Richard agreed. He stood up and walked over to the basement. "Hey, guys. It's just a few minutes until the launch...you coming up?"

Ed and Max bounded up the stairs. They finished the work hooking up the new generator and rigging up another chair. Ed was ebullient. "Is it showtime already?"

Max stood watching the broadcast. "At least they'll get great ratings. If I remember correctly, it will take ten minutes for the missiles to strike the asteroid.

Ed nodded. "Yeah, that sounds about right. Well, here goes nothing!"

The room grew silent, save for the TV announcer. "*If unsuccessful, the asteroid will strike almost directly in the centre of Russia, after that, it will be mere seconds until the blast wave engulfs the Earth.*" The final minute countdown began.

"*Five, four, three, two, one...*" The missiles launched all over the world towards the celestial invader. The TV newscaster was silent. All eyes around the world watched as the deadly weapons tracked their way through the bright blue sky.

Ed leaped up from the chair to the front door. He ran outside to watch the action. "Damn! You can't see any of the missiles from here. Too bad Canada doesn't have any nukes." He ran back into the house.

Richard finally broke the silence. "Ed, do you think God is watching this?"

Ed thought for a moment, pondering the question. "Hard to say, really. Depends upon how you look at things, I guess. Whomever he or she is, you have to think they have a very dark sense of humour, or are just plain mean."

Samantha thought for a moment before remarking, "Something like this happening makes you wonder about everything, really. I mean, if there is a God, and he did create us, why would he want to destroy us...it seems kind of pointless."

Max offered his opinion. "If there is a God, and he truly is trying to test us, what better way than creating a truly hopeless situation? It's the only means of really determining how a person will react, when they face their own death."

The flickering screen of the TV showed multiple images of streaking tails of light flashing like fireworks through the blue sky. It was a spectacle both terrible and beautiful, thought Ed. The attacking force of missiles battered the asteroid with incredible force. The impact filled the sky with an impossible light, surpassing that of the sun. Viewers outside averted their eyes during the event, to avoid retinal damage. A deafening sound shook the house. It was the largest explosive force in the history of the world. It rivalled the moment of creation, in its all-encompassing light.

The announcer on TV began to speak slowly and haltingly, with neither enthusiasm nor joy. Overcome with emotion, he searched for the right words. "*It seems...friends...that the last hope has failed...the asteroid was simply too large to destroy...it is difficult to know what to say at this point...may God have mercy on all our souls.*" His weary head fell as the camera pulled back. A moment later, the image on the screen faded away. The TV station ceased broadcasting.

Ed was first to break the uncomfortable heaviness that enveloped the room. "Well, definitely not the outcome we were hoping for, but honestly, I'm not surprised, really. What can I say? Mother Nature is a bitch! Let's get going on plan B."

The others in the room were dumbstruck by the realization that their world was ending. Samantha looked into Richard's gaping eyes. "Well, so much for that idea. I have to admit, I didn't actually think it would work."

Richard nodded. "No, me neither, but still, it's hard to believe that it's really the end, that this is really happening."

Max remarked, "Unfortunately this is happening, despite all our misgivings, our doubts, we have to accept the reality that is presented to us. I think we'd better get going, there's not much time left, for any of us." They all departed, one by one, towards the dark basement below. Ed opened the heavy black door to his once top-secret laboratory.

Max entered the black room and turned up the lights. "We really don't have a lot of time here."

Ed laughed. "Yeah, barely enough time to kiss our sweet asses goodbye, for us two schlemiels, anyway. At least you two have a chance." Richard and Samantha saw the two heavy steel chairs. Ed gestured towards both of them. "Okay, you two lovebirds, it's showtime. Grab a chair, it doesn't matter which one."

They both sat down together, side by side, their hands clenched together tightly. They both looked over at the other and held a long, poignant gaze. Neither said a word. Richard could clearly see the terror in her eyes. "Don't look so freaked out, you've basically done this before. Remember the alternative."

"Are we doing the right thing? I mean this is crazy, isn't it? Suddenly this all seems strange, like déjà vu, maybe? I don't know...I can't explain it properly."

Richard shook his head. "I'm not sure I follow..."

Ed stood boldly before the two intrepid travellers, arms folded behind his back. "The time has come, it's now or never. Speak now or forever hold your peace...or something like that. I guess that's for marriages, isn't it. I just want you two to know, there is no guarantee here. I want you to understand exactly what you're getting into."

Both Richard and Samantha looked at each other, then at Ed. Richard spoke for both of them. "I don't think we really do understand what we're getting into, but I guess we have no choice."

Ed nodded. "Fair enough, but I hope at least that you trust me."

Samantha answered, "Honestly, I don't know you enough to trust you, but I think Richard does, and that's enough for me. I trust him." They both nodded in unison, assenting.

Ed grinned. "Okay, then, I will begin."

Ed seized hold of a semicircular metal apparatus that hung above the chair. An identical device was attached to Samantha's chair. Each piece was connected to thick electrical cables that snaked across the floor. Ed began with Richard. He affixed the metal headpiece to his willing volunteer's head. He duplicated the feat with Samantha. He gestured to Max. "How we doing, Max? Are they hooked up properly?"

Max nodded. "All good here."

Ed seized a frighteningly large syringe from a nearby metal table. He held it up to the light and squeezed the air from the cannister. He administered his strange concoction of drugs directly into Richard's arm. He proceeded to repeat the procedure with Samantha. She winced as the long, sharp tip of the needle penetrated her arm. The dose was more massive than any he had before attempted. Max was at the other side of the room, slowly increasing the power of the plasma-field generator. Ed ran over to help his colleague.

The room bristled with brilliant spikes of electricity. The still air crackled with sound and vibration. Ed spurred on his friend. "More! Increase the energy output to maximum!"

Max's brow furrowed in doubt. "Are you sure?"

Ed threw his arms up in desperation. "Yes! It's time!"

The floor beneath them rumbled. Ed wondered if the cause was his infernal machine or the asteroid impact. Richard and Samantha sensed the vibrating power flowing through their bodies. The metal apparatus affixed to both their heads pulsated with energy.

Suddenly a blinding flash of light bright as the sun enveloped the room. Like a bursting, expanding singular moment of creation, it obliterated the darkness in the room. Ed and Max both stared at the now empty metal chairs in disbelief.

"I have to say, Max, I didn't really think this would work...I mean, I hoped it would."

Max agreed. "That's for sure. They're both gone, just like the monkey. I wonder where they are now?"

Ed looked over at Max. "You know, if you want to, I could send you, to wherever the hell they are."

Max smiled. "And leave you to clean up this mess? Nah…I've had a good run. I say let the cards fall where they may."

Ed and Max stood for several moments in the now darkened room. "Hey, Max, I guess we're going to go out like old Adolph, hunkered down in the bunker, awaiting the inevitable end. We might as well stay down here, not that it'll make much difference of course."

"That's strange, actually," said Max. "Shouldn't we be gone now, I mean, shouldn't we be dead?"

Ed was also somewhat perplexed. "Maybe they had the timing off a little. Maybe the missile attack did work? I did feel that rumble earlier. No, we both watched it. That's not right."

"Ed, do you think we should leave the basement, and check upstairs?"

"I think we should wait a little…let's see how this plays out."

PART TWO

CHAPTER 9

Dorian bolted upright from his bed, as if electrocuted. He shook his head to clear away the heavy cobwebs. His thoughts raced, as he attempted to right his wildly spinning mind. He grasped desperately for some shred of reality within the miasma of his confusion. He struggled out of bed in a comatose state. He steadied himself on the side of the bed, as his legs wobbled back and forth. His house seemed strange to him, as if he had awoken in the wrong building altogether. Yet it was not completely alien, a part of him recognized it. He thought back to the previous day. His mind was a complete blank slate.

He looked over to see that somebody had been in his bed. He knew it to be his wife, yet he could not recall her face, or her name. He remembered that she was always up early to exercise at the gym. Instinctively he looked over at the wall-screen in his bedroom. The image flickered to life. It was Eve. "Hey, Dorian, what's up?" Eve was in her bathroom, sipping a coffee.

Dorian walked up to the screen and touched it. "You know, I was just going to call you. I had the most bizarre dream. It's really hard to describe, like nothing I've ever experienced. It was like I was this different person, with a whole other life. It felt so real."

Lilith walked into view on the screen wearing a thick, blood-red robe, also sipping a coffee. Dorian watched her casually caress Eve on the backside. Eve wore a silk sky-blue peignoir set. She replied to Dorian, "So you had a weird dream, too? So did I."

Dorian walked from his bedroom to the kitchen. The automatic wall-screen flickered on. He set about making some coffee, and some toast. He continued his explanation. "Yeah, you were in my dream, it's all beginning to fade already. I remember I worked in some boring advertising job, you know, office work, and everything was old-fashioned. You were an actress, Eve, but then everyone was going to die for some reason, some kind of apocalypse, and there was this mad scientist, a stereotype character, like from an old black-and-white TV show. It was nuts."

Eve did not say a word for several moments. She stared at the wall-screen in disbelief. She chose her words carefully. "This is going to sound even weirder...but I think I had the exact same dream. Does that make any sense?" Eve gazed at Dorian, as if seeing him for the first time in a completely new light.

Lilith came over and put her arms around Eve, pulling her close. Eve recoiled from the touch, alarming her. "Uh...what's the problem? Why so touchy?"

Lilith was annoyed, and commanded the wall-screen to shut down. She made one last remark to Dorian. "Is it okay if we call you back, Dorian?" Dorian nodded as his image flickered away. She turned back towards Eve. "Why are you giving me the stink-eye? This isn't about that stupid dream you had, is it? I mean, get over it. Did I do something to you?"

Eve gave her a circumspect look. "Did I tell you about my dream?"

Lilith shrugged. "No, I just overheard you and Dorian talking about it. Anyway, I've got a busy day; actually, I think we both do."

Eve walked into the kitchen and refilled her coffee. The wall-screen flickered on to the news channel. She thought about her incomprehensible cold reaction to Lilith's touch. Her feelings towards her wife had suddenly changed drastically. The realization that Lilith was correct was overwhelming. Her wife had done something terrible to her in this dream, but the specific details remained beyond her grasp. She rationalized that her bitter feelings were imaginary, yet the pain and resentment Eve felt was all too vivid. Lilith joined her in the kitchen. Eve caressed her arm. "Lill…I'm so sorry, it just feels so strange. It's like this dream really happened. I feel like I barely know you at all."

Lilith pushed Eve's arm away from hers. She fumed with rage. "What the hell are you talking about? We've been together for two years, and one crazy dream wipes that out? You just need to calm down."

Eve felt bewildered and betrayed. She no longer felt quite like herself. "I'm so sorry, Lill. Just let me get myself together…just forget it." She offered the apology only to mollify her furious wife. In her heart, she realized that nothing in her life would ever be the same. She felt turned inside out, backward, and upside down. Eve left Lilith and returned to the bedroom to change. She searched her closet for something to wear. All of her clothes seemed strange and unfamiliar. She grabbed an iridescent powder-blue dress, and quickly dressed.

✷

Ed opened the heavy black door leading from the dark basement. He cautiously pushed it open. Max followed him closely. The two scientists made their way hesitantly up through the murky darkness. Ed gingerly pushed open the door to the living room, fully expecting to find a chaotic, hellish maelstrom above. As they stepped onto the main floor, they were amazed to see that nothing whatsoever had changed. Ed was shocked, and Max was speechless. Ed shook his head and stammered out, "What the hell…happened? Did we get the impact time wrong… maybe it's still coming?"

"Hard to imagine that. Let's go look outside."

Both men ventured outside and returned in disbelief. Nothing had changed, and the asteroid had disappeared from the sky above. Ed picked up the TV remote and clicked it on. The middle-aged male anchor was deadly serious, and spoke deliberately. "*Experts are baffled, as the deadly asteroid has disappeared completely, with no logical explanation. As you can see here, after the failed missile launch, we see the asteroid continuing on its course...there is a blinding flash of light, and then nothing, as if it were plucked from the sky by some unseen Godly hand. We know nothing more at this point.*"

Ed and Max both watched in utter confusion. Ed shook his head. "Max, this is going to sound crazy...but did that huge flash of light on TV remind you of anything?"

At first, Max did not see the connection. "I'm not sure what you're getting at, really."

"Didn't that blinding white flash of light look just like the one we saw when Richard and Samantha vanished?"

Max slowly began to see his reasoning. "Yes...perhaps on a much larger scale. You're not suggesting..."

"I am. That's exactly what I'm suggesting, however nuts that seems. Let's check the chronology to be sure."

The newscaster continued with an upbeat tone. "*Beyond all expectations, life seems to be slowly returning to normal, all over the planet. There almost feels like a new sense of hope and renewal has swept over the world.*"

Both Max and Ed returned quickly to the basement. Ed sat down at the computer monitor and turned it on. "I can hardly believe we didn't fry the machinery this time. Everything still seems to be working okay." Ed squinted at the video record of Richard's and Samantha's departure. Max stared over his shoulder. He carefully watched the time counter and recorded the exact moment of the flash on a notepad. Both men ran upstairs to watch the news again. The two times of the blinding flash of light were identical. Both events occurred at precisely 11:11 a.m., EST. "Max, do you realize what this means?"

Max was still in utter confusion. "Absolutely not, this makes no sense. How could one event somehow be connected to the other?"

"And yet it happened. Somehow by sending Richard and Samantha through that portal, or whatever you want to call it, we must have opened some sort of interdimensional gateway, and that asteroid got pulled through also. So, by saving them, we inadvertently saved humanity in the process."

"Ed...the science just doesn't add up, but what about the other time?" Ed at first did not fully comprehend the question. Max continued, "I know we're just speculating at this point. I'm referring to the experiment with your magical monkey, you must have opened up the portal then also."

Ed slowly began to understand the argument. "Are you suggesting that by opening the portal that first time, I introduced the asteroid into our reality?"

Max nodded. "Inadvertently, of course, but it seems you have at once doomed all of humanity, and then saved it."

Ed had difficulty grasping the gravity of the declaration. "Talk about playing God. Makes you wonder about sticking your nose where it doesn't belong."

Max agreed. "Ed, I hope you've finally learned your lesson."

Dorian finished his breakfast in a state of utter bewilderment. He vaguely recalled a need to go to work. The nature of which was a complete mystery. He left his apartment and travelled down the elevator into the expansive, gleaming, clean lobby. Several people rushed by him, presumably also on their way to work. He stood outside the towering apartment complex and stared up at the impressively large glass-enclosed structure. Dorian suddenly recalled a massive asteroid in the sky. Looking up, its absence was perplexing to him. He struggled to recover more details of his vivid dream.

His reverie was broken by a passerby. The older man had thinning grey hair and small, round glasses. He spoke with great animation. "Dorian, man, are you still asleep? You're going to be late for work. Come on, we might catch the last tube if we hurry."

Dorian did not recognize the person, but smiled and followed him. They travelled as always along the pneumatic tube expressway to his office at the Perimeter Institute. Dorian exited the cylindrical compartment after three stops. He waved goodbye to the distinguished man as he walked away.

His surroundings were strange and alien to him, yet he still seemed to know the way. He felt like an actor walking through an incredibly detailed movie set. Dorian walked through the revolving glass doors and into a gargantuan lobby with cathedral ceilings. He gazed down the hallway at strange banners hanging on the walls. He pulled out a security badge from his pocket and swiped it a large metal rectangle. The machine beeped and an LED light turned green. He strode over to the elevator and waited inside the car. He could not recall his floor. An extremely attractive woman wearing a tight black leather skirt and a crisp white blouse entered the car.

She smiled seductively. "What's wrong, Dorian, still half-asleep?" She pushed the button labelled thirty-three. They stood in awkward silence as they both stared at the red numbers slowly increasing. The car stopped and the alluring woman exited. Dorian gawked at her shapely behind as she walked away. She turned around and waved at him, seemingly aware of his attention.

He nodded at a few people before finding his office. He gazed out the polished glass window at a similar office, in an almost identical building across from him. He heard his videophone ring. The face of a beautiful blonde woman appeared on the screen. Dorian recognized the face immediately, but struggled to recall her name. "Hey, honey, I didn't even hear you get up. I had a weird night...really weird. I'll tell you about it later. You have a good workout?"

Alice was an intimidating, towering blonde goddess of a woman. Her confident, piercing sky-blue eyes dominated the image on the screen. Her toned body neatly contained her generous, feminine curves. Alice was well-educated, witty, and very conventional in her political and social views. She worked as a receptionist at a large, downtown advertising firm. "Yeah, it's crazy here already. You look like crap, did you sleep at all?"

"Gee, thanks for the compliment! Maybe, I don't know, like I said, I'm a little messed up." He tried to alleviate her concerns. "I'll be fine... don't worry about me."

"Poor baby. Did you have a nightmare?"

"Something like that." Dorian maintained a cool composure, unsure of which card to play. "I'll call you later...love you." His image flickered away. Alice instinctively felt something was amiss with her husband.

Dorian's computer flickered on automatically. He stared at the screen as if mesmerized. Dorian had apparently worked at the Institute for several years, although, he had no recognition of this time. His latest project involved the development of experimental propulsion systems and interdimensional gravitation field technology. He was currently focused on a plasma-field generator. He was collaborating with several other colleagues, including Eve and her wife, Lilith.

He opened a file on his computer and stared at a complex array of equations. Soon his mind wandered back to his perplexing dream from the previous night. The image of Eve's beautiful face consumed his thoughts. He called her name into the videophone and slowly her image materialized before him. The background behind her face was unfamiliar to him. Eve's expression was serious. "Dorian, are you okay? I know I'm not...not by a long shot. I have no idea what's going on. Do you?"

"Where are you? You're not at the Institute. Listen, I hope it's not weird, me calling you like this. I just didn't know who else to call. This is hard to explain. It's like I've had my memory erased...or replaced?"

"Yes! That's it, that's how I feel! What's going on, Dorian? Why is it only us that feels this? Lilith thinks I'm crazy, but honestly, she's a complete stranger to me. If anything, she's giving me a really weird vibe, like she's done something horrible to me...but I can't remember. I know that makes no sense."

Dorian listened with great interest, his spirits were buoyed by the fact that another person understood his confusion. "We have to meet...I have to get out of here. I noticed this weird-looking church on my way here. I think it's just around the corner; it had this huge yellow eight-pointed star."

"Yeah, I saw it, too. I know exactly where you mean. I'm apparently at some new test site. I have no idea what they're actually doing here. I'll be there in ten minutes."

Dorian nodded. "Okay. I'll have to make up some excuse to get out of here."

The image of Eve's face slowly faded. Dorian locked his computer with a spoken password and left his office. He breezed by his attractive blonde secretary Betty. "Alice, if anybody needs me, I just need to grab something from my car."

She stared back curiously. "Alice? I think you're confusing me with your lovely wife, although I certainly don't take that as an insult. And what do you mean *car*? I didn't think you even owned one. You always take the tube."

Dorian realized his mistake and corrected himself. "Sorry, yes, Betty, I was just thinking about my wife...I meant, I just need to run out to get something to eat." He was clearly flustered by his errors.

Betty inquired, "Are you feeling okay, Mr. Steffen?"

Dorian feigned a casual smile. "Oh sure, I just didn't sleep well, nothing to worry about."

The stunning, highly polished secretary nodded and flashed her pure white teeth.

✷

Max and Ed sat on the leather sofa watching TV. The news channel anchor intoned, "*Slowly, around the world, life is beginning to return to normal. The rioting and looting that had plagued cities has largely been contained. Most areas of the world are slowly returning to their usual routine. People are waking up to the realization that the world is not going to end anytime soon. Still, many questions remain. How did this asteroid suddenly disappear into thin air, and why was NASA so late in first identifying this deadly threat? We are pleased to have an expert on the subject from NASA to discuss this. Dr. Nauhaus, what is your explanation for recent events?*"

A very distinguished, grey-bearded, professorial man appeared on the screen. "*Hello, Peter. Thank you for having me. This asteroid Apophis really is an enigma to us all. Normally we have a fairly accurate, comprehensive inventory of all the celestial objects in, or around our solar system. Yet this one literally appeared out of empty space, and returned from whence it came, from nowhere to nothingness.*"

The anchorman queried, "*So there is no logical explanation for the sudden vanishing, Dr. Nauhaus?*"

"*Honestly, it's like nothing we've ever encountered before. Almost like God decided to suddenly pluck it from the sky. Obviously, there is some logical, rational explanation. We just haven't discovered it yet.*"

"*Well, thank you for joining us this morning, professor. So, who knows, maybe it was the power of prayer, of people all around the world, of all different faiths, praying together that somehow made the difference.*"

Edward and Max watched in utter disbelief. "Ed, do you think we should tell people what we've done?"

"Are you nuts? Where would we even begin? Honestly, I'm not sure where we even go from here."

Max responded with a furrowed brow, "And what about Richard and Samantha. Do we dare try and bring them back?"

"And risk upsetting the balance of the universe again? I think I've opened enough temporal-spatial rifts for one lifetime. I don't think so, my friend."

"So, we do nothing, doom them to some unknown fate? We don't even know if they're still alive."

Ed was adamant. "Isn't that everyone, really? Do any of us know our fate? I really don't think we have any choice here. We sent them away in good faith. I was trying to save their lives. I don't see how we can try and retrieve them...if that were even possible. Still, we definitely have to try something, we have to do some detective work, find out more about both of them. Who knows where it might lead? We might be missing something crucial."

"I agree with you, opening the portal again is way too dangerous, but who knows, they both seem like intelligent people, maybe they'll find their own way back."

Ed shrugged. "Well, I honestly doubt that very much, but who knows? In the meantime, I guess it's business as usual for you and me tomorrow, more obnoxious students, with their endless questions."

Max nodded. "I guess you're right, I'm going to head home, and try to get a good night's sleep for a change." Max left Ed's house and headed home on the subway. Edward sat back down on the sofa and stared absently at the wall. His mind wandered as he ruminated upon the whereabouts of his two new friends.

✷

Dorian left the Perimeter Institute and walked down the many flights of stairs. It was a beautiful sunny morning. He instinctively looked up, trying to find the asteroid in the sky. Its very absence was again jarring. The unfamiliar city was teeming with focused, well-dressed people walking quickly. He crossed a street and found a strange, fast-moving walkway system. He watched as others around him casually walked on to the metallic moving panels. He carefully mimicked their behaviour. He remembered passing the nearby church that morning. Its tall spire and brightly lit star figured prominently in the skyline. It was close enough that he didn't have to take the elaborate tube system. The strangely futuristic city around him was altogether unfamiliar. Gleaming, immensely tall, angular buildings and silent electric vehicles moved by him. The sky was a deep azure blue. Dorian noticed that the air itself smelled differently. It felt clean, free from the smog and grit he was accustomed to in the city.

Huge advertisements, blinking brightly from moving billboards filled the sky. It was impossible to ignore the constant barrage of ads, noticed Dorian. He looked up to watch them more closely. One featured a beautiful blonde woman, wearing a canary yellow dress enjoying a coffee at the Berliner coffeehouse. Another showed a bank ad for Deutschland First National, and many others that were perplexing to him. The clothes he wore were entirely unfamiliar. His pants were bright ruby red, and very loose fitting. His shirt was emerald green, and glistened in the shining sun. He watched a young man speed by him on the fastest lane of the walkway system. He wore a T-shirt with a design that read "*Aldebaran Lions*." He noticed the massive church ahead of him. He slowly disembarked from the moving walkways by progressively moving to the slower lanes.

Dorian gazed at the monumental, towering white cathedral with the brightly lit eight-pointed yellow star. The imposing building resembled a grand parliament more than a church, with its overbearing, totalitarian proportions. He slowly made his way up the endless concrete stairs. He looked back to search for Eve. She apparently had not arrived, thought Dorian. He desperately hoped that nothing ill had befallen her.

He grabbed hold of the handle to the heavy black steel doors and entered the holy place. The interior of the church was like most other churches, with long rows of carved dark wood pews in the nave. Dorian looked around and found himself alone in the silent space. He apprehensively walked toward the altar and noticed a glaring difference to the church he knew. Dominating the altar was by a towering, shining gold stature of a Babylonian goddess. He recognized the statue as Astarte. Although he was not an expert in mythology, he knew this particular deity. The twenty-foot goddess stood fully naked and proud, staring menacingly forward. Her arms were held aloft, with one hand holding some strange implement. The terrifying figure struck Dorian with fear and awe.

He turned around as he heard footsteps behind him. He was relieved to see Eve walking up towards him. She stood beside him, staring at the impressive idol. "This doesn't seem quite right, does it? I mean, I recognize the statue, but don't most churches like this usually have something different at the altar, like a crucifix, or something?"

"Yes, you're totally right; something is way off. This place gives me the creeps. Let's get out, we shouldn't be here."

Eve nodded and turned around to see a tall figure in a thick, black cloak walk towards them. He stopped and sank to his knees several feet before them, and slowly laid his arms to the floor, prostrating himself before the holy goddess. A huge black hood obscured his face. "Welcome, friends. I've not seen you at our cathedral before. Are you visiting from another district?" The elderly, avuncular clergyman spoke with a forthright, direct manner that alarmed both Dorian and Eve.

Dorian struggled to find a response. "Yes, of course. We were both in town, and we saw this beautiful cathedral; we just wanted to look around. I hope that's okay."

The old priest seemed puzzled by the answer. "So, have you not yet been indoctrinated into the faith? I ask, because I noticed that you did not prostrate yourself before the most holy goddess when you arrived, as is the law."

The stern priest carefully scrutinized and judged both Dorian and Eve. Eve attempted to break the awkward silence that descended. "You know, we were so tired, I think we just forgot. I'm so sorry, we meant no offence." She motioned to Dorian as she tried her best to imitate the priest's gesture of fealty towards the goddess. Dorian carefully mimicked Eve, kneeling and reaching his arms forward. They both immediately got up and headed for the door. The dour priest glared ominously at them. Eve blurted out, "We really are in a hurry, I hope you understand."

They walked briskly towards the entrance, almost at a run.

The angry priest called out harshly, "See here, this is highly irregular, you have not followed the sacred protocols. Stop at once!"

Suddenly, two menacing black-hooded figures appeared out of nowhere. Dorian and Eve broke into a full run towards the exit. Dorian heaved open the heavy black door, as Eve barely slipped out. The church guards seized hold of Dorian, just as he tried to leave. The hooded men pushed close the door and forcibly dragged Dorian back into the church. He heard Eve's plaintive voice call his name as he struggled against his captors. He attempted to escape their grasp. One guard removed a long, shining metal shaft from inside his black cloak. He extended the metallic device towards Dorian's head. The weapon shot out a bluish-white electric tendril of energy that immediately immobilized the prisoner. Dorian felt his body seize up in pain, then nothing. His crumpled body lay immobilized upon the cold, checkerboard church floor. The guards dutifully followed the priest, dragging the limp body away.

CHAPTER 10

Ed awoke early the next morning to a beautiful, clear spring day. He went through his usual morning routine and stood in his kitchen sipping strong coffee from his *Doctor Who* mug. Ed was proctoring an exam in the afternoon, and he was in no mood to arrive early. He picked up the phone and dialled his friend's number. "Max, are you up?"

"I am now...I guess...what's wrong?"

"Nothing exactly. I mean, other than the fact that the entire balance of the universe seems off-kilter. Something is wrong, but I can't quite put my finger on it."

"What do you mean? Things are slowly getting back to normal, but it won't be immediate, that's to be expected."

"Max, I'm not sure precisely, I know that the asteroid is gone, so that threat is no longer here, but something still doesn't feel right. Call it a gut feeling. I think I'm going to do a little investigating, keep your phone close, I may need you."

"Need me for what?"

"If I knew that I wouldn't need to investigate. Just keep your eyes open, and I mean wide open."

"Okay, then, you go play Sherlock Holmes. I'm going to the university, Ed, I have to oversee an exam. You have fun."

Ed grabbed his cell phone from the table and got dressed. He found Richard's business card in the pocket of his tweed jacket. He looked at it intently. The card somehow looked different than he remembered, but he could not figure out why exactly. He decided that Richard's place of business would be the first stop in his investigation.

Ed drove his yellow Volvo wagon into the downtown core. The prevailing chaos in the city was slowly dissipating. Life was gradually falling back into the usual routine, almost as if nothing at all had happened. Ed thought it strange how quickly people dismissed the near Earth-shattering event. He also realized that nothing had actually happened. Ed began to question his own recollection of recent events. The rebirth of hope left many malcontents feeling bitterly disappointed. Ed eventually found the downtown office where Richard worked. The advertising company was located in a towering, gold-tinted glass skyscraper on Bay Street. The blazing morning sun refracted against the brilliant, shining exterior. Ed shielded his eyes against the searing, blindingly bright light.

Ed found a parking lot nearby and walked amongst the busy people hurrying to work. He pushed through the revolving door to the spacious lobby. A long security desk filled the back wall. Huge tropical plants filled the space. Ed stopped at a large glass rectangle in the centre of the space and searched for the location of the firm. He made his way to the busy elevator. The invigorating smell of coffee filled the air as he stepped in. He pushed the button for the twenty-third floor and waited. He exited the doors to see a bevy of impeccably polished and manicured women rushing by him. A tall, distinguished-looking man wearing a blue pinstriped suit regarded him with suspicion as he entered the room. He walked up to a smiling, striking blonde receptionist. She wore a simple sky-blue dress with a white sash and a white ribbon in her hair.

"Can I help you?"

Ed was slightly flustered by the attractive woman, and fumbled with his words, "Uh...yes...I hope so...I'm looking for a friend of mine that works here...Richard York."

The woman's expression changed slightly. "And you say he works here? On this floor? That name doesn't ring a bell." She then reached down to her desk and picked a strawberry tart from a tray. She took a bite. "I know these aren't good for you, but they're delicious, would you like one?"

Ed thanked her and took one. He swooned in delight. "You're right, this is exquisite, thank you." Ed reached in his pocket and proffered Richard's business card.

Alice took the card and examined it closely. "Well, this does look sort of like our business card, but the logo is wrong, I don't recognize the yellow star. I'm pretty sure he doesn't work in this office, maybe he's new?"

"No, no, he's worked here for years, at least that's what he told me. He mentioned you by name." Ed was at an impasse.

Alice was sympathetic. "This is very curious, what did he supposedly do here?"

Ed explained that Richard was an executive of some sort. Alice listened and called the manager of the department. She picked up the phone and explained, "There's a gentleman asking about a Richard York...we don't have anybody by that name working here, do we? No...I didn't think so."

Ed thanked the beautiful blonde receptionist and walked away feeling dejected and deeply confused. He walked out of the office and left the building. He headed for his car, and took his phone out. "Max, are you busy? This is so weird. I just left Richard's office, and they've never heard of him. I know this is the right place, it's like he never existed, or the memory of him has been erased."

"What do you mean by erased? What are you suggesting exactly? Are you quite sure you're in the right place? There must be some sort of logical explanation. What about Samantha? Why don't you try and find out something about her?"

"That's a great idea, Max. I'll talk to you after your exam."

"Don't you have to watch an exam later?"

"Yeah, I almost forgot. I'll be back on campus soon. I'll call me you this afternoon." Ed put his phone back in his pocket. He was spooked, and it was not a feeling he enjoyed.

Ed walked down the less busy downtown streets. He looked up at the beautiful spring morning. The absence of the asteroid in the sky was still jarring. He found his parking lot and got into his car. He started it up and paid for his ticket as he drove away. His plans gone awry, and he was now improvising. He stopped by a bagel shop he knew well and walked in. It was an old establishment that had sat on the same land for seventy years. The walls of the small restaurant were covered in old black-and-white photos of the early city. A long Formica counter wound around the back. Behind it were old-fashioned glassware and a metal milkshake machine. An ancient-looking menu hung on the wall behind. A tired-looking middle-aged man stood behind the counter, marrying the ketchup bottles. Ed looked up at the menu and ordered a coffee and bagel with cream cheese. After his order arrived, he took it and sat down at a nearby table.

An old Jewish couple sat at a table across from him. The elderly man spoke loudly, with a thick Yiddish accent. "Mildred, I tell you, God has spared us from this apocalypse. It's time to rejoice, not complain!"

The woman, presumably his wife, replied indignantly, "Meh! I still think we're all still doomed. I think it's some kind of trick!"

Ed smiled and thought about his long conversation with Samantha, before the experiment. He had asked her many questions about the science-fiction set where she worked. Ed recalled her mentioning that the show was filmed in an old abandoned factory down by the lake. Ed finished eating his bagel and coffee. He left the shop and returned to his car. He knew the city very well and easily found the set location. He parked close to the building and walked up, not knowing exactly how he would proceed. He stopped short as he noticed the faded, huge yellow eight-pointed star painted above the entrance. He stared at the strange symbol, knowing well how it featured prominently in his occult studies. The ancient sigil resonated loudly in his mind. He felt as though the symbol held the key to the mystery unfolding before him.

Ed walked into the building and saw a few people milling around the craft-service table. He hesitantly ambled up to a young girl carrying a clipboard and wearing a headset. The girl wore her hair in dreadlocks and sported multiple piercings on her face. Ed found her appearance quite repulsive.

She chewed gum as she spoke to him. "Hey, can I help you with something? Are you looking for someone? This is a closed set, you can't just walk in here, you know."

Ed was clearly out of his element, and was unusually diffident. "Uh…I'm looking for an actress that works on this show, her name is Samantha, she plays Eve on the show. She's a friend of mine. I haven't been able to reach her. It's very important that I find her."

The young woman took her eyes briefly away from her phone to scan her clipboard. "Well, I know everyone working on the show and you must be mistaken. Eve is played by Marsha Hare, so, not sure what to tell you. Are you sure it was this show?"

Ed had no answer. The girl shrugged and continued fiddling with her phone as she walked away. She turned around and called out abruptly, "You have to leave. Don't make me call security. If you want an autograph, you can wait outside, like everybody else."

Ed stood alone in the darkness, more confused than ever.

✷

Eve looked back to see the heavy black doors of the cathedral slam shut. She realized that she had no chance of saving Dorian on her own. She ran down the long procession of stone steps to the road. The tube station was close by, she recalled. She ran quickly past strangely dressed people and the bizarre architecture of the buildings around her. She walked towards the tube station with no clear destination in mind. Her mind raced with fleeting images from the previous night's dream.

Yet the more she thought about it, the more real it seemed. Recent events were inexplicable to her. It felt to her as if another person were occupying her mind. In the dream, she imagined she was an actor, and something terrible was about to happen. Try as she might, she could not hold on to the dissipating fragments of the dream. They melted away like vapour as soon as they materialized. Dorian's whereabouts and safety was foremost in her mind.

Eve carefully watched the other passengers in the tube station. They waved their wristwatches at an electronic sensor to enter. She followed their lead. She sat down, avoiding eye contact and attempting to blend in with the crowd. Eve gazed around the smooth, shiny interior of the tube compartment. Her wristwatch buzzed. She looked at the image on the screen.

The angry face of Lilith stared back at her. "Why aren't you at work? People here are talking!"

Eve stared at the image and struggled to think of an answer. "I... wasn't feeling well..."

Lilith did not believe the lie. "What are you talking about? You were fine this morning. Where are you now?"

Eve shot out in a panicky voice, "I have to go...I'll talk to you later." She found the button to switch off the video watch. She tried desperately to collect her scattered, confused thoughts. She felt her heart pounding violently in her chest. Eve fought back tears as her breathing grew more pronounced. An alarm sounded on her wristwatch, warning of a serious health condition.

A passenger sitting across from her noticed her distress. "Are you okay?"

Eve feigned a casual response. "Oh, I'm fine, just relationship problems, you know."

The woman smiled back and warmly nodded. Eve stared at her reflection in the window, and did not recognize the face staring back at her.

✷

The two hooded black guards dragged a barely conscious Dorian to the altar of the cathedral. The priest stared down at the limp body. He spoke to his guards. "I've called the authorities, take him outside, and see if you can find the woman he was with." The underlings carried out the priest's orders. A sleek, silver metal police vehicle was waiting at the steps of the church. It hummed softly above the perfectly smooth road. Bound and gagged, Dorian was unceremoniously tossed in the back as the door slammed shut behind him. The vehicle sped away, along an electric current, towards a massive concrete government building in the distance. Dorian was barely conscious of his surroundings. He felt the vehicle stop after a short ride, as they arrived at the imposing church building. The two guards emerged from the back and roughly pulled him from the vehicle. Dorian shook himself to consciousness as his feet scraped along the ground. He looked up to see a yellow eight-pointed star etched above the entrance of the towering edifice.

Dorian struggled as they dragged him inside the building for processing "Where are you taking me? What have I done?"

The two guards remained silent. They pushed Dorian through a long dark hallway towards a heavy black steel door. Dorian looked up to see two huge banners, emblazoned swastikas, hanging from the ceiling. One guard waved his wristwatch over the console by the door and it slowly opened wide. Dorian looked around in astonishment at a dizzying array of computers and electronics, very similar to those at the Institute where he supposedly worked. He faintly recalled the same plasma-field generator present in his own lab. It was at once familiar and completely alien to him. An aching dread consumed his mind. Dorian spied a massive black steel chair in the centre of the room. The purpose of the elaborate, experimental equipment was somehow well-known. He struggled mightily as the two guards fastened him to the chair with biting steel clamps and thick black leather straps.

He yelled at his captors, "You can't scare me! I've done nothing wrong! None of this is really happening! It's all just nonsense in my head!" Dorian was losing his mind. He shrieked in sudden recognition, as he knew why he was in that chair. He had been there before. His plaintive wail of anguish echoed through the cold empty concrete halls.

*

Ed returned to the university to oversee the afternoon exam. The campus slowly returned to normal, with students busily studying for final exams. Later in the day, he met Max in the cafeteria for a coffee and snack. They both sat down across from each other at the table. Ed picked at a blueberry muffin. "Max, none of this makes any sense. It's like Richard and Samantha never existed. Nobody other than you and me has ever heard of them, it's as if they were simply erased, like some redundant program."

Max looked quizzically at him. "And you're absolutely sure you were at the right places, where they each worked?"

"Completely sure! Here, let me show you." Ed reached into his pocket, searching for Richard's business card. "I know I have it somewhere...it can't just disappear."

Max looked weary. "So where does that leave us? What about their family? Do we know anything about them?"

"No...I can't remember either of them mentioning it. There must be some trace of them somewhere."

Max replied dejectedly, "I don't know, Ed. I wonder if this might be something we should just leave alone. I mean, I want to save them as much as you do, but I wonder about upsetting the balance of things any further. Maybe there's a reason they're not here. Maybe they're not supposed to be here."

"How can we just leave them? Wherever they are, it's my fault. I'm not giving up. I'm going to figure this out. If for no other reason than

I must know the scientific explanation for all this. I refuse to live in a world of magic and nonsense!"

Max remained unconvinced. "Well, I do see your point, but I'm not sure where you go from here. I'll help in any way I can."

Ed was more determined than ever to unravel the mystery. He waved goodbye to Max as he left the cafeteria for his office. He had no other commitments that afternoon. He absently finished grading some papers. His attention wavered. The whereabouts of Richard and Samantha consumed his thoughts. He left the university as the sun began to set.

Darkness fell as he drove back home. Etched deeply in his mind was the image of the yellow eight-pointed star. The connection, if any, between the Aldebaran corporation and the disappearance of his friends from this reality remained elusive to him. Ed picked up some groceries on the way home. He thought about dinner. He threw a frozen chicken pot pie in the oven and sat down on the sofa. He flicked on the TV and absently flipped through the channels. Ed found the show Samantha worked on, *Outer Edge*. He was impressed by the high level of scientific knowledge the show included. He decided to watch the entire series from its first episode.

Ed picked up the phone and dialled Max's number. "Max, what are you up to?"

"Nothing exciting, probably the same as you...just going to make something to eat."

"Why don't you come over? I've got plenty of this chicken pot pie. Maybe I'll make some wild mushroom risotto to go with it, make it a meal. Maybe we can even figure out this Scooby-Doo mystery we have on our hands, if we work together."

Max laughed a little. "I'm pretty sure even Velma and the gang couldn't figure this one out, but okay, I'll be over. Don't eat everything before I get there!"

Ed turned off the TV to prepare the mushroom risotto.

CHAPTER 11

Eve walked through the bustling downtown core of the busy city. She noticed many pedestrians standing atop elaborate floating scooters that glided effortlessly along the ground. Others moved along rapid walkways, but most just walked. It all grew increasingly strange to Eve. The crushing, unearthly silence fell heavily upon her. She recalled a cacophony of vehicles, horns, and traffic. Eve also noted the mute, deadly quiet commuters. Nobody uttered a word of either greeting or frustration. The urban throngs shuffled by like cattle, with cold, expressionless faces. She imagined she was in a solemn church, or watching a performance by some virtuoso at some immense concert hall. None of it seemed real to her. She looked up into the clear azure sky.

Eve wandered around aimlessly, felling exhausted and terrified. Finding Dorian was her first priority, but how to do so remained a mystery. A massive official-looking building, with a huge red swastika emblazoned outside stood before her. The sight filled her with dread. She searched for some sort of anchor, some point of recognition that would guide her way. Curiosity drew her towards a towering, shining gold-tinted skyscraper of immense height. Its sharp metal pinnacle penetrated the white, pillowy clouds above. On the ground floor, she recognized the familiar green goddess logo of the coffee company. The image of the green flowing hair, along with the intoxicating scent of bitter strong coffee awakened her senses. The site of a familiar landmark calmed her immensely. She walked into the coffee shop and sat down. A few people sat together in pairs, but most sat alone. Every person around her was lost within their own self-absorbed world, staring into their various screens. She was desperate to have a coffee, but the payment procedure eluded her. She watched a customer walk up and wave their arm across a device. The video watch beeped and lit up a bright green, and the person ordered the beverage.

Eve decided to try her luck with her own wristwatch. She walked up to the counter to order a coffee. The barista was a young East Indian man, with thick, wavy black hair, creamy coffee-coloured skin, and large, deep, expressive brown eyes. She was about to order, when a large man in a hooded black cloak appeared beside her. Eve instantly recognized the garment as the same one worn by the guards at the strange church. She froze in fear as the towering man turned to scrutinize her. Eve was about to flee, when the heavy-set man smiled broadly and spoke, "God, I never know what to order, either. So much pressure! I mean, do we really need a hundred different types of coffee? How do you choose? Whatever happened to just plain old black coffee, am I right?"

The sound of the familiar voice filled Eve with joy and relief. She turned to him and blurted out far too loudly, "Ed! I can't believe you found me!"

The man smiled, but was confused. "My child, you must be confused. My name is Father George. Are you quite all right? You seem very agitated. Why don't you go sit down, I'll order something both of us."

Eve was more confused than ever. Although she somehow knew the man, she could not recall how. The large, ebullient man returned with two steaming, aromatic cups. He handed one beverage to Eve who eagerly accepted the enticing offering. "This smells heavenly! What is it?"

"This is one of my favourites. I think they call it a cinnamon chocolate latte. I just ask for the usual, they kind of know me pretty well here."

The soothing scent of cinnamon and chocolate wafted over her. It recalled to her a cozy log cabin in winter. The familiar scent of the bitter strong coffee calmed her frazzled nerves. She lifted the huge cup to her lips and took a long sip. The elixir flowed over tongue, down her throat, and warmed her body. She wiped away the creamy froth that covered her upper lip. "I can't thank you enough, this is just what I needed. It's been a very strange morning for me."

The affable man sitting across from her was also enjoying the coffee. "Call me George, I mean, you're supposed to call me Father George, but you don't look like a tattletale. I'm not one for formality. So, you seem to think I am somebody named Ed...this is strange, but I feel like I've met you before also, but exactly where or when I couldn't say. An instance of déjà vu, perhaps. What did you say your name was?"

Eve was hesitant to reveal too much to the stranger. "Eve...I mean, I'm supposed to be Eve, but I don't feel like her at all. I feel like I'm someone else just pretending to be Eve. People call me Eve, so I guess that must be who I am. I feel like there is somebody else inside of me struggling to get out. I guess that doesn't make much sense."

The large, floppy-haired man smiled. "This is strange, what you say, but certainly not that unusual. Have you taken any medications? You know I could prescribe some for you now; the right medicine will fix anything that bothers you. These are indeed odd times we live in. Let me tell you something I really shouldn't. Just yesterday a massive asteroid appeared out of nowhere, and could have potentially wiped out the planet. Of course, we have the planetary defence system that neutralized it, but without it, we'd all be dead...imagine that. Obviously, the public could not be told of such things, it would only cause unrest. The only reason I know anything is because of my position at the Perimeter Institute."

Eve was dumbstruck. "Yes…I remember the asteroid, we were all going to die, it was going to destroy the Earth, but I assumed it was just a dream I had."

George was intrigued. "So you say you remember these things from a dream? This is strange. The asteroid incident was not released to the public, as I mentioned. Only people at the Institute would know about it."

"The Perimeter Institute! That's where I work…I think, but I thought it was just made up. It seemed like some sort of cheesy sci-fi show, with all the crazy futuristic technology, like somebody's idea of what the future would be like, you know?"

George listened with great interest. He took a long sip of coffee. "So, if you work there, you must know Lilith."

"Well, yes, we're married, although I can't figure that out, either. All of this is so odd to me. I really need your help."

✷

Dorian continued to struggle against his captors. A large metal spiked helmet descended from above. He looked up to see a blinding white light halo around the device. It came to a stop and fit itself snuggly around his cranium. On either side of the throne-like metal chair were two huge pulsating columns with massive rounded tops. They bristled with electricity and energy. Bright blue tendrils of spiked electricity shot between the devices. A deep, growing hum filled the room as the instrument gained power. Dorian was dizzy and exhausted. He watched the two black hooded figures operate the controls in the background. After a few minutes, Dorian noticed another figure enter the chamber. He watched a very shapely blonde woman walk towards him, wearing a bright, canary yellow cloak. The two operators bowed in reverence as she entered. His mind felt fuzzy and unfocused, as he desperately attempted to maintain his consciousness.

The cloaked figure in yellow stood before him and removed her hood. A brilliant, thick shining cascade of blonde hair fell around her shoulders. Dorian was awestruck by her angelic, luminous, unearthly beauty. Her delicate skin glowed with health. Her strangely serene, dazzling azure eyes were at once calming and frightening.

The intimidating woman stood imperiously before him with a gaze of cold calculation. Dorian noticed a tight yellow dress underneath her cloak. He tried not to stare at her massive, heaving chest as it undulated with her breath. She brought her face close to his. "Who are you? Your identification chip lists you as Dorian Kindred. Yet the mind scan reveals a very different story. You believe you are somebody named Richard York. Who is this person, and how do you explain this?" The seductive interviewer fixed him with a penetrating stare.

Dorian blurted out the first thing that entered his mind. "Maria? Is that you? It's me!"

His inquisitor angrily responded, "I am the lead examiner, and my name is Maria Orsic. How do you know me? It is not your place to question me!"

The name meant nothing special to Dorian. He struggled to disentangle the confused knots in his mind. His firmly held notions of reality evaporated like a ghostly mist. He scrambled to collect his thoughts.

His inquisitor continued her questioning. "Answer me! Who are you? What are you doing here? What is you mission, and who are you serving?"

Dorian began to cry out of sheer exhaustion and despair. Tears welled up and flowed down his weary face. His head drooped to his chest, and his mind went blank. His entire body collapsed in complete capitulation to the icy-blonde goddess.

✷

It was a warm evening in the bustling city. Everywhere people continued playing their various roles as if nothing unusual had ever transpired.

Talk of the near-cataclysmic asteroid had disappeared completely. Ed sat alone on his sofa consuming his dinner. He was watching his program when there was a knock on the door. Ed called out loudly, "Max, is that you? Come on in."

Max entered and made his way immediately to the kitchen. He helped himself to the wild mushroom risotto. He ate as he walked into the living room and sat down on the sofa. "Not bad this. Did you make it from scratch?"

Ed shook his head. "No, just a mix."

Max looked at the TV. "We're watching that *Outer Edge* show?"

"Yeah, so you remember when you were on the set, with your plasma-field generator, did you notice anything unusual?"

Max was still chewing his food. "Well, other than the miraculous reappearing monkey trick...not really, I guess."

Ed continued. "Okay, so I've been watching this show from the beginning, but I've never noticed all the strange occult references. It's like it was supposedly shot in an alternate timeline or something, or alternate reality maybe, I don't know. There are all these interesting German influences. You know how they write those what-if books, about what would have happened if the Nazis had won? That sort of thing."

"Yes, I do see that, now that you mention it. But it's just a made-up show, I never really gave it much serious thought."

"People today, reading history books, seem to think that the Allies winning World War Two was a forgone conclusion, but that wasn't the case, as you well know. It easily could have gone the other way, had fate decided otherwise."

Max nodded. "Yes, all very true, so what else?"

"Why is there all this strange ancient goddess worship stuff on the show? I mean, who wrote this? It's almost as if the writers were trying to convey some sort of hidden message. Look at the names of the characters: Eve, Lilith. I mean, what's really going on here?"

Max slowly realized the implications of Ed remarks. “It is all very odd, but like I said, it’s just a show, right?”

“What if it’s more than that? There has to be some sort of motivation for all these obscure occult references. Even mentioning some of these names and themes can have a demonstrable influence on the viewer. Those holding the true seats of authority know this all too well. My question is this, why have they allowed this seditious material to exist at all?”

Max pondered the profound ramifications of Ed’s reasoning. “Either the powers that be don’t know, or don’t care. Maybe we overestimate our power as humans, in the end.”

“Or maybe they want us to underestimate our true power. Max, have you felt any different since we emerged from my lab, our basement bunker, as it were?”

Max looked puzzled. “What do you mean?”

“It’s hard to explain, but I don’t quite feel like myself, like some part of me is missing. I feel like a reflection some strange, inverse mirror.”

Max gazed at his good friend. He did not wish to admit to Ed, or himself, that he felt exactly the same. The two professors sat silently beside each other on the leather sofa. They continued to watch the bizarre program, now with a heightened degree of interest.

✷

Eve and George finished their coffees and left the busy downtown café. They walked side by side along the heavily travelled walkway. Eve implored the stranger, who now seemed more like her friend, to help her find Dorian. She explained how he had been detained, and wondered if he would know how to find him. “You must help me. I don’t know another person in this world.”

George listened intently. “I do believe, Eve, that fate has brought us together, and that for some reason, I was sent to help you, my child. I will do what I can. Now, why is it you have no recollections of your life here? It's almost like you're a different person."

Eve nodded eagerly. "Yes, that's exactly it. I am a different person. Everyone here calls me Eve, but that's not who I am." Eve struggled to find the crucial piece of information in her mind. "Wait...it starts with an S...Samantha! Yes, that's it. My name is Samantha!" For the first time in a long while, Samantha experienced a moment of pure clarity.

George was pleased but confused. "Okay, that's a start, but do we know who Samantha is? And how is it she finds herself in this particular reality?"

Samantha continued. "Little fragments are returning. Yes! I just remembered. Dorian...that's not his real name either...it's...Richard! Yes...Richard! He's alive, but we must help him, he's in big trouble. Two men in black cloaks took him away in some sort of police vehicle."

George listened with a concerned expression. "Those would be the watchers. They are everywhere. They enforce the law; he must have committed some infraction."

Samantha pleaded with the priest. "Yes, but don't you see that neither of us belong here, how could we know your laws? We really shouldn't be here!"

"What do you mean by *here*? Are you from another province, another country within the Republic?"

Samantha shook her head. "No, you're not understanding me. We don't belong in this reality! If we can get to Richard, then you'll understand. He'll back up my story. I'm not crazy!"

Samantha was very fortunate to have met George. He happened to be a very powerful and open-minded member of the church's inner sanctum. He understood the inner workings of the church and government with complete assurance. The two institutions were seamlessly intertwined. George spoke into his wristwatch and made some inquiries as to the whereabouts of Richard. He was able to glean his location, and discovered that Richard was a prisoner. George relayed the information to Samantha. They rode a moving walkway to the massive church building.

They walked up the grey stone steps of the overwhelming edifice. The eight-pointed yellow star shone brightly above. Samantha recognized the symbol from the cathedral she had visited earlier that day. Suddenly in a flash of insight, she recalled noticing the image on the building at the television set. Small details from her alternate identity emerged from the fog of confusion. They passed through a maze of security. George was easily able to pass through and vouch for Samantha. She looked around the pure white building. She noticed the same huge golden goddess statue of Astarte that she had seen in the church earlier. Samantha was transfixed by the glimmering, azure-blue jewel eyes of the goddess.

Two female figures rushed by her wearing ruby red cloaks over downward cast faces. George ushered her along the cold, concrete halls, trying hard not to arouse suspicion. Samantha looked up in horror at the towering swastika banners hanging from the ceiling. George finally found the room where Richard was being held captive. He pulled open the heavy black door, after gaining security access with a wave of his arm over the black panel. They approached the beautiful, blonde inquisitor, who was standing tall above Richard.

Samantha's eyes suddenly lit up with joy. She cried out loudly, "Richard! Are you okay?"

Richard was dazed and barley cognizant of his surroundings. His head lolled back and forth, and his eyes were barely open. "Who's there?" Even in his beleaguered state, the name struck a chord. His brow furrowed as he slowly gained full consciousness. "Yes...that is my name! Richard! And you're Samantha, and is that Ed with you?"

George walked over to the imposing yellow-cloaked blonde woman. She acknowledged his superior rank within the organization with a slight bow. They spoke in hushed whispers. Maria pushed her case, but realized that she was overmatched. "I can't stop you from assuming responsibility for this prisoner, but you do realize a report must be completed. She grabbed a tablet device from a nearby table and scrolled through the screens to find the appropriate form.

She handed the device to George, who examined it and waved his hand over it in acknowledgment. "Of course, this all seems in order. May I ask what you have been able to gather in the way of information from the mind scan?"

"He is not who he seems, or rather, he is who he imagines himself to be. He is not Dorian Kindred, but rather some person named Richard York. It's actually all very unusual, I don't think we've ever had a result like this…it's almost as if he doesn't belong here, like he's from another world. I realize that makes no sense."

George nodded. "You're right, it doesn't make sense, but it does confirm what this woman here has told me."

Maria's beatific face smiled. "We must get to the bottom of this. If this man is not Dorian, what has happened to him? How could any of this happen?"

George shook his head. "Honestly, I do not know at this point, but I do intend to find out."

CHAPTER 12

Ed bolted upright from his bed. He shook his head to clear away the cobwebs. His sleep had been troubled and dream-filled. Scattered images from his Discordian, chaotic dreams flooded his mind. His sleep patterns grew increasingly sporadic and unpredictable. The previous night he had consumed a massive dose of melatonin and other compounds in an attempt at a good night's sleep. Ed felt his cognitive abilities decline as his insomnia grew more troublesome. Ed stared into the bathroom mirror as he brushed his teeth. He did not fully recognize the face staring back at him. The visage seemed to him a poorly rendered facsimile. The idea filled him with an existential dread.

He shuffled to the kitchen, wearing his burgundy wizard robe. He picked at some toast and coffee, and eventually left for the university. He glanced at the sky above, which was dark and overcast, with rain forecast for the afternoon. He pulled up to the parking lot in his yellow Volvo and walked into the venerable old stone building. Ed noticed a group of students he recognized and waved at them. They returned his greeting in kind. The familiar routine of his schedule reaffirmed his resolve. His first lecture was in ten minutes, and he headed for the lecture hall.

He arrived to find a nearly full room, populated by eager first-year students, not yet jaded by the deadening scholastic grind. Ed proceeded to write on the massive blackboard when a female student spoke up.

"Professor, Could I ask a question?"

Ed turned to the direction of the soft voice. He smiled and looked for her in the crowd. His face was ashen when he spied the familiar face. He haltingly asked, "Please, miss?"

The girl replied shyly, "It's Erin, Erin Murphy."

Ed gestured with his arms. "Please, stand up, you have a question? Go right ahead."

The slim, blonde-haired girl wore old, torn jeans and a university sweatshirt. She was clearly nervous as she hesitantly spoke up. "Well, sir, professor, what do you think happened to the asteroid? It doesn't seem like anybody really knows."

Ed smiled stiffly. He realized that a truthful answer was impossible. He decided upon a generic, meaningless response. "Well it's hard to say...I don't think we will truly ever know what really happened. Perhaps God has smiled upon us, and the prayers of everyone around the world were heard." Even he blanched at his own insincere words. The girl shrugged and sat down, clearly not impressed by the half-hearted response. Ed resumed his lecture without further interruption.

Ed met up with Max later in the day, at the cafeteria. "Hey, Max, how did your class go?"

Max was less than enthusiastic about his students. "You mean with the brain-dead zombies staring at their phones, whilst I drone on about subject matter none of them could begin to comprehend?"

"So...the usual?"

"Yeah, I guess so. It's a living, better than digging ditches. How was yours?"

"Well, it's strange. I could have sworn classes were done for the semester, but I suppose not. This girl, very pretty, asked me about the asteroid. I gave this pathetic answer...embarrassing really. But that's not all. This girl, she looked so much like Samantha. It could have been her daughter. Frankly, I was shocked."

Max listened intently. "Do you think you were seeing what you wanted to see? We both want to find her, and Richard, of course. In any case, I think your answer was fine. What are you going to do? Tell people the truth?" Ed nodded. Max continued. "So, did you make any progress on finding our lost friends? What about that *Outer Edge* show? Did you find out anything there?"

Ed picked at a plate of macaroni and cheese, and sipped on a coffee. "Well, you've watched it, I guess it hits a little bit too close to home, for me personally."

"Yes, I honestly noticed that also, it's almost like something you might have written with all the weird occult and German references. It's like a projection of your own imagination. Why are you so fascinated by those things anyway?"

Ed mused for a moment before answering. "It probably has something to do with my father, he taught German, and there were always all these books around for me to read. As for the Occult stuff, I don't know, I've always been drawn to the dark side...call it the Darth Vader in me. Ultimately, it's purely an intellectual pursuit, at least that's how I see it."

Max listened intently. He ate a meatloaf platter with French fries. He devoured it eagerly. "Isn't it strange, though, to watch something that you had considered private, buried deep within you? I mean the *Outer Edge* show."

"I don't know, I just want to find out what happened to them, and also why I feel so strange. What's your afternoon look like? Do you any time off?"

Max replied between bites. "Sorry, no can do. I'm booked with student meetings and I have to get some marking done."

Ed was displeased. "Okay, I think I might have better luck if I show up on the set of the show with you, at least they know you, but I'll have to make do. There's something or somebody there that knows what's going on. I'm sure of it."

Ed completed his work that afternoon, and left the university. The sky overhead was still dark and brooding with threatening clouds. He drove his yellow Volvo back to the set of the *Outer Edge* TV set down by the water. He parked his car and walked up to the old brick warehouse.

Ed walked slowly into the darkness. He noticed a few people milling about a table full of food. He walked over to the craft-service table and recognized the assistant he had spoken with previously. As before, she wore a headset and carried a clipboard.

Dinah acknowledged him immediately. "You were here yesterday, are you a cop or something? You know you can't just wander in here."

Ed seized the opportunity and decided to improvise. "I'm actually a private detective, I'm sorry I didn't mention that earlier. I'm investigating the disappearance of somebody that worked on this show, Samantha Steffen."

The heavily tattooed girl nodded. "Yeah, and remember I told you last time you were here, there's nobody working on the show named Samantha and there never was. You're going to have to leave."

Instinctively a head turned towards the conversation at the mention of the name. Ed stared back at a set of piercing green eyes scrutinizing him intently. A seductive, raven-haired woman swooped over to him. Her unblinking intense gaze immobilized Ed to the spot where he stood. Ed felt his force of will melt away with the power of her intoxicating, rapturous attention. She stood before him in a form-fitting red leather skirt and top. Ed struggled to avoid examining the generous shape of her body. The commanding woman stood in absolute silence, like a gilded statue.

Ed stammered out a question to break the unbearable tension. "Your perfume is quite...quite arresting...what is it, may I ask."

The woman suddenly dropped her imperious demeanour. "I'm so glad that you like it. It's called *Poison* by *Christian Dior*. My name is Selena, and who are you?" Her deep, thick sultry voice poured over him like sweet syrup.

He felt his heart begin to pump as she drew closer. He felt her warm breath on his face. His face grew flush. "I'm Ed...I'm a private detective. I'm looking for Samantha Steffen."

Selena's luminescent emerald eyes sparkled with wit. She smiled knowingly. "No you're not. You're just pretending to be a private detective or maybe you're pretending to be a professor, who knows? I suppose we're all pretending to be this person or that. Is anybody ever really who they say they are? Maybe your name is Ed, or maybe it's George. If you want to find out what happened to Samantha, follow me."

Ed was mesmerized by the enchanting creature. She exuded pure confidence and a heavy scent of sex and danger. He accepted her intriguing invitation, despite his better instincts.

✷

George was successful in securing the release of Richard. After taking possession of the prisoner from Maria, he and Samantha released him from the heavy metal chair. He breathed a heavy sigh of relief.

Samantha fell into his awaiting arms. She looked up into his teary hazel eyes. "We made it, we're still alive! I don't really understand how it happened, but we're here, wherever here is."

Richard was overjoyed, but still deeply confused. "It's almost as if we've assumed the identities of other people. I know that doesn't make much sense."

Samantha listened carefully. "No, you're absolutely right. For a while there, I thought I was the character from *Outer Edge*, Eve, and you were Dorian from the show, but then we both suddenly woke up, and remembered who we really are."

George interrupted them. "This is all very fascinating, but we have to get out of here. I am not all-powerful, and we will be questioned. We need to get out of here, pronto."

Richard agreed. "Ed, where are we going?"

Samantha corrected him. "This is actually George. He just looks like our friend Ed."

The three left the concrete interrogation room and hurried down the long hallway. Richard continued. "So is it possible that George is actually Ed? Maybe he just needs to wake up like we did."

George shook his head. “Sorry to disappoint you, buy I am me.”

Samantha wondered, “Is it possible we’re in some sort of parallel reality, or alternate dimension…or something like that?”

George replied, “This is most definitely a possibility, and likely probable. You see, this is precisely the sort of research you two were working on here at the Perimeter Institute, or at least your two alter-egos were. You were attempting, along with many others, to open up a portal to another dimension. It would appear that your work, or their work, has succeeded.”

Richard remained unconvinced. “No, I have no recollection of any of this. Don’t you see that this reality is not real; the one that we came from is the actual, base reality. This one is just something fabricated from someone’s imagination.”

“Richard is right. None of this is real; I’ve never worked at any Institute, and I certainly don’t understand how to create some sort of alternate dimension.”

George attempted to summarize. “It is clear that neither of you belong here. That could be a problem. Somehow you have upset the balance of this reality, I feel that. The question then becomes, why are you here, and what happened to Eve and Dorian? The church has been studying these matters, the idea of opening a portal to another dimension.”

Richard was intrigued. “For what purpose?”

“I’m afraid that information is highly classified, and above my pay grade, and I can tell you, that is pretty high indeed. As much as I want to help you, I need to find out what’s going on myself. There are dark forces at work within the church that would seek to undermine its very core…its very being. This faction must be stopped, and maybe you two are the key. We need to do some serious investigating, and it is essential that you two maintain your identities in this reality; that is, Eve and Dorian.”

Ed immediately fell under Selena's spell. As if entranced, he followed her dutifully from the set of the *Outer Edge* TV set. He stared at Selena as she strutted from the old brick building towards her fiery red sports car. She stopped before the Italian sports car and waited for him to catch up. "Here's my baby, get in."

Ed stared in admiration at the impressive, luxurious car. "Wow, a Ferrari! I should take my car. I don't want to leave it here."

Selena rebuffed his comment. "You don't want to ride in that old thing, no offence. Have you ever been inside a Ferrari?" Selena climbed into the sensuous, soft tan leather seats. "We'll pick it up later, it's fine here."

Her deep emerald green eyes froze Ed in place. He had no intellectual defence against her overwhelming feminine allure. He found himself climbing into the passenger seat of the inviting machine.

Selena started the intricate machine with the touch of a button. The powerful engine roared to life like a slumbering beast. Ed drank in his sumptuous surroundings, as he secured his seat belt. "Wow, this is something else."

Selena threw the vehicle into drive with a powerful thrust forward. Ed had never felt such force, and it drove him back, deep into the plush leather seat. He instinctively grabbed hold of the seat with both hands. "It's got quite a kick, doesn't it? It's a little peppier than my Volvo, I must say."

Selena smiled with satisfaction. "That's what 600 horsepower feels like. Worth every penny. I enjoy power and speed. We should eat, you do eat, don't you?"

Ed nodded. "Sure, whatever you say, but I thought you were going to tell me about what happened to Samantha?"

"All in good time. Patience is a virtue, my dear professor. So where to eat? I know a great Thai place. You like Thai food?"

Ed, diverted by his hunger replied, "Sure, Thai sounds great."

The lithe red Ferrari darted in and out of the downtown traffic. The car leapt past the other vehicles like a jungle cat. It was a sultry Friday night, unusually warm for late May. The city was completely back to normal, with people enjoying the nightlife. The vehicle came to a screeching halt before a large neon sign that read, "Thai Village."

Ed exclaimed, "Wow, you're quite the driver. You drive Formula 1 or something?"

Selena looked bemused. "I like to push things to the limit. How else do you find your breaking point?"

They both exited the car and walked up to the restaurant. Huge wooden palm leaves and large tiki statues decorated the entrance. A beautiful black-haired smiling Asian woman led them to a table by the window. They opened the menus provided to them and began searching, while the server waited. Selena immediately ordered a drink. "I'll have a Wild Turkey on the rocks."

Ed smiled. "The lady knows her bourbon. I'll have the same, thanks."

The young woman smiled and left the table. They returned to their menus, glancing up at each other. Selena began, "I know you've never been here. Do you like spicy food? I usually get the red seafood curry here, it's divine."

Ed nodded and closed his menu. "I am in your hands, that sounds fine."

The waitress returned with the drinks and took their orders. Ed took a sip of the dark, rich bourbon. "Okay. The reason I came to the set, to find out about Samantha, how do you seem to know so much?"

Selena was unfazed by his insistent tone. "Sometimes, it's best not to know too much, especially about matters that don't really concern you. I only provide information on a need-to-know basis, you see. You want to know where Samantha is, and of course Richard."

Ed was perplexed. "How would you know about Richard? I didn't mention him."

"I don't know everything, Ed, but I know a lot...a lot more than you. Let's just say that I am aware of your secret work, and we are aware that you opened a portal to another dimension, something we have been working on ourselves for quite some time."

Ed put down his drink and moved back from the table in shock. He stared at the strange woman, completely speechless. Finally, he collected his thoughts. "Who are you exactly? You are clearly much more than just an actress. How can you possibly know so much? How could you know about my work? It's…it's impossible. You're just some woman."

The raven-haired seductress laughed loudly. "Oh you little, little man, if you actually had any idea of what was going on, of who actually is in charge, I'm afraid your tiny male brain would explode!"

The server returned with two appetizing, fragrant plates of food. The pungent scent of spice and sweetness filled the air. Ed frowned at his dinner companion. "So clearly there is more going on here than I first thought. And it doesn't sound much like you're going to volunteer any information. Is that correct?"

Selena giggled. "Do you ever shut up? You must love the sound of your own voice. Is that it? Why don't we eat, and maybe I'll tell you more later."

Ed relented, and looked down with delight. "Well, this looks delicious." Ed was pleased for the change of conversation. He was genuinely leery of his gorgeous dinner companion. He was unaccustomed to intellectual bullying, especially at the hands of a female. He breathed in the wonderful, complex aroma of the dish before him. He identified the spicy chilies, the delicate lemongrass, and the strong curry. He took a generous bite of the scallops and noodles, and savoured the panoply of flavours on his palate. "You were right…this is superb…great choice."

Selena was also enjoying the delectable meal. "So glad that you are enjoying it. To me, pleasure is everything. If it doesn't feel good, why do it, right? I do what I desire. Morality is for boring people."

His inquiry into the whereabouts of Samantha and Richard faded from his mind. He decided it was best to make peace with the enigmatic woman. The extraordinary nature of his dinner companion dawned on him. He would need to change his tact, he thought as he ate. Selena consumed her food with great relish, and offered up her considerable charms along the way. All the while, she coldly sized up her prey, with a detached feline countenance.

✷

George, Samantha, and Richard hurried down the long concrete steps of the massive building. George stopped and looked back surreptitiously. "I don't think we're being followed, but we need to hurry." They left the Church headquarters and headed for the Perimeter Institute. They walked briskly along the moving walkway, George cautioned them both, "Best not to run, it will only draw attention."

He knew the city transportation system better than most. They boarded the pneumatic tube system by swiping their respective wristwatches. George looked ruefully at his watch. "Problem is, the authorities will know our whereabouts now, but it can't be helped."

Samantha was concerned. "Are we safe?"

George shrugged. "Maybe for now, but not for long."

Richard gaped at the technological ingenuity of the system. "This is so impressive, I mean, there was always talk in my world of building something like this, but this technology is decades away, where we come from."

George listened with interest. "You have nothing like this? It seems as if you have come from not just another place, but another timeline."

"Yeah...we're still getting around in the old underground subway system. To us, it's like you're living in some kind of futuristic sci-fi show. It's really strange how much this place reminds me of that show you were working on, *Outer Edge*...right?" Richard asked.

Samantha nodded. "It is a little weird. It's almost like we walked right onto the set of the show. It's so futuristic, almost too futuristic, like from one of the dumb sci-fi shows from the fifties, like *Twilight Zone* or something. They imagined everyone would be driving flying cars by the year 2000."

George listened carefully. "Fascinating. We also had similar types of entertainment, yet somehow our worlds have diverged markedly."

Richard's wristwatch chimed. He looked down to see the image of his wife from his present reality, Alice. Her face wore a stern frown. "Where are you? Why aren't you at work? You weren't sleeping on the job again, were you? You know if your boss catches you again, you'll be fired!"

Richard scrambled to find an answer. The woman he gazed at was his receptionist at his advertising firm, Alice. He also had a vague recollection of being married to the woman. The memory of her seemed to dissipate in the misty recess of his mind. He stammered out a response to her question, "I...had an appointment, with my doctor." He moved his wrist to show the image of George, who dutifully nodded in agreement. The strikingly attractive blonde woman scrutinized the man for several moments.

"Hello, Alice, yes, I am discussing some important health issues with your husband here. It's sort of confidential stuff, I'm sure you understand," said George.

Alice stared back inquisitively. "Why is your doctor dressed like a priest? Dorian, why didn't you tell me about this earlier? You're acting very strangely. I'm coming down to see you."

"No, that's really not necessary." Before Richard could finish speaking, she ended the conversation. Her image slowly disappeared from the screen.

George shook his head. "That's not good. Will she come to see you at the Institute?"

Richard replied, "I'm not sure what she'll do. I don't even know her, except I do...sort of. She's the receptionist at my work, in my real life. I know that doesn't make any sense."

The three fugitives arrived at the Perimeter Institute in the downtown core. It looked very similar to the church headquarters. It was a massive, totalitarian-inspired concrete building. It might have emerged from the mind of Albert Speer himself. A huge eight-pointed yellow star shone from the entrance. A golden many-armed Shiva idol danced in the sunlight outside in the elaborate central fountain. Surrounding the impressive structure was a perfectly manicured French garden, replete with geometrically shaped bushes and trees. Richard was awe-struck by the breathtaking beauty of the scene. He asked George about it, before being cut short.

"Richard, we don't have time for travelogue details. All in good time. I'm more interested in finding out what exactly is going on, and keeping you two, safe." George then carefully led them inside, advising them to cloak their identities. "Keep your heads down, surveillance is everywhere. We were able to get out of the church, but no doubt a report was filed, nothing goes unnoticed here. We have to assume that they are looking for you, Richard."

George looked back as they approached the security entrance. Two guards dressed in long black robes stood on either side of a metal rectangular security barrier. "Now remember, you two both work here. Just act naturally. Use your wristwatches on the device there." All three were granted access to the building without question. They walked down the corridors of the impressive institute, with heads down. Richard recalled where Dorian's office was located. They all entered and shut the door.

George sat down at the computer. "Here, Richard, sign on to your computer."

Richard sat down and stared at the screen. "I can't remember my password!"

George was frustrated. "Well, you better remember. Listen, I can never remember mine, maybe you wrote them down somewhere. Look around."

Richard began frantically searching the messy desk. He finally found a notebook under the desk. He read it out and typed in the password, "Wonderland." The computer screen flashed to life.

George took his seat. "Good work, now let me try to find out what we need." He typed furiously at the keyboard, attempting to access the computer files. "There must be some record of somebody accessing information about the interdimensional portal. Somebody here is working behind the scenes, trying to sabotage the work we're doing."

Suddenly the door to the office flew open. Lilith strode in confidently, followed by three guards. She wore a ruby red hooded cloak. "Hello there, Father George, and what is it you're doing here exactly? You are out of your element. Why are you abetting these two fugitives?"

George stood up defiantly. "They have committed no serious crime, and they are under my authority."

Lilith dismissed his objections with a wave of her hand. "First of all, my authority goes far beyond yours. Strictly speaking, this is none of your business, little man. You are all charged with sedition and heresy. My authority in this matter is absolute, take them away."

The three black-cloaked guards, armed with long electric prods, stood menacingly before them. George shook his head in defeat. "We are outnumbered and outgunned. We must go with her."

Samantha called out to Lilith, "It's me! Eve! Why are you doing this Lilith?"

"What a joke! You're not Eve! I admit it took me awhile to figure out what was going on. You were acting so strangely this morning. That made me suspicious. Anyway, you'll find out everything in good time. Guards, follow me!"

Richard reached for Samantha's hand as they left the office with George. The three fugitives followed Lilith down the long hallway.

✱

Ed and Selena finished their sumptuous meal and were well satisfied. Ed was consumed with great doubt, when his phone rang. He looked down to see that Max was calling him. He excused himself politely from his dinner guest, and moved aside. "Excuse me, I need to take this. Hey, Max, what's up?"

"How did your visit to the TV set go? You were going to call me. Did you learn anything?"

Ed replied softly, "Listen, I can't really talk right now, I sort of met somebody on the set, she definitely knows something. In fact, I think she knows everything about what's going on. She's one of the actresses, the one who plays Lilith. She might be the key to this whole thing. Let me call you later...I have to go."

Max tried to reply, "Be careful—"

Before he could finish his thought, Ed hung up. He put the phone away and caught up to Selena who was standing before her sports car. They both climbed into the cockpit of the voluptuous red vehicle. Ed was impressed by the luxurious interior. "It is a little fancier than my Volvo, although I doubt it's as safe."

Selena chuckled. "Life is not about safety, it's about excitement and thrills, don't you think?" She reached over and gently stroked his thigh.

Ed's face flushed as he stammered out, "I should really go get my car."

Selena shrugged. "You don't have to worry about your old bucket of bolts; that lot is well-lit, there's security overnight, it'll be fine. Why don't we go to your place? I bet you have all kinds of interesting toys there." Her seductive voice and lascivious gaze were more that Ed could withstand.

"Okay, the place is a mess...it's just me there."

Selena slammed on the gas as the sleek red car shot out into traffic. "All the better. Don't you worry, I don't bite, relax." Selena darted quickly in and out of traffic, with little regard for other drivers.

Ed sat anxiously in the passenger seat, feigning a casual demeanour. He glanced over at the plunging neckline of the driver. Her intoxicating scent caused his heart to race. She looked over at him sympathetically. "You okay there, tiger?"

Ed grinned broadly. "Oh, I'm great, maybe just a little indigestion. That food was a little spicy." He nervously stammered out the directions to his house. They arrived shortly after with an abrupt stop in

Ed's driveway. Selena climbed out of the car. Her tight red skirt hugged her hips snugly. Her curvaceous body moved catlike towards the front door. Her stiletto heels clacked loudly in the driveway. Ed tried not to stare at her as she walked ahead of him.

She stopped at the door. "It's just you here, is that right? I know you mentioned that you were once married. Nice place, cozy, not too big."

Ed opened the door, stepped in, and invited her inside. "I know it's not much, but its fine for me. Sorry about the mess. Yeah, it's just me here."

Selena replied flirtatiously, "So that means you're available?"

Ed's face flushed red. "Um...can I get you a drink? I'm just going to have coffee myself."

Selena declined the coffee. "Do you have any strong stuff? I could go for some bourbon, if you have it."

Ed moved to the kitchen to prepare the drink. The coffee machine dripped as he poured Selena a generous portion of bourbon. Selena accepted the libation and sipped on it. She sat down on the leather sofa. "Is this Jim Beam?"

"Yeah, you know your bourbon. Funny thing, I used to have a terrible time sleeping, bad insomnia, I could never have coffee this late, but I had one last night and it didn't even bother me. It's like my insomnia just disappeared since the whole asteroid scare. Do you want some dessert? I might have some chocolate ice cream." Ed talked too much when he was nervous.

Selena only half listened to him. "You have quite an impressive bookshelf. Do you mind if I look around?" She stood up and walked around.

Ed encouraged her. "Not at all, look around as much as you want."

She grabbed a book from the shelf. "This is interesting, *DMT: The Spirit Molecule*. You do have a wide array of interests, don't you? Are you interested in psychedelic drugs, or just the effects they have?"

Ed explained, "This is all part of my research. Drugs, of the recreational variety, don't interest me, although psychedelics have some unusual and novel properties. Insomnia and other sleep disorders are some of my areas of expertise."

"Is it now? Have you been having trouble sleeping, Ed?" she asked slyly.

Ed pondered the question for a moment. "Well, like I mentioned earlier, the last few days I've been sleeping fine. I wonder why that is?"

Selena laughed knowingly. "Yes, that is a mystery."

Ed was mystified by Selena's mirthful response. He sat up abruptly and walked into the kitchen to pour his coffee.

Selena put the book down. She called out to Ed, "Do you mind if I look around the house?"

"No, not at all, no secrets here."

Selena replied sharply, "I think we both know that's not entirely true." She wandered through the house and eventually found herself in the bedroom. "You certainly have an interesting crew of characters on your walls: Maria Orsic, Crowley, Einstein. Curious, do you study the dark arts, magic, and the sort?"

Ed heard her from the bedroom and joined her. "I study a lot of things. For me it's purely academic, of course, I don't really believe in all of that magic mumbo-jumbo."

Selena laughed. "Nothing is purely academic, and there is no purity in this world, only a compromised, diluted mess of half-baked truths. I think you know a hell of a lot more than you let on, professor."

Ed was taken aback by her frank tone. "I'm sure I have no idea what you're talking about, and what you're getting at."

Selena stood proudly beside the bed, staring into Ed's dark eyes. She was well aware of the uplifting effect she was having on him. Ed's indignation at her accusing tone was overtaken by his carnal desires. Ed's body was immobilized by the fast-rushing blood coursing through his body. His chest heaved, sucking in huge gulps of air. He stared straight ahead, like a deer caught in a bright headlight. He waited for her to act, to get an indication of her intentions. He was deeply worried about embarrassing himself in the presence of the intoxicatingly attractive woman. Ed's mind raced, and his breath quickened as he imagined seizing hold of her soft, warm hips.

Like a cat with a mouse, Selena suddenly left the bedroom, dashing his hopes at once. "So, is there anything else to this place? You must have a basement. I bet you've got all kinds of interesting toys down there, that you hide away from prying eyes."

Ed was reticent, but did not wish to appear uncordial. He desperately wished her to stay. "Well, I have been working on some rather cutting-edge stuff. Honestly, I shouldn't even be talking about it to you. It's sort of *Outer Edge* stuff really, most people wouldn't even understand it."

"You're a fan of the show, are you?" Selena opened the basement door and walked down the stairs.

Ed was close behind her, and unlocked the heavy black steel door. "Yes, it's a most interesting show indeed. Do you ever have any input on the scripts?"

Selena walked casually into the Ed's lair. "Of course, I do. Did you think I was just some silly actress? I write most of it myself. It's a fascinating little reality that I've created. I mean the show. But don't you think every show, every book, every dream, is its own possible reality? Do you understand what I mean, Ed? There are an infinite number of realities, and it's just a matter of which one you choose to inhabit."

Selena sipped on her bourbon as she meandered around the dark room. "This certainly is a classic mad scientist lab you have here, and still with all the prints. You have Madame Blavatsky, Richard Nixon, and some Hindu gods. Is that one Shiva?"

Ed nodded. "I guess I do have some odd tastes."

She ran her hand over the head of the many-armed golden Hindu idol, sitting on a desk. Selena walked over to him and looked directly into his eyes. "You aren't actually mad, are you, Ed?"

"I...I don't think so, are you?"

Selena laughed. "That's for me to know, and for you to find out...if you have enough time, that is."

Selena walked seductively over to the mysterious looking black metal chair in the centre of the room. She brushed her hand across the thick black leather straps and the rounded, hard metal helmet. "What a terrible-looking chair. It looks like something from a horror movie, or a medieval torture device. Do you like to torture people, Ed?"

Ed was indignant. "No, of course not. It's simply an experimental instrument I was using." He walked over to join her by the provocative device.

The raven-haired beauty ran her slender hand slowly down Ed's chest. "All in the name of science, and your god of course, isn't that right, Ed? Of course, it's not exactly clear which god you follow, is it? So how does this crazy machine work, anyway?"

Ed could not resist the allure of her rich, syrup-sweet voice. "Well, I guess I can show you how it works." He walked over to the computer table and set his mug of coffee down, and walked back to the chair. He sat down in the metal chair and began explaining. "You see, as I mentioned upstairs, I have been experimenting with the effects of DMT, melatonin, and ayahuasca."

Selena moved very close to him. He could feel her warm breath on his neck, as her soft breasts brushed lightly against his chest. Ed's heartbeat quickened as he stared up into her deep emerald green eyes. Selena surreptitiously clasped Ed's arms to the chair, without his notice. His eyes focused upon her cleavage, he failed to see her lash his legs to the chair. "Is this sort of how it works, Ed?"

Ed was fixated upon the soft, undulating flesh straining against her top. The intoxicating scent of her vanilla sweet perfume flooded his overwhelmed senses.

Ed looked down to see that he was firmly strapped to the chair. He laughed good-naturedly. "It's a little tight…just wanted to see how it works, eh?"

Selena smiled. "Don't you worry, you'll be just fine, relax, I'll take care of everything."

Ed began to struggle against the restraints. "Okay, very funny, you can let me go now." Selena said nothing, walking over to the computer table. Ed was extremely agitated. "You need to let me go right now! Who exactly do you think you are? You can't treat me like this! I'm a well-respected professor!"

Selena pronounced loudly. "Hardly! Nobody will even notice you are gone, will they? You asked me who I am...Selena? That's just a name I'm using at the moment. I go by many names: Lilith, Inanna, Astarte, Ashtoreth...all just meaningless names...different masks hiding the same face. Ed, you seem more intelligent than most men, which means you're more dangerous. I've been attempting to open a portal between our two dimensions for quite some time. You have succeeded where many before you have failed. You've actually helped me more than I can say, helped me in reaching my ultimate goal, the final solution, as it were."

Selena stood imperiously above him, flaunting her power and strength. Ed stared up into her luminescent green eyes. He struggled against his bonds, but to no avail. "I...don't understand...you're saying you are not human...what are you then?"

"Human? As if! I am your goddess, and you will worship me as such! Now all I need you to do is keep quiet. I'm going to send you on a little journey."

Ed was terrified by his captor. "What are you going to do, kill me?"

Selena made a mock-sad face. "No, no, little man, I'm simply going to send you to another reality, another timeline, if that's easier for you. You know, there are many, right? You've become somewhat troublesome in this one. I'm going to send you to an unusual one. All possibilities are permitted, thine will be done."

"You can't do this! Someone will stop you!"

Selena ignored his warnings, as she toiled at the computer table. She took some time to find the compounds, and loaded them into a large syringe. "Oh, Ed, nobody knows you're here, you live all alone. You could be down here for a week, for all eternity, and nobody would know, or care. Just think, you'll have a whole new identity. Don't worry, in time you'll completely forget who you are, or were."

Ed realized that resistance was futile. "Will I see Richard and Samantha?"

"No, you already exist in that reality, in a slightly different form...a variation of yourself, if you will. They're alive, by the way. They're in a very interesting reality now, one that is firmly under my control. You would recognize it, of course, it's a manifestation of this one, but more advanced. I'm sending you to a very backward reality, one where you can't do any damage. They don't even have electricity yet. In time, you will adjust, they do have your precious coffee, though, and bourbon. Of course, interdimensional travel is not an exact science, fate always rules the day. You might end up anywhere at all."

Ed was no match for a being of her stature and power. Foolishly, he let his guard down, tricked by her considerable feminine wiles. He held out hope that he might still rescue Richard and Samantha, although any sort of actual plan eluded him. Selena plunged the hypodermic needle into his arm. Ed winced in pain. His hands curled tightly around the metal arms of the chair. The irony of being finally undone by his own machine was not lost on him. She smiled as she walked over to the computer and initiated the plasma-field generator. The air crackled with electricity. The power continued to increase as the large metal columns pulsed with energy. Suddenly there was an explosion of blinding white light. It was a light as bright as the moment of creation.

CHAPTER 13

George, Richard, and Samantha followed Lilith down a long hallway. The three guards were close behind. Samantha looked up to see an enormous portrait of Adolf Hitler hung along the wall. The ceiling was festooned with German flags and an unfamiliar angular sigil. Samantha whispered to Richard, "Is this really happening? I mean, what is this place?"

A guard roughly jabbed her in the back with his prod. "Silence!"

Lilith led the group through a door, down a short staircase to a basement. They all entered a large dark room behind a heavy black door. Lilith locked the door behind her. She spoke sternly to George. "You are obviously aware of the research we have been doing. It's why you have been helping these two, isn't it? You have some idea of what we're doing, but the motivations and reasons are unclear to you. I have big plans for Richard and Samantha here, but that's for later. For you George, your big scene happens now...aren't you a lucky duck! You're going to be the star of the show!" With that, she motioned for the guards to grab hold of George. He was a large man, and it took all three of them to subdue him.

Samantha motioned to aid her new friend, but was quickly rebuffed their captor. "Don't bother, Sam. I could have you on the ground in moments. You might actually like me on top of you!" She winked slyly at the confused woman.

Samantha stared hard at the strange woman. "Richard, I feel like I know this woman, but I can't place her. She certainly seems to know me and you. What are we going to do?"

Richard was at a loss. He put his arms around his distraught beloved. "I think we have no choice, right now. I've been shocked by those metal prods the guards have, and believe me, it was not fun."

The guards dragged George to a large metal chair, with black leather straps, in the centre of the room. Both Richard and Samantha were well acquainted with the machine. It was almost identical to the one they had experienced in Ed's basement. On either side of the device were two tall bulbous metal shafts.

George was familiar with the device, but had never before been strapped down into it himself. He knew of its purpose and operation. The guards firmly strapped George into the chair. They tightened the heavy leather straps against his struggling arms and legs. A lustrous metal bowl was lowered down onto his head. His hands curled tightly around the metal arms of the chair. He pleaded with his oppressor. "Lilith, you don't have to do this. This is all just one big misunderstanding. We can work this out, I promise!"

The imperious woman chuckled. "Oh, I think you know we've gone too far to just let you go. You know too much already."

He realized that escape was impossible, as he finally relented and went limp. Lilith sat down to a computer and initiated the machine. She turned to another table and filled a needle with the elixir. The air in the room began to crackle with electricity, as the thick metal columns on either side powered up. Sharp icy-blue tendrils of energy shot back and forth between the two shiny metal shafts. Richard made a move towards the chair. The black-hooded figure pushed him down harshly.

George lifted his head from beneath his cloak. "What are you doing with me, Lilith? Do you know where you're sending me? You at least owe me that much."

The powerful feminine creature walked slowly over to the prisoner. "I'm sending you to a place where you can't bother me anymore. Don't worry, you won't be dead, but you'll be in a place so technologically backward, that you'll be long dead of old age, before you could ever get back here."

George listened, "I don't care what you do with me...what about these two? What are you going to do with them?"

Lilith smiled. "I have very special plans for them, and believe me, their precious, interdimensional romance will be dead and forgotten! They will never be together; happy ever after is a myth, and a boring one at that." She took the hypodermic needle full of the DMT, melatonin, and ayahuasca compound, and plunged it deeply into George's arm. He winced in pain.

Lilith walked back to the computer for the final command. "Say goodbye to your friends, George, you'll never see them again, not exactly like this anyway."

A blinding white flash of light consumed the room. Then there was another brilliant, blasting flash, and another, and another. The entire room shook as fiery bolts of electricity shot everywhere through the room. Icy-blue spikes of energy shot from the two metal columns. Samantha fell accidentally into the plasma field. She immediately vaporized into nothingness and disappeared. Fire swept over the floor as the ceiling above began to crack and fall. A massive steel beam fell hard onto Lilith's head, knocking her unconscious. The guards scattered from the room. A fire-suppression sprinkler system shot water from the ceiling. Richard miraculously avoided any injuries. He ran over to George. His eyes were bloodshot and his pupils fully dilated. He stared in bewilderment up at Richard. He was dishevelled and confused. "What happened?"

Richard released the prisoner from the metal chair. He was soon free and looked up in utter disbelief. "My God...Richard...it's you! It's me...Ed!"

Richard was dumbfounded, not comprehending what had occurred. He instinctively grabbed him and pulled him from the hellish, fiery room.

They spilled out into the hallway to find a chaotic scene. Guards and robed officials were scattered with people running here and there. Oddly, Dorian's wife Alice met them in the hallway outside. Not knowing what had happened to him, she had earlier come to his office to investigate.

"Dorian, what the heck is going on? Who is this?" She gestured towards Ed.

Richard had no easy answer to either query. "Honestly, I have no idea what's going on. I thought this guy was somebody named George, now he tells me he's my friend Ed." Richard suddenly looked around in shock. "Where is Samantha? Wasn't she following us?" Richard turned to head back into the room.

Alice cried out plaintively, "Dorian, you can't go in there! You'll be killed!"

Richard ignored her imprecations and ran back into the dangerous burning room. He spied an unconscious Lilith beneath a steel beam. He searched the room and found no trace of Samantha. He yelled loudly, "Samantha! Where are you? It's Richard!" The desperate man fought his way through burning debris and mangled wires, searching in vain for a trace of Samantha. She was nowhere to be found in the nightmarish space. He ran back out to the hall. "She's gone! She's completely gone! How can that be?"

Alice shook her head in utter confusion. "Who are you talking about? Do you mean Eve? Was Eve in there?"

Ed grabbed his head with both hands. He shrieked, "My God! My head is killing me! What's going on? Where the hell am I?" In his mentally debilitated state, he struggled to understand what had happened. The many powerful drugs coursing through him muddled his mind.

At the precise moment that Lilith initiated the interdimensional plasma-field generator in the alternate reality, her alter-ego Selena had initiated the same process in her own reality. The incredible confluence of events sent Ed to one reality, and George to the other. The opening of both portals at the exact same moment destroyed both devices in both realities. Lilith remained unconscious on the floor. The two men stood in the hallway, trying to unravel recent events.

Richard looked at Alice. "You must understand, however crazy this sounds...I am not who you think I am. I am not Dorian."

She shook her head vehemently. "No, I know my own husband, but you're not acting like him really. Something is different. You say your name is Richard?"

Richard continued, "Yes, but did you see a woman with blonde hair run out here? You would know her as Eve, but she is actually Samantha. We can't find her. I realize this is all very confusing, but try to stay with me. Anyway, I know you're not going to believe us, but we're from an alternate reality. This is Ed, and somehow, we have lost my Samantha. Lilith was trying to get rid of us all." Ed's face was drenched in sweat. His vision was clouded by brilliant colours and vivid shapes. "We need to find Samantha, and she's not here."

Alice grabbed Richard's arm. "There will be guards here any second, we need to get out of here."

Richard did not want to leave without his beloved. "I can't lose her again! We need to find her!"

Ed attempted to calm him down. "We have no way of knowing where she is now. Somehow, she must have been caught in the plasma-field. She could be anywhere. Nobody has ever been caught within the actual field itself. It exhibits temporal-spatial properties that even I don't understand. Our best chance of getting her back is to stay alive, and out of government custody."

The fire grew into a raging inferno, caused confusion to reign throughout the complex. Lights and alarms flashed and rang out everywhere. In the ensuing chaos, the three were able to slip past security. Outside the towering complex, a bevy of fire-fighting vehicles arrived. Heavy, dark smoke poured from the entrance out into the pristine, clean air outside. A growing group of curious onlookers gathered outside.

Richard tried his best to explain their dire situation to Alice. She was only slightly less perturbed. " If you're not my Dorian, where is he? How do I get him back?"

Richard was sympathetic. "I wish we had more information. I'm not sure anybody knows exactly what is going on."

Ed slowly regained his cognitive function. He picked up his thought. "Alice, you know Dorian was experimenting with some very high-level, very dangerous research. Well, somehow, a dark cabal led by Lilith hijacked his research. Quite frankly, we're not exactly sure who, or what she is. She is clearly not what she seems, and she is most dangerous. It's possible she is not human, at least not in the way we understand. Both Richard, Samantha, and myself are from an alternate reality, or possibly a different timeline."

Alice had some difficulty processing the dizzying information. "It is a lot to take in, but I can't see why you would lie. I will do everything I can to help, and hopefully you can help me get my Dorian back." Alice urged them to follow her to the pneumatic tube system. "Keep your heads down and don't look at anyone. Try to keep your faces away from the surveillance system." Alice possessed an expert knowledge of the city transport system and showed them the way. She strategized in her head, searching for a place to hide, as she planned their next move.

✷

George found himself bound and stuck in the heavy steel chair, as he slowly regained consciousness. The laboratory around him was in complete disarray, as if decimated by a massive projectile attack. A small fire burned on a table as equipment lay strewn across the floor. Beside him was an unconscious figure that he recognized as Lilith. She wore a tight red leather dress, which jarred with his recollection of her. The more he looked at her, with her differing hairstyle and appearance, the more he realized that it was not Lilith. It might have been her doppelganger, thought George. As he appraised his situation, he realized he was no longer at the Institute, but somewhere unfamiliar. The powerful intoxicants injected into his body muddied his thought process. As he pieced together the events in his mind, he theorized that he was now in an alternate reality. His predicament was a difficult one, he thought. He had no means of escape, and the small fire in the room was slowly growing.

Suddenly George heard steps above him. Somebody was in the house, he thought.

There was a voice at the stairs to the basement. "Ed? Are you down there?"

George called out, "Down here!" He heard steps coming down the staircase, and then watched the basement door open.

A professorial-looking older man walked over to him. "Ed?"

George looked up at the quizzical face. "Not exactly...my name is George, and who might you be?"

"Well, I'm Max, and you say you're not Ed, yet you look almost like him, but not quite. So what's going on here?" Max noticed the small fire and the attractive woman splayed across the floor before them. He recognized the woman from the set of the TV show, *Outer Edge*. He had noticed her when he had worked on set with his plasma generator. He continued, "Whomever you are, or claim to be, we need to get out of here." He released the captive and grabbed a fire extinguisher. He easily put out the fire. "Okay, come with me, you can explain later."

George pointed down at the woman. "What about her? Should we just leave her here?"

Max shook his head. "I'm not exactly sure what's going on, but I feel very strongly that it has something to do with her. I think we need to get far away from her."

They both left the dark laboratory and went upstairs. Max urged him out the door and into his small, borrowed Fiat car. Max quickly drove away as George attempted to explain recent events. Max listened with great interest and concern. He drove back to his apartment. He was terrified and uncertain of how to proceed.

✷

Samantha bolted upright from her bed as if electrocuted. She awoke in a luxurious, soft queen-sized bed. She wore beautiful sky-blue pajamas, with little fluffy clouds imprinted on the smooth cotton fabric. A man who looked a little like Richard looked over at her. He had dark, slicked hair, parted to the side. He wore an impassioned, almost comically animated expression. He spoke quietly, but with purpose. "Sam… you expect me to believe that you're a witch?"

Samantha stared back in abject confusion. She felt like herself, yet she was not herself. "What are you talking about? Who are you? How did I get here?"

The perplexed man continued his questioning. "Sam, this whole witch thing, are you sure this isn't something you just dreamed up in your head?"

Samantha had no answer and got up out of bed. She looked back at the strange man. He threw his arms up in the air and continued to mutter to himself. She glided effortlessly down the staircase to the kitchen. It seemed old-fashioned to her eyes, with garishly bright coloured appliances, an exposed brick wall, and white countertops. She looked around at the strange surroundings that were completely alien to her. Somehow, she knew where to find the coffee percolator, and where to find the coffee. Suddenly, a wave of realization washed over her like a warm ocean breeze. Her surroundings recalled a pleasant memory of watching a TV show as a child. She remembered spending countless hours staring at the bright screen, wishing she were the mother in the show. It provided a necessary escape from her difficult childhood and her alcoholic father. The warm, passive comfort of watching TV always calmed her nerves and soothed her mind.

Samantha roused herself from her reverie. Her husband, or at least the man who was acting as such, joined her in the spotlessly clean kitchen. He wore a dark grey business suit, with a thin black-red-and-gold-striped tie. He was an unremarkable, slender man in his early thirties. Samantha became increasingly familiar with her new husband. He appeared to her the perfect personification of a respectable 1960s father.

The agitated man continued his nonsensical rant. "Now I don't know what's going on with you, Sam, but I need you to get it together. You do remember that Barry and his wife are bringing over some very important clients for dinner tonight. Everything has to go perfectly if I'm going to land this account, and for gosh sakes, none of this witch nonsense!" He took a large sip of coffee and put the cup and saucer down.

Samantha was still acclimatizing to her new surroundings. Almost automatically she blurted out, "Now take it easy, Dorian, I'll take care of everything. It'll be ready for when you get home." Her voice sounded odd, and almost alien in her head. It was not her voice, as if a stranger had invaded her mind. She cast her eyes around the kitchen as her husband prepared to leave for the office. "Hold on, Dorian, let me get you a travel mug."

He looked back quizzically. "What are you talking about, Sam?"

She thought to herself that the item might well not exist in this reality. "Oh...never mind, sweetheart." She followed him to the door. He kissed her and climbed into his blue sedan parked in the driveway. He waved again and drove away to his office. She called out cheerfully as he drove away, "Have a nice day at the office!"

✷

Richard, Ed, and Alice raced through the city within the pneumatic transportation pod. It shot through a translucent Plexiglas tube built just above the ground. Richard and Ed were astonished by the incredible futuristic city. A huge emerald green tower dominated the skyline. Snow-white electric vehicles moved silently along the perfect roads. Shining golden skyscrapers shot proudly into the clear azure-blue sky above. Ed was deeply troubled by the prominent red, white, and black swastika and yellow star symbolism that punctuated the cityscape. Only Alice knew of their destination.

"We can't go anywhere public; facial recognition cameras are everywhere. They most likely have already identified us." She pointed out the window. "Look at that!"

A large white rabbit was hopping madly beside the compartment, as if late for an appointment. Suddenly, a monstrous black raven swooped down to seize the rabbit. Alice looked on in horror, worried about the defenceless creature. The black bird grew closer and closer. Luckily, the terrified rabbit escaped by hopping into its hole. The frustrated bird flew away.

Ed looked around, examining his ominous surroundings. "This place is like some kind of totalitarian nightmare. You have so much advanced technology. It's a Nazi dystopia, yet also so warm and inviting. It's a paradoxical reality, this."

Richard remarked, "This almost looks like some sort of reality that you might have created, Ed, with all the obvious Germanic influence."

Ed replied, "Well, the Germans got some things right, and a lot of other things wrong, but at least the trains ran on time."

Richard then addressed Alice. "This is going to sound strange, but I actually knew you in my own reality."

Alice gazed at him with her beautiful, sparkling blue eyes. "Really? How curious. Were we married?"

"No, no, nothing like that. You were working as the receptionist at my advertising company."

Alice wore a tight white skirt and white heels. On top she wore a perfectly ironed cornflower-blue blouse, with a white, frilled patch in front. Alice tilted her head to the side. Her long, straight blonde hair fell past her shoulders. "That is indeed curious. That is just what I do for a living now."

Ed attempted to make sense of the situation. "Alice, you may well prove to be the hidden piece of the map that may lead us out of this labyrinth. The fact that you exist unchanged in both these realities is most odd. You are very clearly unique in some manner. Where are we headed?"

"We have a family cottage out in the woods. Dorian and I were headed out there soon, actually, for a summer vacation. At most, it will keep us away from government security for a while. I really need to find out where he is, I miss him so much." Her saddened face was etched with worry.

Richard nodded. "We need to figure this whole mess out. We'll get Dorian back, and Samantha, and then somehow get back to our own world. Ed, you remember that show *Outer Edge*, right?"

"Yeah, sure, it's my favourite show. What about it?" Ed asked.

Richard continued his thought. "Well, have you noticed how much this city, this whole reality, is just like the show? I mean, even the characters are the same. In that last episode, remember how Dorian was transported through that portal?"

"Now that you mention it, yeah. What the hell is going on anyway? Why didn't I figure that out?"

Richard continued. "The key is to understand what's going on, right?"

Ed nodded. "That may be easier said than done. There exists this strange theory I once read about. It was proposed by the author of *The Hitchhiker's Guide to the Galaxy* books, Douglas Adams. It states that if ever anyone discovers exactly what the universe is for, and why it is here, it will instantly disappear and be replaced by something even more bizarre and inexplicable."

Richard listened intently. "Speaking of disappearing, how is that you exist? I mean, Samantha and I narrowly escaped being blown to bits by the asteroid. How are you still here?"

Ed looked down at the ground. He began sheepishly, "Well, about that...I was going to tell you, but I wasn't sure how to start. You see, the asteroid never did hit the Earth."

Richard stared in disbelief. "That's impossible. We all watched as the missile strikes fail."

Ed continued, "Listen, Rich, I'm not going to tell you that I understand it, but somehow, the asteroid miraculously disappeared from the sky. No explanation at all. Earth, and everybody living there, is fine." Ed intentionally left out the important fact that he himself might have caused the asteroid to appear in the first place.

Richard shook his head. "So all of this was for nothing..." He cast a suspicious eye at his friend. The transparent pod raced through the tube to the end of the line.

✷

The sky above was cloudless, approaching midnight. A bright half moon shone high in the sky. It was a warm night with a slight breeze. Max pulled up to his apartment building. He parked the car and the two men entered the building, saying nothing. They rode the elevator to the eleventh floor. They exited and walked down the hallway to Max's domicile. Inside the small apartment, Max motioned for George to sit down as he went to the kitchen. He grabbed a diet soda.

"Can I get you something?"

George looked around quizzically at the sparsely decorated room. He picked up a picture of a younger looking Max and a beautiful girl. "Who is this?"

Max walked over and held the frame. "That was my fiancée, Savitri. We were both in university. She became ill, we were married just before she passed. I guess really she was my wife, although it was only for a month."

George nodded. "I'm sorry, that must have been terrible for you. Now listen, I hate to change the subject, but we have to figure out what's going on here. We don't know each other, and yet I feel like we've met before somehow."

Max agreed with his assessment. "Yes, I feel just the same way. It's as if you're a different version of my friend Ed. You could be his twin.

What's with the cloak? You look a little out of place here. What is it you do?"

George went on to explain his work and position within the church. He detailed where and how he came to be there. Max found his story utterly fascinating. "So, obviously at the precise moment that Ed was sent to your world, you were sent here. I wonder how he is doing?"

George tried to unravel the tangled knot of complicated events. "Well, if that is what happened, then he is with friends, at least I thought of them as friends, Richard and Samantha."

Max was ecstatic. "My God! They're alive! That means there might well be hope for us all." Max proceeded to detail the manner of Richard and Samantha's strange escape.

George listened with great interest. "So what you're saying, is that this world was about to be obliterated by an asteroid, and then it miraculously disappeared? You see, in my world, we just obliterated a massive asteroid that would have hit the Earth. Our planetary defence system easily eliminated the threat. Is it possible the asteroid itself opened some sort of wormhole?"

Max pondered the remark and walked back to the kitchen. "Well, there are certainly a lot of moving parts. Regardless of what's going on, we still have to eat. Do you want a sandwich or something? I feel like I'm losing track of time."

George nodded. "I rarely say no to food. I'll have whatever you're having, thanks."

Max prepared two sandwiches with ham and cheese, tomato, lettuce, and mayonnaise. He carefully cut each sandwich in half and brought them to the coffee table.

George picked up a sandwich and took a large bite. "Delicious, thanks. Nothing like a tasty sandwich, and this is real ham, right? We have mostly that protein substitute in my world, it just doesn't taste the same."

Max also munched on his sandwich, as he flipped on the TV. "So do you still watch TV in your reality?"

George nodded. "Yes, of course. It's a little more advanced than this, but I remember these old sets. We have a three-dimensional set-up. It's pretty cool."

Max flipped to a news channel. "See, it's as if nothing happened at all...no news at all about the asteroid...everything is back to normal. I'm starting to even wonder if it actually happened at all." He continued to flip through the channels, until he came to one of his favourite shows, *Outer Edge*. Max explained what was happening on the show.

George was perplexed. "You say this is a TV show, but this is my world, this is literally a mirror of what happened recently. There are slight changes, though, and the characters are off in small ways. What does this mean?"

The two men sat watching and eating their sandwiches. Max sat up. "So, this is the latest episode. You say this is what happened in your world. Whomever wrote this seems to have a small understanding of neuroscience, but there are mistakes. We have to find out who's behind this, who wrote this, and who's pulling the strings, as it were. We have to investigate, if we're ever going to get you back, and get my friends back."

✷

Samantha watched Dorian drive away in a 1965 baby blue Chevy Malibu. She experienced a strange feeling of déjà vu, as if she had lived through the moment before, but in slightly different circumstances. She recalled the sporty vehicle from a distant, faint memory. Everything around her seemed very real, and also not quite real, she thought to herself. She grabbed hold of the door, and it was solid to the touch. If this was not actually happening, she mused, it was certainly a convincing simulation. Her previous life slowly faded away in her mind like a ship pulling away from a receding shoreline.

Automatically, she assumed her new role as housekeeper. She returned to the kitchen and planned the dinner party for that evening. She pulled out several pots and pans.

Suddenly, a middle-aged woman appeared in a flash of smoke before her. She wore a long, sheer seafoam-green and purple dress. Her bountiful, curly red hair sat heavily upon her clownishly made-up face. Her demeanour was abrasive and imperious as she spoke, "Sam, why do you persist in this drudgery, in this dreary mortal world. You could have all this done in an instant, as if Dum-dum would even know the difference."

Samantha instinctively knew how to answer the loud woman. "Mother, you're just going to have to get used to the fact that I'm not going to do any magic in this house. I'm married to Dorian."

The older woman shook her head in disgust. "Why you ever did that is a complete mystery, believe me." With that last remark, she left in a puff of smoke, just as she had arrived. The bizarre encounter struck Samantha as being perfectly normal.

Samantha returned to her dinner preparations, when she heard the front door open. She walked out to see her dark-haired twin sister Selena. The raven-haired woman wore a shiny red jumpsuit, which hugged her curvaceous frame tightly. She spoke with a sardonic voice. "There you are, sister. You almost lost me with this last attempted escape, but not quite. You're much more clever than even I had imagined. How's that cute mortal husband of yours?"

Samantha stood transfixed by the strange woman, who seemed so familiar and yet so alien. The seductive visitor walked quietly and confidently up to Samantha. She grabbed the blonde-haired woman and forcefully pulled her close. Samantha's face blushed red. Her head flooded with emotion. She struggled against the unwanted advances. Selena pushed her lips towards hers and reached down to grab her chest. She felt Selena try to flick her tongue into her tightly closed mouth. Samantha's body instinctively reacted to the powerful stimulation, as her chest heaved against the soft fabric of her dress.

Samantha regained her composure, as her mind caught up to her body's desires. She recognized the unwanted violation and, with a sudden surge of realization, pushed her aggressor away. "You're Selena! I know you now!"

Selena smiled knowingly. "Well, of course I am, we're twin sisters! Why wouldn't you know who I am?"

Samantha shook her head. "No...No...I mean you're Selena from the show, you're an actress...from *Outer Edge*...the show I was working on...you came into my hotel room...you tried to rape me!"

"Oh, Sam, you're silly! I was just playing around, trying to get a rise out of you. You're such a square, loosen up!" The dark-haired creature raised her arm above her head and snapped her fingers. With that, she vanished as quickly as she had appeared. Like a ghostly image fading in the dark, she was gone.

Samantha felt broken and crushed by the strange encounter. It was the same terrible sensation that she had experienced in the hotel room days ago. Her sanity was sent reeling as her grasp of reality gave way. She felt her mind fall backward, away from herself. She collapsed in a heap on the carpeted floor. She lay motionless for an indeterminate amount of time. Eventually she regained consciousness and returned to the kitchen to begin preparations for the dinner party. Samantha slowly accepted the reality in which she found herself. Despite her despair, she felt it important to complete her duties as a wife. Samantha wanted so much to present a successful dinner party, and impress Dorian's important clients.

✷

Ed, Richard, and Alice rode the tube system to the end of the line. There were only a few people standing by the entrance by this late hour. They exited the transport tube system, taking care to avoid others. Hidden surveillance cameras and government agents were everywhere. They kept their heads down to avoid recognition.

Alice looked back and spoke in hushed tones, "Don't follow too close! They're probably looking for a group of three."

Richard nodded and fell back a few steps, as did Ed. Alice led them out of the tube system to a walkway transport. Richard and Ed followed her lead, as they carefully stepped aboard the fast-moving walkway. Despite the urgency, Ed gazed in awe at the amazing technology. "This is like some cool futuristic spread from *Time* magazine from the 1950s. You know, with the electric cars and shiny new buildings. It's the future we all hoped for, that never happened, except for the Nazi stuff, of course."

Richard agreed. "It's like the future as I imagined it, but as you said, without the weird goddess-worship. It's almost like our Christian God doesn't exist here."

Ed frowned. " It's just different gods here, it's definitely not a Judeo-Christian world. If anything, I'd say this is a more God-oriented world than ours."

They passed by a huge black, red and white swastika emblazoned on the front of a towering building. A strange, angular V-shaped sigil monument sat at the entrance. Alice noticed their keen interest. "That's the Aldebaran parliament building over there. Impressive, isn't it?"

Both Richard and Ed looked at each other with confusion.

They reached the end of the walkway system and made their way to a fleet of identical vehicles. The cars, secured and connected to a central charging unit, hummed quietly. Alice knew to walk up to a vehicle and wave her wristwatch over the sensor. A small red light changed to green with the motion. Alice motioned for them to get in. "We're not going to get very far undetected, now that I've scanned this car, they'll be able to track us easily."

Ed wondered, "It must use some form of GPS, similar to what we know. I wonder if we could mess it up somehow."

Alice shook her head. "No, they would know, they always know. The artificial intelligence system is infallible, although it does occasionally get the odd detail incorrect."

The three fugitives fled through the night in the smoothly-shaped white vehicle. The immaculately clean highway was deserted, but for them. They were soon far beyond the bounds of the great city.

Alice punched in the directions as the car sped along at top speed. "We'll take this exit here, and then ditch the car. We'll have to walk the rest of the way and stash all electronics, especially the watches. It's a bit of a walk, but we can do it."

The car came to slow stop in a clearing not far off the exit. It pulled up to another central charging station and automatically plugged itself in. She removed her watch and smashed it against a large rock. She removed Richard's watch and performed the same destructive motion. From this point on, Alice knew there was no electronic surveillance in the woods. The extensive satellite system could still pinpoint their present location, but no farther.

The independent and capable Alice led the way along a narrow path through the dark woods. Ed and Richard followed closely behind. Ed asked, "Just what kind of wonderful adventure are you taking us on here? Do you know where you're going, Alice?"

She smiled agreeably back at them. "Don't worry, I know this path like the back of my hand. We've been coming here since I was a little girl."

Ed looked up at the panoply of brilliant stars above. It was a clear, warm night, and the Milky Way was visible above. A bright half- moon shone down on them. He recognized many of the constellations. "Well, at least I still recognize the stars, at least that's one constant. There's Orion and Sagittarius over there."

Richard looked up wistfully as he spoke. "Do you think Samantha is out there? Or is she somewhere right in front of our eyes, just out of reach?"

Alice fell back to them. "You must really care about her. We'll find her, and Dorian."

Richard listened and replied, "You know, I really do love her. I've never felt this way about anybody else, not even my ex-wife. I hope she feels the same. Sometimes I feel like fate is keeping us apart, after bringing us together; it makes no sense to me. It's almost like we're both being punished for something. I don't know what exactly."

The bright, twinkling stars above in the clear night sky continued to chart their progress.

Ed listened intently. He grabbed a large stick from the ground and used it as a walking stick. The woods were silent save for the sound of their shoes crunching the leaves and twigs beneath. A coyote cried out in the distance. The pungent aroma of spruce trees and nocturnal bushes filled the warm night air. "Yeah, Rich, we're in a pickle, that's for sure, but we're not done, not by a long shot. We'll find Samantha, and we'll get your Dorian back, too, Alice."

A large white rabbit hopped along the path ahead of them. Overhead a huge black raven swirled above them. It marked their passage with keen interest, while keeping an eye on the racing rabbit below. The three runaways hiked along the trail in the woods for another hour. They eventually found themselves at a large cottage by the lake. The property was dense with tall trees and brush. The impressive cedar-shingled dwelling featured a large deck overlooking the beautiful still water.

CHAPTER 14

Max bolted upright his from bed with a shock. He looked around in amazement at his suddenly unfamiliar bedroom. He said out loud to himself, "Where am I?" His confusion slowly dissipated and he regained his composure. George spent the night on a pull-out sofa bed. He woke up groggy and disoriented.

Max walked out to the living room. "You know, it's the strangest thing. I can't remember what day it is. I'm pretty sure I don't need to go to the university, though. I guess it must be Monday. Did you sleep okay? I know it's not the most comfortable mattress."

George got out of bed with some difficulty. "It was okay. I've slept on worse. I was having the strangest dreams. It's starting to fade already, but it was something about living in a world without reality, it was frightening. There was an estate with a towering maple tree out back. Beneath the tree, there was a woman reading a book to girl. The girl was blonde and wore a blue and white dress, with a white ribbon in her hair. Suddenly, a huge black bird swooped down from high in the tree. The girl fled, and whilst doing so, fell into a deep hole, and tumbled down it. Then I woke up. It was weird, and it seemed so real."

Max was curious. "That is strange, but you know, just a dream." Max went into the kitchen to make coffee and search the fridge. "Are you hungry? Do you like bacon and eggs?"

George nodded appreciatively. "You mean real bacon and real eggs? Sounds great, I'm famished."

Max placed the bacon in the frying pan. The wonderful smell of the sizzling meat soon permeated the air. The acrid aroma of strong coffee also filled the room. "Is scrambled okay for the eggs?"

"Yeah, it's been so long since I've tasted real eggs."

They both ate their breakfast in front of the TV, mostly watching the news. Max switched off the TV and walked into another room in the spacious apartment. He switched on the computer. The primitive device shocked George. "I remember using something like this when I was a kid. It's so old."

Max shrugged. "It's pretty fast by today's standards, I guess." Max typed away quickly at the keyboard. "I'm trying to get some information on this *Outer Edge* show. It looks like it's done by some company called Ashtoreth productions. Its office is actually in town, on King St. West. Check out the web page, all these strange, ancient symbols: the eight-pointed yellow star, and the golden Babylonian goddess. Weird. What do you think it means?"

George studied the page. "Well, this just looks like something from my church. But what's it doing here in this reality?"

Max was perplexed. "Somebody is in charge, pulling the strings, a puppet-master, don't you think? I mean somebody that somehow exists in both realities. Does that make any sense? We need to find out more about this Ashtoreth productions, find out who's running the show, no pun intended."

George nodded ruefully. "Honestly, I hope you're wrong. This would be a most disturbing development."

✷

Samantha worked away diligently in the immaculate kitchen. She was preparing a fancy crown of lamb with roasted potatoes, carrots, cauliflower, and asparagus. There was also a delicious wild mushroom risotto slowly simmering. The tantalizing aroma of slow-roasting meat wafted through the house. Suddenly, a huge plume of smoke appeared in the kitchen. It was again her mother Eudora, wearing the same long flowing green dress. "Samantha, really. Why do you persist in acting long some sort of common slave?" She waved her arm imperiously and an impressive, three-layered strawberry cream cake materialized on the counter. "There, do you see how easy that was?"

Samantha automatically thought to dispense with the magical creation by throwing it in the trash. "Now you know what I told you about magic in this house. I don't like it!"

Eudora was petulant. "But now that it's made, why destroy a perfectly good cake? It's not poisoned, for goodness' sake."

Samantha smiled. "Do you promise it won't hurt them in any way?"

Eudora made a gesture with her hand on her face. "Witch's honour, it will not kill anyone. If I wanted to get rid of Dum Dum, I would simply turn him into a toad. It would be an improvement, if you ask me." Eudora grinned broadly and vanished in a grand flourish, just as she had arrived.

At precisely 6 p.m., the front door opened. Dorian wore a dark grey suit with a thin black, red, and gold tie. Along with him were two couples. One was his boss, Barry, and his wife, Lois. Samantha accepted the coats handed to her, and dutifully hung them in the closet.

Dorian began the introductions. "Sam, Barry, and Lois need no introductions, of course."

Samantha smiled and shook hands with them. Barry leaned in to peck Samantha on the cheek. Dorian continued, "Let me introduce Bjorn and his wife, Agnetha, they're from Sweden."

Barry continued the formalities. "Dorian here is working on a big promotion for their new line of home saunas."

They were both dressed majestically, in fine European clothes. Agnetha wore a bright canary yellow dress, with a dazzling diamond pendant. Green emerald earrings shone from beneath her tumbling blonde locks. Bjorn sported an azure-blue silk suit, with a ruby red striped tie. Samantha was very impressed. "Imagine having a sauna in your own home!"

They all sat down in the living room enjoying cocktails, save for Samantha who was still busy in the kitchen. Lois called out, "Everything under control out there? Do you need a hand?"

Samantha poked her head out into the room. "No. I'm good. We're almost ready!"

The dinner party sat engaged in an animated conversation. It focused primarily upon the differences between Sweden and the United States. Samantha walked into the living room and declared that the dinner was ready. They all moved to the dining room, which sat adjoining the living room. They all sat down, with Dorian at the head of the table, and Samantha sitting directly across. He poured a bottle of wine around the table, and then raised his glass high. "Sam, this looks fantastic!"

The repast was bountiful, sumptuous, and delightful to the eye. The expertly prepared crown of lamb sat impressively in the centre of the table. The appetizing aroma of the roasted meat perfumed the air. Barry was particularly impressed. "Samantha, you've outdone yourself again. You should give my Lois here some lessons."

His wife frowned at the insult, and did not let the remark pass. "Maybe if you didn't spend every other night late at the office, I'd put in a little more effort."

Bjorn chewed slowly on the roasted meat. "This is so delicious, our native Swedish food is much simpler. It is so sad that our children are missing this, they would love it."

His stunning wife, Agnetha, agreed. "Yes, Anni-Frid and Benny are missing out. They are staying with my cousin in Stockholm, while we are here. They are actually taking singing lessons from him. We are a very musical family."

The guests devoured the delicious meal. Samantha and Lois collected the dinner plates and cleaned off the table. Samantha called out from the kitchen, "I hope you all left room for dessert!" Samantha brought out the towering three-layered strawberry cake with much fanfare and anticipation.

Lois followed with a silver tray holding a silver coffee pitcher, and matching silver containers of sugar and cream. The aroma of the fresh-perked coffee permeated the room. Lois carefully poured the coffee around as Samantha cut and served the impressive layered cake. Dorian was particularly proud and pleased by the fascinating dessert. "Sam, this cake looks spectacular, where did you find the time?" He took a large bite and moaned with delight. "This is the best cake I've have ever had."

Their Nordic guests were also thoroughly enjoying the dessert. "My English...not so good maybe...what is word for Kaka?"

The guests continued to marvel at the intricate confection. It featured layers of soft white cake interspersed with sweet whipped cream and fresh strawberries. It was covered in a bright red fondant, with bright white polka dots of whipped cream.

As they continued to enjoy the cake, Samantha finally sat down to allow herself a slice. Suddenly, she watched in horror as her husband and guests slowly shrank in their chairs. They all grew smaller, save Samantha, who had not yet taken a bite. She instantly recognized her mother's fingerprints on the strange occurrence. She angrily stomped out to the kitchen. "Mother, you get out here right now!"

After a few moments, Eudora appeared as usual in a huge puff of smoke. She was dressed in a bright orange bathing suit. "Oh, what is it now. I was just enjoying the sun in Monte Carlo."

Samantha was furious. She stormed back to the dining room to retrieve her mouse-sized husband. She carefully picked him up from the seat of the chair and returned to the kitchen. "You know perfectly well what now! You didn't poison the cake, but you've obviously enchanted it!"

Eudora was nonplussed. "Oh, really! I should think you'd be pleased. He's so much nicer to look at, and easier to deal with. All I said was it wouldn't kill anyone, and it hasn't."

"Now you change them all back this instant! And make sure none of them remember any of this!"

Eudora entered the dining room and undid the damage caused by her enchanted cake with a grand flourish of her arms. The guests reverted to their usual state, and all was back to normal. Samantha watched carefully. "That's better! Now get lost before I have to explain you, too!"

Eudora sniffed. "Well, there's no need to be rude!"

The dinner party continued in the living room with some coffee and conversation. No mention was made of the bizarre transformation. Soon the guests left for the evening, well satisfied, and none the wiser. The unfortunate episode forgotten, all returned to normal. Like a morning mist, or an unpleasant dream, it faded away into nothingness.

Dorian helped Samantha clean up in the kitchen. "I've got to say, Sam, that was a wonderful dinner. You're wonderful!" He kissed her on the cheek.

They both headed upstairs to prepare for sleep. They separately brushed their teeth and dressed for bed. He wore dark blue-striped cotton pajamas. She wore sky-blue pajamas with white polka dots. Dorian leaned over to kiss her goodnight. "I love you, Sam, even if you are a witch." He fell asleep quickly, satisfied by the success of the dinner party and the sumptuous meal. Eudora's shenanigans remained completely unknown to him.

Samantha became increasingly comfortable with her new domesticated role in life. In her previous life, the idea of living as a dutiful, submissive jobless wife would have been anathema to her. The memory of her former self slowly fell away. A part of her missed the fiercely independent woman she once was, yet she enjoyed the feeling of being secure and protected. As she fell asleep, the tumultuous and terrifying events of her recent past seemed to melt away, like a beautiful cake melting in the pouring rain.

✷

The three fugitives admired the impressive cottage in the woods. Ed looked up at the black, star-filled sky. "I wonder if one of those satellites up there has spotted us yet?"

Richard shrugged. "I certainly hope not." He was dumbstruck as he gazed at the impressive building by the lake. "This looks just like our place, our family cottage."

Alice was quizzical. "No...this has been my family's cottage since I was little. That is curious."

Richard walked up to the cedar-sided walls. "It's just as I remember it, but I suppose many cottages do look alike just as complete strangers can look alike. Yet it seems identical in almost every way."

Ed offered his opinion. "You're right, memories fade from childhood. We remember things as we want to, not necessarily as they were. Let's not worry about that, and thank our lucky stars we have a place to crash for the night. Let's get inside."

Alice found a little three-legged table on the porch. Its top was solid glass with nothing at all on it. She lifted up the table to find a small key taped to the bottom of one leg. She seized the small key and walked back to them. "Thank God the key is still here."

An enormous red and white polka-dotted mushroom sat beside the porch. Alice exclaimed, "Look at his beautiful mushroom! Might we have it for dinner?"

Ed shook his head vehemently. "If we eat that, we certainly won't have anything else to worry about...we'll all be dead!" Ed reached down to another small patch of mushrooms. "Now these ones, we can definitely eat." He plucked several brownish-grey mushrooms and examined them closely. "I'm a bit of an amateur mycologist. Now these have a little psilocybin in them, a mild hallucinogenic. I've tried them; quite tasty, very relaxing. Sometimes they can unlock hidden doors within the mind, and of course, there are small side effects, but they act differently on different people." Ed proceeded to forage the small patch of fungi, careful to not disturb the roots.

Alice smiled and continued to the entrance of the cottage.

They all walked in to a finely decorated living room. For a cottage, it was quite well-appointed. Richard immediately recognized the canoe paddle hanging over the fireplace, and the buck's head trophy on the facing wall. "I remember we had a small boat, my dad named it Carol, after my mom."

Alice commented, "My father Charles loved this cottage so much. He was actually a writer, but he published under another name. He did a lot of his deep thinking up here."

Ed noticed the large fireplace. "I'm pretty handy with fires, it's not that cold, but it might cool down tonight. I'll get it going."

Alice opened the pantry to search for something to eat. "Maybe there's something in here that's not poisonous. there's a can of beans and wieners. not sure how old it is but it might be edible."

Richard nodded. "Are they magical beans? That sounds good to me." He was amazed at the incredible similarity to the cottage of his childhood. "Can I help you make it?"

Alice declined the offer. "I think I can manage, as long as I can find a can-opener somewhere."

Ed came over and handed her the mushrooms from his pocket. "Maybe you could wash these up and fry them?"

Alice took them and washed them up in the sink. Alice was a take-charge sort of woman; adventurous and fearless. She missed Dorian very much, but tried to make the best of the difficult situation.

Richard was impressed that the cottage had electricity. "I have to admit, my cottage didn't have power like this. We used to have to run a gasoline generator to get the lights running. Is it solar power that runs this place?"

Alice nodded as she prepared the simple meal. Ed managed to get a small fire started. Richard came over to warm himself. "You know, it's just a matter of time before they eventually find us here."

Ed poked at the fire with the stoker. "I realize that. We'll just have to deal with the situation as it happens. In the meantime, maybe we can regroup, plan our next move. You know, Richard, in all this confusion, I never did apologize for what we did to you and Samantha. I can't help feeling responsible for all that's happened. Especially since it turned out to be unnecessary."

Richard returned a quizzical look. "What exactly do you mean? You saved Samantha and me, that's something."

Ed shook his head. "No, you don't understand. Think about it. How am I here, if the asteroid hit the Earth? That's what I'm trying to tell you. It never did hit. Everybody survived. Max and I sent you away for no reason."

Richard was dumbstruck. "No...that's impossible, it was our only escape, that's what you told us."

Ed resisted the urge to explain that he had somehow caused the appearance of the asteroid in the first place. "It was a miracle. Let's just say that if we hadn't sent you, everybody on Earth would be dead."

Richard remained mystified. "Maybe someday you'll explain exactly what it is you're saying." He wandered around the strangely familiar old cottage. "I remember we used to have an old box of DVDs in the closet over there. He walked over and opened the door. He looked down and found the box of DVDs precisely as he had recalled them. "How strange...exactly as I remembered." He picked up the box and brought them over to the TV. "Alice, do you have a player that will still play these?"

Alice walked over and found an old-fashioned DVD player. She plugged it into the paper-thin TV on the wall.

Richard rummaged through the box. "These are a bunch of old shows we used to love watching, you know, shows from the '60s and '70s."

The comforting scent of the burning wood spread through the room, along with the calming warmth. The smell of beans and the mushrooms filled the kitchen. Ed declared, "That smells good. So Richard, any decent shows there to watch?"

Richard found a favourite old DVD. "I know we shouldn't be watching TV at a time like this..."

Ed shrugged. "Who knows, maybe we'll get some inspiration." Richard held up a DVD. "Look at this one. You remember the one about that guy married to the witch and then they suddenly changed the actor playing the husband, with no explanation? That was weird, like nobody would notice. You're probably too young to remember this one, Alice. Ed, don't you think it's strange that a TV show from our reality also exists is this reality?"

Ed nodded. "Yes, I do remember that show, and you're right, it doesn't make sense. None of this does, in fact."

Richard replied, "What do you mean?" Ed continued. "I'm not exactly sure right now. I'm still trying to work it out in my mind. The number of strange coincidences, they're adding up, to the point where I think something entirely different is going on here. Let's just say that I'm not prepared to accept the reality of this situation."

"What choice do we have? This all seems real to me, as real as my life before this place. How can we tell the difference?"

Alice was busy preparing the bowls of food. Richard found the controls for the DVD player and the episode began. The animated opening credits showed a beautiful blonde witch in a kitchen, preparing a meal. A burst of smoke appeared as the husband leaned in to kiss her. The familiar theme music brought back pleasant memories for Richard, watching the show as a child.

Alice entered with the food. The bowl of fried mushrooms sat in the middle. She watched the show along with the two men. Ed offered Richard the mushrooms, after helping himself. "Here, try a few, they'll help you relax."

Richard helped himself and passed the bowl to Alice. "Some for you?"

Alice declined. "Usually I love trying new mushrooms, but I think I will stick to the beans tonight...my stomach feels a bit odd."

They all enjoyed the simple dinner. Ed was especially hungry. "Thanks, Alice. Comfort food, just what we all needed." He looked over at Richard, sitting across from him in a leather chair. "I hope Max is okay. I won't even begin to explain how I ended up in that metal chair in the basement. It's a little embarrassing. Actually, it's a lot embarrassing. Let's just say that I was investigating what exactly happened to you and Samantha. I ran into one of the actresses on the *Outer Edge* show, Selena. Suffice it to say, she is not what she seems. In fact, I have no idea who or what she is, but I have my suspicions. She is very, very dangerous. I certainly hope we don't run into her again."

Richard listened intently while still watching the TV screen. Suddenly he stopped eating and put down the bowl. He pointed animatedly at the screen. "Ed! Look at that...the actress in this show...that looks like Samantha, doesn't it?"

Ed was not watching the program. He was not a fan of the show. "You mean the character. Her name is Samantha. Sure, that's a minor coincidence. It's not that uncommon a name, though."

Richard shook his head. "No, I mean that is my Samantha! Look closely!"

Ed put his bowl of food down to take a closer look. "Holy crap, Richard, you're right!"

Alice had no idea what they were talking about. "Are you saying your Samantha is that woman there, the actress? That doesn't make sense. I've never watched it, but this is just a show we're watching, right?"

Richard leapt to his feet and paced the room. He was extremely agitated. "This is freaking me out, Ed, what's going on? How can we save her? I'm not hallucinating, am I?"

Ed tried to mollify his distraught friend. "Okay, Rich, calm down, this is a mess, but I'll figure this out. Somebody, or something, might be attempting to confuse us. Let's watch this episode, maybe there's a clue as to what's going on."

The three fugitives ate their food and watched the episode with great interest. It was a typical episode where Samantha busily prepared a fancy dinner for Dorian's boss, Barry, and some important foreign clients. Her mother, Eudora, attempts to sabotage the dinner with an enchanted cake. Richard switched the TV off after the end credits. "So, what did that teach us?"

Ed noticed his frustration. "Did you notice the character of Selena? She pops in to bother Samantha periodically. I would swear that's the same woman that tried to kill me earlier, but ending up sending me here instead."

Alice also recognized the woman. "That woman on the show that plays the twin sister, she looks identical to one of my husband's co-workers Lilith. Weird coincidence, I guess."

Ed was not so sure. "There are no coincidences, really, only patterns beyond our comprehension. I think Lilith, Selena, they're all the same woman. I realize that it makes no sense, but there it is. When we are left with only one conclusion, however improbable, we must accept it. I think she may be the one behind all this confusion, maybe she's the one controlling things."

Alice was unconvinced. "How could one woman do so much damage, and have so much power? Are you saying that she exists in all these realities at once? How is that possible?"

Ed listened carefully, weighing his thoughts, and burying his face in his hands. "Friends, I don't think this is any ordinary woman. I think we might be facing dome sort of demon, or ancient goddess, however crazy that sounds. This ancient force has gone by many names since the dawn of civilization: Lilith, Ashtoreth, Inanna, and now perhaps Selena. She is darkness itself, and there may be no way to stop her."

The three companions sat dejectedly in the living room. They switched off the TV, as they began to internalize their desperate situation. Richard asked Ed, "Can I finish these off?" Ed gestured with his hand, lost in thought. Richard ate the mushrooms that remained in the bowl.

Ed asked suddenly, "I need something sweet. Do you have anything like that?"

Alice stood up and checked the pantry. "There are some old jam tarts in the fridge, but they're probably quite stale. I can't imagine how long they're been here."

Ed accepted them and lifted open the plastic package. He took a deep sniff to check for rot. "They smell edible, barely." He began munching on a raspberry tart and talking. "So, Rich, you've read my article, and you know what's going on, at least somewhat. The key is the pineal gland; it's something the ancients understood. The Egyptians knew it, the Babylonians, you name it. It's lost knowledge, that I've been trying to reacquire. It clearly plays a crucial role in the ability to move from one reality to another. Clearly this Lilith, or Selena, or whomever she is, has existed for a very, very long time. Maybe she's immortal, maybe she's is an adept."

Richard listened carefully. "Do you think she's a god?"

"No...not in the way you're thinking anyway, but she will not be easy to defeat, that much is certain. It will require cunning and determination. I hope both of you are up to the task." Ed continued to eat the raspberry tarts as crumbs scattered over the floor. "Make no mistake, her goal seems to be nothing less than absolute control over all realities in all dimensions. Still, tomorrow is another day, and fortune favours the brave. I suggest we sleep on it, and start fresh in the morning." Ed stood up and threw several logs on the fire to keep it going in the night.

Alice led them each to a separate bedroom, providing them with blankets and pillows. Richard was mentally and physically exhausted, and felt comforted by the soft, luxurious bed. Alice dressed and came by his half-opened door. She wore pink flannel pajamas with feet. Her long-flowing blonde hair framed her angelic face. She looked in, with her fine-featured face. "Goodnight, Richard, I really hope we find your Samantha."

Richard sat up and smiled. "Don't you worry, we'll find your Dorian, too. I somehow feel like the two are connected somehow, you know?"

Alice walked into his room. "I think we're all connected on some level. The problem is finding the right level, finding the right frequency maybe?" She turned, with nothing more to say. Alice returned to her bedroom, as Richard turned over to fall asleep. Ed was already travelling to dreamland in his room.

CHAPTER 15

George and Max got up from the chairs in front of the computer. Max walked over to the window and looked out. The sun was shining brightly in a cloudless blue sky. "What time is it, anyway? Did I say it was Monday this morning? I feel like we've been in this room forever. I should be at the university today, but something is telling me to stay here and figure this mess out." Max walked over to the TV. "This *Outer Edge* show has everything to do with what's going on. You said earlier, when we were watching this, you said it looked like your world, and mirrored events that happened in your reality. Let's see what else there is to find out."

Max found the latest episode, which was not present previously. The storyline involved three fugitives fleeing from an authoritarian regime. It depicted a highly advanced, technocratic society. The government appeared of Germanic origin, as if the Nazis had won the last world war. The escapees were travelling along a complex pneumatic tube system. They exited the clear pod and found their way to an electric vehicle installation. Max pointed animatedly at the screen. "Did you see that? It looks like Ed, Richard, and some other blonde woman...I don't recognize her."

George spoke up. "I do, that's Dorian's wife, Alice!"

The episode continued, showing the three fugitives finding a cottage in the woods. The scene then cut back to the road. Several figures entered a large white vehicle at the electric car installation.

There was a red-robed woman and several black-hooded guards. They sped along the highway.

George pointed excitedly at the screen. "That woman in red, that's Lilith! She's the one that sent me here, to this reality! She's the one we have to worry about!"

Max suddenly stood up and turned off the TV. "I don't understand any of this, but we have to do something, we can't just sit here and watch them get caught!"

"But I don't understand. You said this was an entertainment show we were watching, not reality."

Max threw up his arms in exasperation. "I'm not sure that there's any difference at this point. We just have to accept that somehow, what we just watched is actually happening."

George made a suggestion. "All of this seems to concern Ed. Why don't we go over to his place, there must be some kind of clue."

"Yes. What time is anyway?" He walked over to the window and stared out. It was pitch-black. "Wasn't it just daytime, I mean, just a few minutes ago?" He glanced at the clock on the wall. "Apparently, it's three in the morning, I need to get some sleep first."

George agreed. Max slogged off to his bedroom after helping George pull out the sofa bed.

Max awoke the next morning feeling rested. He put on his robe and slippers and shuffled into the kitchen. He prepared the coffee and turned it on. The aromatic scent of the strong brew wafted into the living room. George awoke with a start and staggered out to the kitchen. "Max, I could really use some of that. I clearly need some new clothes. I'm definitely not going to fit in around here wearing this robe. Do you have any I could borrow for today?"

Max shook his head. "You're welcome to help yourself, but I think they might be a bit small." Max poured George a strong coffee. "You like some cream, right?"

George accepted the large mug with a gracious gulp. "Thanks...perfect."

Max considered going over to Ed's place. "You know, Ed would have clothes that fit you, I mean, you're basically twins. We should head over right away."

They both finished their coffees as Max returned to the bedroom to get dressed.

Max walked ahead of George to the elevator. They both entered as Max pushed the button. He turned to George. "It is the most extraordinary thing. I honestly can't recall what day it is. It might be Tuesday?"

They both left the apartment building. Max looked up. "I remember that there was something in the sky, that shouldn't have been there, but I'm not sure what."

They walked the few blocks to the subway. They entered the station and rode towards Ed's house. Max asked, "So, you recall we were watching that *Outer Edge* episode last night? You mentioned that the woman in the red robe was Lilith. Well, something just jogged my memory. I know that woman by the name Selena. Clearly, they are the same, although I realize that is impossible.

"You think this Selena and Lilith might be the same person?"

Max shrugged. "Who knows? Somehow it seems that you and Ed are the same person."

They arrived at the house. Max immediately noticed the absence of Ed's yellow Volvo. Max found the front door open. He called out loudly, "Ed! Ed, are you here? You check upstairs, I'll check the basement. Help yourself to some of Ed's clothes in his bedroom. I'm sure he won't mind."

George wandered around the house, finding nobody. He found a bedroom closet and rummaged for some clothes that would fit him. He chose a green plaid shirt and some brown corduroy pants to wear.

Max searched the basement as George joined him. "She was right there, on the floor, Selena, now she's gone." Max walked over to the table to search for clues. "Check those notes over there, look for something having to do with his DMT-pineal gland experiments."

Max and George rifled through notes and files in the dark laboratory. After a few minutes, Max noticed a DVD with an eight-pointed yellow star drawn crudely with a marker. He slipped it into the computer drive. They both sat down to watch.

The image of Ed, speaking into the camera, came into view. "*If you're watching this without me, it means that something has gone wrong. My research into the occult, the Aldebaran corporation, goddess worship, the Vril, and the possibility of travelling to other dimensions, has led me to believe that somebody, or something is conspiring to take control of all these realities. Who, or what this entity is, is not entirely clear to me, except that it is clearly female. I have not shared this information with anyone, not even my good friend Max. Max, if you are watching this now, tread with great caution.*"

Max shook his head ruefully. "This is worse than I thought. Ed mentioned to me once, his interest in the Aldebaran corporation. He believed that the beings from Aldebaran possessed cognitive powers far beyond our comprehension. Ed was attempting to harness this understanding for his own dark purposes. He believed these beings were capable of creating entire timelines, whole new realities, in their image. Essentially these beings are what we think of as gods."

George nodded and watched the screen in amazement. "I see what you mean, he looks just like me, but slightly different, even his field of research mirrors mine."

Max nodded. "Mirror, perhaps a black mirror; an apt description indeed, for I believe that you exist in a mirror reality, or to put it another way, our reality is a reflection of yours. Which one can claim to be the base reality? How many other mirror realities are out there?"

"A strange world we live in, isn't it? We truly are gazing through the veil of Maya."

Ed's video image continued. "It is clear from my research, that the human pineal gland is the key to understanding this trans-dimensional reality. This organ may act as a conduit or portal to other worlds. Perhaps the gland may be a long-forgotten vestige of our godlike ancestors. This is indeed ancient knowledge, the Sumerians knew it, and the Egyptians, and now we our slowly rediscovering this missing puzzle piece. Yet in order to access this singularity, it is necessary to utilize some sort of triggering mechanism, some old and some new. The hallucinogens ayahuasca, DMT, along with the hormone melatonin, energized with a powerful electromagnetic plasma field, appear to open this gateway. How precisely this portal operates is beyond my understanding. If you are watching this, Max, and perhaps who knows else, you must learn how to use this trans-dimensional gateway to our advantage. You must beware of the Goddess Ashtoreth, and the myriad of dark aliases she might assume."

Max and George found the video thoroughly fascinating. Much of it was already known to Max, as he had helped with the research. He was uncomfortable with the metaphysical and occult underpinnings of Ed's work. Neither man noticed as Selena walked calmly into the room. She skulked around in the dark, looking for a suitable weapon. She seized hold of a large brass statue of the Goddess Kali that she found by a window. She slowly walked up behind George and smashed the back of his head with great force. He immediately collapsed in a heap on the floor. Max turned around in shock to see the feline, grinning face of Selena. Her bright green eyes flashed with delight. The slender, frail man attempted to shield himself from the next blow. She raised her arm high and brought the weapon down hard upon his skull. It landed with a sickening thud against the side of his head. Blood poured down his face from the open wound. He fell back onto the computer table, as Ed's voice continued to divulge the secrets of his research.

Selena looked down casually at her latest victims. She walked over to the computer and watched the screen with great interest. She listened intently to his explanation. "You were so very close to stopping me, professor, but it seems like the last move in this chess game is mine. Your friends here, or what's left of them, will soon be eliminated. You have nothing left to teach me, little man." Selena watched as the video ended and continued with her diabolical plan. She heaved each of the men into the damaged steel chairs in the room. She secured them with the heavy leather straps. Max was barely conscious. His blood-soaked head flopped back and forth in the chair, as the thick, ruby red liquid pooled at his feet. George was still unconscious from the blow. His large head, with its sweaty, dark hair, hung forward listlessly.

Max struggled to regain control of his senses. He attempted to see through the trickle of blood flowing over his eyes. "What are you going to do with us? You know the plasma-field generator on this apparatus was overloaded...it doesn't work anymore."

Selena shrugged. "Look at you two fools, Tweedle-Dee and Tweedle-Dummer. You're a silly little monkey, that's really all you are, a slightly more evolved little monkey. Obviously, you haven't studied Ed's research as closely as I have. You must have at least some sort of idea of what I'm planning. It's all about the pineal gland, it's the key. Now, transporting you two to another reality, that's just a temporary fix. To truly get control, and to get rid of all you pesky scientists, it will be necessary to implement the final solution."

Max was bewildered. "Are you suggesting you're not human? Are you going to kill us?"

"Never mind, I doubt you'd even understand. I am an adept, I've learned epigenetic self-transformation. You might say I'm a little bit smarter, a more elevated version of yourself. Humanity 2.0, if you like. I suppose that I must seem like a god from your primitive perspective. Now, killing you would still allow you to exist in other realities through the manifestation of your pineal gland. It possesses unique abilities that permit the mind and body to transcend both time and space. I'm going to surgically remove the pineal gland while you're still alive. This will permanently destroy your existence for all time and through all parallel realities ."

Max was terrified by the bizarre explanation Selena left him to gather the necessary instruments for the sinister procedure. Ed's extensive animal testing meant that plenty of medical utensils were available for her use. She carefully placed all the razor-sharp, shining steel objects in a tray before the two men. Max could only stare in horror at his impending torture. The polished steel blades glinted in the darkness. George thankfully was still unconscious and avoided the excruciating anticipation. He remained in a coma-like mindlessness.

✷

Samantha bolted upright from her bed, as if electrocuted. She felt a massive surge of energy flowing through her limbs. She looked over at her slumbering husband. He was wearing the same dark blue-striped pajamas, yet as she looked more closely, she realized it was not Dorian. It was Richard. She began to shake the sleepy figure. "Richard! Wake up...is that you?"

Richard slowly began to open his eyes. He looked around in bewilderment. "What the hell?" He looked across the bed. "Samantha, is that really you? How did I get here? Where am I?" He wore an expression of joy mixed with confusion. "I thought I lost you again...what's going on?"

Samantha threw her arms around him, her face glowing with happiness. "Who cares, I'm just happy to have you back, that's all that matters to me. Let's not question things, okay? Not yet anyway."

They embraced tightly, as Samantha's warm soft body slid easily into his welcoming embrace. They gazed deeply into each other's eyes, becoming completely lost within the other. They kissed passionately, oblivious to their surroundings. After what seemed to them an eternity, Richard pulled away. "Last thing I remember, I was eating a bowl of magic mushrooms and then I went to sleep. I was with Ed and Alice, you know, the receptionist from my office, only it wasn't actually her, or maybe it was. It's all quite confusing. We were at her family cottage. Only, it looked exactly like my family cottage. We were watching that show from the sixties, the one with the witch...and then as we watched, we realized that we were actually watching you, not the other actress, although it is amazing, the similarity."

"Curious. Did we talk about this before? I honestly can't remember. Do you think this might be some sort of dream we're in?"

"No, how could we both be in each other's dream? Dreams are never this detailed, and you can't argue in a dream, there's no logic or reason. I've studied dreams and dream architecture, and it possibly could be a lucid dream, but whose dream is it we're in? Am I dreaming you, or are you dreaming me? Or maybe we're in somebody else's dream? How can we escape from a dream?"

Samantha was just as confused. "Where would we escape to?"

Richard seemed puzzled. "Well, we do want to get back to our real lives, to reality, right? I'm an advertising man, and you're an actress."

Samantha was unconvinced. "Richard, obviously you have forgotten why we tried to escape in the first place. You remember the asteroid? The Earth and our lives are gone."

"No, that's just it. I spoke to Ed. He's still alive! Everybody is! Somehow the asteroid never hit the Earth."

Samantha stared in disbelief. "That's impossible! We didn't actually see it hit the Earth obviously, but it must have. Anyway, even if the Earth is still there, what was so great about our lives there? You've always found your job boring and difficult, and I'm just a struggling actress at best. Why couldn't we just stay here? It's so nice, we'll have hilarious adventures every week. It would be like living in a real TV show, what could be better? I'm Samantha and you can be Dorian, and my crazy mother, Eudora, will show up sometimes."

Richard frowned. "No, this isn't real. Just recalling old memories from a TV show is not reality."

"What's the difference? It could be real for us, if we both believe in it wholeheartedly."

Richard could not accept their newfound paradise. "I'm sorry, Samantha. You know I love you, and I want to be with you more than anything in the world, but something is wrong here, it doesn't feel right. What if we're being tricked into thinking all of this is real?"

"Who would do that?"

"Lilith, Selena, whatever you want to call her. What if she's behind all of this…this false reality?"

Samantha remained unconvinced. "How do we even know there's anything left to go back to? The world we knew could still be gone, maybe Ed lied to you. How well do you really know him? Maybe this is all there is left, our own two minds."

A tapping at the bedroom window interrupted their discussion. It was a large black raven seemingly insistent upon entering the room. They both stared at the intruder, wondering what to do. Richard got out of bed and walked over to the window. The black creature's empty, dark eyes stared menacingly into his own. "I remember this bird. It's like he's following me for some reason. He was at my office, at my house. It's like he's trying to communicate something. I want to find out. I should finally let him in." He motioned to lift the window to grant access to the nocturnal visitor.

Samantha suddenly shot out, "No! Don't open that window! Don't let it in!"

Richard, seized by an ineluctable need to let the dark intruder in, lifted the glass barrier. A huge blast of icy cold air blew in as the window flung open. An ancient, chilling darkness poured into the room, enveloping them completely, extinguishing all vestiges of light. Both Samantha and Richard were speechless, standing alone and in the empty black void. They closed their eyes tightly to slow the icy-cold pain.

They both suddenly awoke in the darkened basement. A single light bulb hung precariously from the ceiling, barely providing illumination. A menacing figure emerged from the darkness and stood before them. Selena wore a tight red floral dress. "I hope you don't mind, sis, I borrowed this from your closet. It's a little boring, but when in Rome."

Richard and Samantha were both completely unaware of how they arrived there. "What...how did we get here?" Richard stammered. "What are you going to do with us?"

They both struggled against the tight, heavy leather straps on the cold, metal chairs. Selena walked forward and ran her hand over Richard's thigh. "We're just in your basement. It is a little musty and dark down here. Really, Sam, you must do a better job of housekeeping, I thought you were supposed to be the perfect little housewife? You two really have caused me so much bother. It's fascinating how neither of you understand how very, very special you both are. There is something absolutely unique about you two, a one in a billion combination, you could say. You each have the unique ability to create a fully formed reality from nothing more than your imagination. Alone, this talent is not that dangerous, but two people can themselves create a stable reality. Remarkable, really, you primitive humans, it's a talent that not even the gods possess." Selena's words merely served to confuse her prisoners.

Samantha struggled to loosen her bonds, to no effect. "Are you going to kill us?"

Selena laughed. "No...well, yes, but much more than that really. I'm going to utterly destroy your being, obliterate the precious bond of love between you two. That infinitesimal chance, a twist of fate, that brought you together, all for nothing, as it turns out." Selena called out loudly, "Dr. Mumbai...emergency...come right away!"

A flamboyantly dressed man with a large, elaborately waxed mustache suddenly appeared. He wore a brightly coloured floral shirt with pink Bermuda shorts. "Who has dared summon me?"

Selena smiled broadly at him. "Dr. Mumbai! I am in need of your medical expertise. Technically, I am capable of performing the procedure, but I could use your help." She snapped her fingers again and a small table appeared before them. A clean white linen sheet covered the top. Its surface showed a myriad of shining surgical steel instruments with razor-sharp blades. She continued, "In order to permanently remove you from existence itself, Dr. Mumbai and myself will be removing your respective pineal glands. You might know a little about this, Richard. You did know something about Ed's research, did you not?"

Samantha looked plaintively over at her fellow victim. "Richard, I don't understand any of this. How are we going to get out of this? How do you know so much about Ed's research?"

"I really don't know much, and I understand even less. He did tell me a few things."

Selena and Dr. Mumbai chatted casually by the table, examining the instruments. Dr. Mumbai held one of the blades up to the failing light. "These really are the most excellent blades, and very sharp indeed, although, we could certainly use more light down here. Would that be possible, my dear?"

Selena snapped her fingers, and a large medical floor lamp appeared before them. She looked over at her helpless prisoners. "That's much better, now we can actually see what we're doing. In any case, this will all be over soon, and you can get back to your vacation."

Richard pulled hard on his straps, to no avail. He looked over helplessly at Samantha. "I...don't know what to do. Can you think of anything to get us out of here? I mean, you are a witch, right?"

Samantha thought for a moment and understood his intent. She attempted to wiggle her nose to free them. Nothing happened. Selena smirked at her. "The magic doesn't work unless you actually believe you're a witch. But the fact of the matter is, deep down you know this can't be really happening, unless it is. You lack the courage. sis, when it comes right down to it...you're as dull as dishwater."

Selena seized hold of a razor-sharp serrated bone saw. "I'd like to say this won't hurt a bit, but it really will. The pain will be exquisite and it will last for all eternity. Pleasant dreams, sis!"

Dr. Mumbai seized hold of a small circular saw and switched it on. The razor-sharp blade whirred to life. "Now, Selena, are you sure this is absolutely necessary? There will be quite a lot of mess to clean up afterwards."

Selena nodded. "Not a problem at all."

The animated physician began, "It will be necessary to first remove the hard skull. I believe I'll begin cutting just about the ear."

Samantha looked over at Richard as a stream of tears flowed down her face. "I'm so sorry, this is all my fault."

Richard's eyes were moist, but his gaze remained stoic and defiant. "Never lose hope...there's many a slip, betwixt a cup and a lip."

Selena laughed. "Okay! Let's get this party started! Start slicing, Dr. Mumbai."

CHAPTER 16

It was very early morning. A sliver of light shone through the drapes of the small bedroom. Ed slept soundly in his mushy old cottage bed. He felt warm and relaxed for the first time in a week. His insomnia had mysteriously disappeared. Suddenly he awoke to a loud crash. He was still wearing his old shirt, as he bolted upright from his bed. He reached down to the floor to retrieve his pants. Before he could do so, the bedroom door opened. A woman wearing a long hooded red robe stood at the entrance. "Lilith…or should I say Ashtoreth?" Ed recognized her immediately.

Lilith giggled. "Ashtoreth, Lilith, Selena, they're all just meaningless, interchangeable identities…it makes no difference to me, call me whatever you wish."

Ed grinned. "I guess I can't say it's a surprise to see you here. Your arrival was expected. Although, it seems we managed to throw a few wrenches into your grand design."

Lilith waved her hand dismissively. " Mere trifles. Although I am nearly omniscient, I do not control fate. You will learn all soon enough. Finish dressing, there is much to do." With that, she departed from the room. As she left, two large, black-hooded guards bounded into the room. She called out to them, "Bring him out here, by force if necessary."

They both seized hold of Ed and dragged him from the room. Ed resisted with all his strength, but the guards overpowered him. Lilith followed them out to the kitchen.

Alice heard the loud commotion from her bedroom. She stealthily peeked around her door and down the hall. She avoided detection and ran to Richard's room to warn him. She found the bed and the room empty. She quietly called his name, "Richard? Where are you? We need to get out of here now." She glanced at the window to see if it had been opened in the night. She briefly considered escaping herself out the window, but realized that Ed's fate would thereby be sealed. Richard's whereabouts remained a mystery. Alice immediately ran back to her bedroom. She reached up for a large case in the closet and pulled it down.

Lilith instructed the guards to check the rest of the cottage. "Find the other two...or maybe, no...it's just the one left here, Richard's, gone isn't he. Get the blonde Barbie doll one. She shouldn't be too much trouble."

The two henchmen walked briskly down the narrow hallway to the bedrooms, electric prods at the ready. The first guard opened the door to Alice's bedroom, to find a twelve-gauge shotgun fixed directly at his eyes. Alice pulled the trigger. The guard's head ripped from the neck, smashing into the wall behind. The hallway behind him was soaked in blood and brain matter. It slowly flowed and dropped onto the floor. The lifeless, decapitated body collapsed on the bloody red floor in a heap. Alice turned the weapon towards the remaining guard, who was still in shock. He managed to counter the attack, smashing the shotgun from her hands with his prod. He then shoved it directly into her abdomen. Alice's body convulsed forward, as her eyes bulged out in pain. She fell hard to the floor with a thud. Her bountiful blonde hair, drenched in blood, splayed over the dead guard.

Lilith regarded the unfolding chaos with cold detachment. "Talk about losing your head! Well, I never really liked him anyway. Come to think of it, I don't think I even remember his name. Although I must say that I may have underestimated blondie there; that was quite well-played. She's a bit of a wild card. She seems to pop up everywhere, at the most inopportune times. I may have to keep a better eye on her."

Ed looked up defiantly from a wooden chair in the kitchen. Lilith held an electrified steel shaft to his neck. Ed shot out, "Where is Richard? What have you done with him? If you so much as lay a finger on Alice...I swear I'll make you pay!"

Lilith smiled. "Oh, I'm quite sure that your new blonde friend doesn't need your help. She's easily the most capable of the group. And don't you worry about your friend Richard, he's under my control, just in a different place. This will all be over soon enough. I'm about to gain control over all these realities, as soon as I remove all your pineal glands. None of you will exist anymore, anywhere. Deleted and exterminated forever."

The remaining guard dragged Alice roughly into the kitchen with Ed. He shoved her onto another wooden chair. Lilith pointed to her. "Make sure you don't take your eyes off her. She's a slippery one. I'll get you some more rope." She barked out more orders to the guard. "She's out for now, go get my instruments from the car."

The guard left the cottage and returned with a large shining steel case. Lilith took hold of it and placed it upon the kitchen table. She pulled open the gull-wing top, to reveal an impressive array of medical tools. She gazed in admiration at her macabre collection of instruments. "Ah, my precious ones! I'm so glad I remembered to bring these with me." She then seized hold of a large black metal device. "Check out this baby! This is a state-of-the-art laser scalpel; this might even cut through your thick egghead skull, Ed!" Lilith put the instrument down to find something else she required.

She walked over to the kitchen cupboards to find some more rope. She pulled open several of them until she found what she was searching for. "Not the best, but this will do."

The cupboard door above her flung open. Suddenly, a blinding flash of light bright as the sun illuminated the entire room. A small monkey shrieked and jumped down from the cupboard onto her head. Its sharp claws sunk deeply into her scalp. Lilith was taken completely off guard. Lilith screamed out in pain. Ed seized the opportunity by jumping up and toppling the guard standing by him. He managed to pick up the electric prod that had fallen from the guard's grasp. Ed pushed it deep into his chest. The instrument administered a powerful electrical shock with a burst of blue, flickering tendrils. The guard convulsed forward and collapsed in a heap.

Lilith screamed loudly as she struggled to pry the shrieking monkey from her head. Blood flowed down her face, obscuring her vision. Ed turned to her and shoved the electric shaft deep and hard into her abdomen. Lilith howled and fell over with a sickening thud. Ed struggled to extricate himself from his bonds. He flung the ropes down on the floor. He moved quickly and grabbed her unconscious body, shoving her forcibly into the wooden chair. Ed exclaimed, "So you can be hurt, that means we have a chance! Maybe you're not as powerful as you imagine." He then grabbed the rope on the floor and tied her tightly to the chair. He looked over at the small monkey now sitting on the floor, its fur matted with blood. "Monkey! I knew you were still alive, and you sure as hell saved the day! What a stroke of luck!" The excited monkey jumped up into Ed's arms. Ed stared into the simian creature's eyes. "I'm surprised you still like me. I wasn't exactly that nice to you when I sent you here, wherever here is. I'm glad you don't hold a grudge."

Alice slowly roused herself from her stunned state. Having missed all the action, she looked around in disbelief. "What the hell happened here?"

"Well, it looks like we have everything under control. You certainly took care of that other guard. I don't think he's going to bother anybody. That other one there, he's just unconscious. Can you take care of him?" Ed motioned to the crumpled hooded figure on the floor.

Alice looked over innocently. "You mean with the shotgun?"

Ed laughed. "No, I don't think that will be necessary. Here's some rope, just tie him tightly to the chair."

Alice glanced quizzically at the small monkey on Ed's shoulder. "So, where the hell did your new friend come from?"

Ed smiled approvingly at his primate cousin. "Not from hell, actually, maybe heaven. Who knows, he's from my world. All I know for certain is that someone or something seems to be looking out for us from above. This monkey saved our lives...maybe a lot of lives."

Lilith slowly regained consciousness. She quickly recognized her predicament. "Hey, Ed, you know we could work this out. I wasn't really going to kill you." She smiled coquettishly at the large man standing above her.

Ed gazed at a large colourful print on the wall in the living room. "Hieronymus Bosch. Your family has excellent taste in art, Alice. I actually have the same print in my office. What do you think of it, Lilith? Three pictures in one, just like the Father, Son, and Holy Ghost. Are you three, Lilith? Or are you just one? What about the other iterations of you? How many are there?"

Lilith ceased being pleasant. "If you don't let me go this instant, little man, I will make sure you spend the rest of eternity in a living hell, far beyond anything your pitiful imagination could conjure up!" Her face was twisted and bloody, in a terrifying depiction of evil and malice.

Bright sunlight cascaded into living room of the cottage. In the clear light of morning, their circumstances improved markedly. Ed looked over at Alice. "It has been a busy morning. I'm starved! Is there any way you could find anything to eat? Even a warmed up can of beans would do."

Alice was incredulous. "How can you be hungry at a time like this? Aren't we still in a lot of danger?"

"Oh, yes, most assuredly, but...you know...you still need to eat, right?"

Alice shrugged. "I guess. I'll see if we have anything left."

Ed smiled appreciatively and calmly regarded the tightly bound, fuming female creature. "It looks like it's going to be a beautiful day! Not for you, of course. I'm not exactly sure what you are, but it's clear you are pure evil, and I intend to destroy you utterly."

Lilith's bright emerald green eyes fixed him with a deathly cold gaze. "Evil? You should know all about that, Herr Doctor. Don't you realize that you helped me get here in the first place? With all your research into other dimensions: Aldebaran, goddess worship, Hitler, the Vril, you were delving into matters that humanity is not meant to understand, you opened a dangerous Pandora's box, or should I say Pandora's reality."

Alice looked over at Ed with concern. "Is that true, Ed? Are you responsible for any of this?"

Ed shook his head. "Perhaps in theory, she has a point. I may have been meddling into affairs that were beyond my purview. But isn't this how all scientific discoveries are made? Einstein's research and theories made nuclear power possible, but also the atomic bomb. There is no light without darkness. The second time that I opened the portal, I was merely trying to save some friends from a miserable, fateful death."

Lilith laughed derisively. "You are quite correct, Ed, about light and dark, and I am the darkness! You can't hope to change your destiny, you can't change fate. That was your mistake! It's not for mere mortals to meddle in such things. You must accept the cards that the gods have dealt; trying to re-deal, or change your fate, just messes up everything."

Ed shot back with a fiery response. "Never! I will never accept a hopeless destiny...even if it comes from God himself! I defy God with this act! I will finally atone for all the mistakes I have made!"

Lilith ruefully realized that she had failed to intimidate Ed. Her emerald green eyes welled up. "What are you going to do?"

Ed regarded her with fierce determination. "I'm going to use these tools of yours to cut open your skull, and surgically remove your pineal gland, and I will destroy you utterly in the process."

Lilith struggled in the chair, her voice choked with fury. "You will not get away with this!" Her teeth clenched as her piercing green eyes blazed with hatred. Ed ignored her words and calmly seized hold of the laser scalpel. Lilith spat in his face as he drew near. The burning hot laser sliced into her head, burning off her raven-black hair in the process.

Ed motioned for Alice. "Could you help me with this? To do this properly, we need to get rid of all this messy hair."

Alice went to the bathroom and returned with some men's shaving tools. "Will this work?"

Ed smiled appreciatively, and accepted the instruments. They both proceeded to shave the head of all its hair. Lilith struggled mightily against the indignity. Her head flung back and forth, until Ed seized hold of it tightly. The black mass of hair littered the floor. Lilith's slick scalp was bleeding from where Ed had begun the incision. "There...you look a lot less intimidating without all that dirty black hair." Ed continued with the surgical procedure. The laser scalpel's bright, ruby red light sliced along a semicircular path around the skull. Deep red blood flowed from the incision and pooled with the black hair on the floor.

Alice was clearly uneasy. "This seems so barbaric. Don't we have any anesthetic to use?"

Ed was adamant. "Unfortunately, she did not think to bring any with her in this bag, I did look. I suppose we could numb her pain with a little booze, although it's more than she would have done for us."

Alice obliged by finding a large bottle of single malt Glenfiddich Scotch in a cabinet. Ed took it and helped himself to a large drink, with a glass Alice provided. He offered it to Lilith. "It is definitely a little early in the day for an alcoholic libation, but this is excellent Scotch. It's more than you deserve, but we're not monsters. Go ahead, have a swig."

Lilith reluctantly accepted the offer as Ed poured the drink carefully into her open mouth. She swallowed gratefully. "All you need is a nice wafer and this could be my last communion."

Ed smiled and ceased his work. He walked over to the cupboard and found a box of unopened Ritz crackers. He opened the box and put a cracker carefully in her mouth. "There you are. Now I'm afraid I'm going to have to continue. From this point on, it's going to be rather messy. Do you have any last words?"

Lilith was subdued by the effects of the liquor on her system. "Well, it's been a good run, I suppose. About four thousand years or so on this rock. I guess is time for a change. You do realize that somebody else will simply take my place. Creatures such as me are an unpleasant necessity...to further the plot, as it were."

Ed listened with some interest, but was undeterred from his task. The red-hot laser cut into the brain matter, as it fell away in bloody chunks to the floor. Lilith's body went still and she ceased breathing. He took the bloody pineal gland and pulverized it violently with a hammer. He then collected the pieces and threw them in the fireplace. "Well, hopefully that will be the end of her, but what do we do now?" Ed heard a strange tapping at the window. The tapping became more persistent. Ed walked over to the window to investigate. He regarded a large black raven perched on the windowsill.

Alice asked, "What is it out there?"

Ed returned to the living room. He poured himself a generous serving of the fine Scotch. He leaned over to offer Alice a drink, but she declined. Ed intoned, "That was a raven, a most inauspicious omen. One should never invite a raven in, it is a summoning of darkness."

Ed enjoyed the fine Scotch as Ed's monkey joined them at the table. The raven continued its persistent tattoo. Ed regarded the small primate fondly. "Without this quick-witted chap, we might well be dead by now, perhaps all of us. Certainly, a stroke of luck, that. One never knows whom lady fortune will favour."

The monkey seemed irritated by the avian intruder at the window. Suddenly, the small but powerful creature seized hold of the bottle of Scotch. He forcefully hurled it at the window. The glass smashed in a loud crash. The black raven flew into the room. The fire snuffed out in the fireplace. All went dark and cold inside the room.

✷

Max looked up to see his tormentor Selena in a crumpled heap, blood flowing from her ears and dripping from her eyes and nose. Beside him, the large man roused himself from his torpor. "Good lord, Max... how did we get here?"

Max gazed at Ed with a mix of confusion and relief. "Ed! You're back!"

Ed stood up and was able to struggle loose from his bonds. He quickly removed Max's ropes that bound him to the chair. They both stood up and looked around the dark laboratory. Ed was silent for a moment, thinking and pondering their situation.

"Ed, what's going on?"

"Max...I just had a terrible thought. I know this is going to sound crazy. Is it possible that we never actually left this laboratory?"

"How do you mean?"

"Well, we sent Richard and Samantha to safety, but I mean, does it make sense that we're still alive? We should be long dead, this laboratory should be destroyed, along with the rest of the world, right?"

Max still was reluctant to accept the argument. "Are you suggesting that none of this is real...that none of this is actually happening?"

"What I mean is, I think that maybe if we leave this basement, we may realize that we're not really here...and be gone forever. It's basically a Schrodinger's cat situation. As long as we don't choose, maybe we can persist in whatever state of reality this is."

Max refused to accept his interpretation, shaking his head. "But how will we ever know if we don't at least look, to see what's up there?"

Ed considered the question for several moments. "I say we leave it up to chance, let fate decide." He grabbed a shiny quarter from his pocket. "Okay, heads we stay here, and tails we leave this basement, how's that?"

Max shrugged. "Not exactly logical, but okay."

Ed carefully examined the image of Queen Elizabeth on the coin. He flipped the coin high in the air. It glinted in the faint light, spinning and spinning ever higher...

✷

Samantha and Richard prepared for the inevitable as Dr. Mumbai's razor-sharp saw approached. Richard was stoic and braced himself for the torturous pain. Suddenly, Selena grabbed her head in abject, searing pain. She let loose a blood-curdling screech. She collapsed in a heap on the floor, as blood flowed from her eyes and ears.

Dr. Mumbai, shocked by the unexpected development was gone with one final summation, "This is where my part in this sordid story ends...at least for this chapter." He snapped his fingers and disappeared in a puff of smoke.

Samantha and Richard both looked at each other in confusion. Richard spoke first. "Someone or something has saved us." He was relieved and let out an exhausted sigh.

Samantha was less relaxed, her brow deeply furrowed in thought. "I don't think we're out of the woods yet. I mean, we're still tied up. How do we get out of this basement? Nobody even knows we're here."

Richard acknowledged her point. "You have me there. Still, at least our brains aren't scattered over the floor, that's good, I guess."

Samantha smiled. "Ever the optimist!"

"So, you're the pessimist then?" Richard continued. "You know, no matter how crazy this seems, we have to accept that this is really happening. I mean, we're talking, and everything seems real, these ropes are hurting my wrists...that's real."

"Yeah, so what's your point?"

"So, where we are now—in this world—you're a witch, right? So why can't you use your witch powers to get us out of here, or at least out of these chairs?"

Samantha pondered the question. "Richard, I just had a terrible thought. Do you think we might still be in Ed's basement? I mean, what if we never really were sent anywhere?"

Richard shook his head vehemently. "Absolutely not! Are you suggesting this is all happening in my head? That's nuts! As long as we're together, we exist. I see you, and you see me. Let's get back to reality and get us out of here. All you have to do is wiggle that nose, I've seen you do it."

Samantha smirked. "I suppose it's worth a try. When in Rome. Although it does seem foolish." She focused all her energy and strength upon her nose. Nothing happened.

"You have to believe. You have to accept that all of this is real. You are an actual witch, and you can do this. Try again."

Samantha complied. To her amazement, her pert nose wiggled. The ropes that had bound her to the chair disappeared. She was free. She quickly untied Richard from his constraints. He beamed at her in admiration. "Sam, I knew you could do it!"

Richard happily jumped up from the heavy steel chair and took Samantha in his arms. They embraced closely and savoured the exhilaration of freedom. They melted into each other with complete abandon. Their lips gently met in anticipation, then grew into a wildly passionate kiss. The perfect kiss seemed to last an eternity.

Samantha finally pulled slightly away and gazed lovingly into Richard's eyes. "That was better than the last time; I can't wait for the next one. Do you have any other amazing talents I should know about?"

Richard felt blissfully dizzy, in a state of amorous abandon. "Nothing and nobody is ever going to tear us apart again; no evil goddess masterminds, nothing. Now let's get out of this dark basement and into the light."

Richard took hold of Samantha's delicate hand. They walked slowly up the basement stairs to the closed door at the threshold. Richard grabbed hold of the doorknob and turned it. The door opened wide. The bright sun shone down upon the gleaming wood floor.

Richard looked over at his beloved. "We're still in our pajamas; let's get dressed and go out for dinner. What do you feel like?"

Samantha looked up, beaming with happiness. "You tell me. Let's just go for a drive and see where fate leads us."

Richard smiled. "Whatever you say, boss. I know, let's flip a coin. Heads we have Chinese, and tails we have Italian, what do you say?"

Samantha agreed. He searched through his pockets until he found a shiny new quarter. He looked at it closely. "It's brand new...1965." He flipped the coin high in the air. It glinted in the bright light...spinning and spinning ever higher...

✷

Her long, shimmering golden-blonde hair cascaded down past her shoulders. A white ribbon held it back from her fine-featured face. She wore a knee-length puffed sleeve blue dress with a pinafore worn over the top, and a white sash around the waist. Around her delicate neck, a shining yellow-gold eight-pointed star pendant caught the suns' early morning rays. Her enormous bed was a dark cherry-red wood, masterfully carved with woodland motifs. The headboard featured large mushrooms, a well-dressed frog, a fish, and a caterpillar. A dazzling display of ruby red, emerald green, and canary yellow windows scattered the sun across the floor. Intricately patterned tiles decorated the walls of her ornate bedroom. The floor was a black-and-white checkerboard that created an illusion of depth. A bright purple striped creature snuggled at her feet.

Another slightly older, statuesque girl with bountiful blonde hair breezed into the room. She wore a long flowing yellow dress, which sparkled in the suns' rays. She wore a shining yellow eight-pointed star gold pendant. It hung down from her delicate neck and finely shaped features. "Alice, you do so love to sleep. I fear one day we may never wake you."

Alice lazily stretched up her slender arms. "I must have fallen asleep. I'm sure I was awake just a moment ago." She gently stroked the creature that sat at the bed. The creature grinned up at her slyly. A regal, stately woman then entered the room. She wore a long flowing purple gown embroidered with brilliant, multicoloured jewels. Alice addressed her. "Mother, I had the most curious dream...quite curious in fact. I was in a distant land, in a different time, and I was not myself, but rather someone else entirely. And then I became yet another person, and then another. It was like a dream within a dream within a dream. There was a very lovely man, and a terribly frightening female. We were in great danger, but somehow we managed to escape. I really didn't want to ever wake up."

Her mother walked over to the bed. "Who is to say you ever did wake up? How do you know this isn't part of your dream?"

The beautiful blonde girl shook her head. "No...this is real...I'm quite sure."

Printed in the USA
CPSIA information can be obtained
at www.ICGtesting.com
JSHW020837081124
73206JS00001B/7

9 781038 319777